Hickville Confessions

A Hickville High novel

Mary Karlik

GPK Publication LLC

This is a work of fiction. Names, characters, places, and incidents are a product of the author's imagination. Locales and public names are sometimes used for atmospheric purposes. Any resemblance to actual people, living or dead, or to businesses, companies, events, institutions, or locales is completely coincidental.

Book Layout ©2013 BookDesignTemplates.com
Cover design by Jenny Zemanek. Cover art by Seedlings, LLC used under license.

Hickville Confessions — 1st ed.
ISBN:978-0-9961556-3-2

ACKNOWLEDGEMENTS

Thank you to Seton Hill University's Writing Popular Fiction program for connecting me with my awesome critique partners John McDevitt, Anita Miller, and Aileen Latcham. Thank you to my awesome editor and friend Shelley Bates. This book could not have been born and raised without your endless patience and guidance. Thank you to my dear friends Kathy Sparrow and Susan Diermann. You listened to me twist and turn this story literally for miles during our runs, walks, and shopping trips. Love ya!

1

Nobody asked the Purity Club girls to dance.

They stood in the corner looking like painted-up losers and Ryan Quinn was smack dab in the middle of the group.

Relax. New beginning. New town. New group.

New me.

If this had been her old school, she'd have put some fire into this party—

Not true. If this had been her old school, she'd have ditched the party for... no, she wasn't going there. Being a member of the Purity Club was the perfect way to atone for the sins she'd committed then. As long as her past remained secret, she'd handle being ignored at the dance.

After the king and queen had been announced, the PC girls were ready to leave. That was fine with her. She was bored out of her mind. Things probably weren't going to get any more exciting at the PC sleepover, but at least she could shed her gown for Soffe shorts and a tank top.

She lagged behind as they crossed the parking lot to Macey Brown's mom's Tahoe. The girls whispered, followed by a round of giggles. Were they laughing at her? Nah. She was just being paranoid. They'd included her in all of the pre-Homecoming stuff. She was the one who'd held back, not sure she was ready to open herself up to a new group.

Once they were in the SUV, Macey cranked up the radio—and it wasn't the Christian rock she usually listened to. They drove around town and sang along to the radio and for the first time, Ryan almost felt like she fit in. Macey parked in front of the courthouse fountain.

"Come on, girls, let's go."

Macey and Katie McDonald exchanged one of those looks that said they had a secret. All the girls laughed—they were in on it too. Uneasiness wafted across the hairs on the back of Ryan's neck. She reminded herself she was being stupid, and forced a grin. "What's funny?"

Macey flashed a plastic smile. "You'll see. Ladies—shoes." They kicked off their heels and climbed out. Katie grabbed a plastic grocery sack with a bottle of dish soap sticking out of the top.

We're going to soap the fountain. PC girls committing minor vandalism? This was not in her change-my-life plan. She didn't need this crap. She should've gone for loner status. But that was easier said than done, and being a fringe member of a marginally popular crowd was better than no group at all.

Macey called out to her, "Come on, Ryan. Let's have some fun."

So they were soaping the fountain. Even if they got caught, how bad could it be? Harmless fun. This was not Chicago. These were nice girls. And as far as they knew, she was a nice girl too. *Stop holding back. Give them a chance.* Ryan slipped from her strappy sandals and drew a deep breath.

All in.

The girls held up the hems of their dresses and climbed into the fountain, squealing and giggling as the cold hit their legs. Ryan stepped over the stone wall into the water, ignored the cold chill that shot from her toes to her head, and joined in the splashing and giggling.

Macey waded over to her. "Ryan, I have to confess that we brought you here for a purpose."

The girls moved close to Ryan.

She smiled, but wariness eased its way into her mind. "What? Is this an initiation?"

Katie McDonald and Carle Davis each grabbed an arm.

So, they're going to dunk me. Relax.

Macey looked back at her with cold black eyes. Her sweet Southern smile was replaced by a sneer. "On your knees."

I can deal. They're just having fun. She dropped to her knees, and sucked in a breath as the cold water hit her torso.

The other girls closed in. Jessica Stern pulled plastic scouring pads from the bag and passed them to the girls. Macey pulled the cap open on the soap. They had crazed looks in their eyes and despite her bravado, the hairs on the back of Ryan's neck screamed that this was not good. "What are you doing?"

"We discovered you've been a naughty girl."

Shit. Shit. Shit. She tried to laugh but all that came out was a nervous giggle. "What do you mean?"

"I'm talking about abusing the temple God gave you. You've abused and shamed your body with sex and drugs."

Her captors tightened their hold. Ryan's heart raced and she tried to pull away, but then it seemed like a thousand hands were on her. They poured soap over her and scrubbed. She screamed and they pushed her under. When they let her up, she coughed soapy water.

Scouring pads scraped across her skin. She twisted and kicked to get away, but they held her down. Macey straddled Ryan and screamed, "You are soiled by the workings of the devil!" She ran the pad above the scoop neck of Ryan's gown. Soap bubbles foamed in the water. "You're evil and unclean." She scrubbed the pad across Ryan's face.

The first pass felt like sand, but she kept working that damned pad. Over and over her cheeks, across her lips, down her neck. It felt as though fire raked across her with each angry stroke.

She's gone batshit crazy. She turned her face to get away from the torture, but Macey clamped a hand on her chin and dug the nylon deeper into Ryan's skin with each stroke.

Jessica yelled, "Stop it, Macey. That's too much!" The hold on her right hand was released and Ryan fought to push Macey off. But the other girls were quick to pin down her arm again. A knee dug into the inside of each bicep. They held her legs by putting pressure on her kneecaps. She fought, but they kept her pinned.

Jessica yelled again. "Macey, she's bleeding. Let her go."

Macey released her chin and looked down on her. The whites of her eyes glowed in the lamplight, giving her a crazy, detached look. She held the scouring pad above Ryan's face and squeezed.

Soapy water mixed with blood showered down. Ryan clamped her eyes shut and prayed the torture would end.

Macey dropped her voice an octave. "I command the darkness in you to come out."

A low, deep growl sounded from somewhere. The girls released her and squealed. She heard splashing as they scrambled to get out of the fountain. Ryan's body shook as she sat up and tried to wash the soap from her eyes. Before she could open them, she heard splashing.

Somebody was slogging through the water toward her.

*

Justin Hayes didn't care that he'd been kicked out of the Homecoming dance, but he was pissed as hell that they treated Eric like a victim. When Coach Graves escorted Justin out, he lectured him about his anger and how he needed to get control of it before he wound up in trouble with the law.

Jesus. How had *he* become the bad guy?

When they got to Justin's truck, Coach Graves put his hand on Justin's shoulder, all fatherly, and said, "Son, think about what I said. You have to learn to let things go."

Justin opened the door and turned to Coach. He wanted to tell him he'd gotten it all wrong. But Justin had thrown the first punch and that was all that really mattered. He choked back all the things he wanted to say and closed the door.

His hands gripped the steering wheel as he fought the urge to slam down the accelerator. He didn't need more trouble. He needed to wrap his brain around the truth that had been revealed tonight. One more thing to add to his big, stinking shithole of a life.

He made a right by the courthouse, where girls in their Homecoming gowns frolicked in the fountain. He pulled up alongside the curb and put it in Park. They'd soaped the fountain. *At least someone was having fun tonight.*

As he watched the scene unfold, uneasiness filled him. Those girls weren't dancing in the bubbles. They looked like they were trying to drown someone.

Holy shit! They're going to kill her.

He jumped from his truck. A deep growl erupted as he ran toward them. The girls screamed and scrambled like rats from a sinking ship. Macey Brown stared at him as she stepped over the rim of the fountain, hatred blazing in her eyes. She wasn't scared like the other girls. She was mad that he'd interrupted.

He pushed past her. Ryan Quinn sat up and splashed water in her face. Her skin was raw and bleeding. He scooped her out of the water. She wasn't crying—she was beyond that. She leaned her face into his chest and her body trembled in his arms. He opened the truck's passenger door and slid her onto the seat.

Macey stood in front of the hood with a pair of shoes in her hand. "You can have the whore. Jesus doesn't want her and neither do we." She chucked the shoes at him.

He caught one. The other thunked onto the windshield. He grabbed the shoe and climbed behind the wheel.

Macey stood on the sidewalk with her hands on her hips. Her prom dress clung to her body and pieces of her hair had come unpinned, making her look even crazier than she was. Katie tried to pull her away, but she wasn't budging. As he drove away, Justin took a last look in the rearview. Macey remained on the sidewalk with her middle finger pointed toward heaven.

Ryan shifted sideways and pressed her face against the seat. "Thank you."

The raw sound of her voice made his gut twist. "Are you okay?"

She nodded. "You're Justin Hayes."

"We have Shop together." They'd never spoken because she and her sisters hung out with Austin McCoy. There'd been no one on this planet he hated more than Austin McCoy—he rubbed his cheek where Eric had managed to get a shot in—until tonight.

He'd noticed her, though—her big blue eyes and the cute pixie haircut. He especially liked the paint-splattered shirt she'd worn on the first day of class. It wasn't screen-printed paint either. These were real splatters. She'd caught him looking at it and with a buttload of attitude had said, "Self portrait." There was something cool about a girl who'd say that.

Even cooler was the way she'd handled Mr. Hesby when he tried to kick her out of class "because girls didn't belong in Shop." She'd stood her ground and talked him into letting her stay. He'd noticed other things too. Like the way she moved when she was cutting wood. It was like watching a dance.

He looked at the girl curled up in the passenger seat. Soap matted her super-short hair and mascara stained her cheeks. *Christ, what did she do to piss those girls off?* "Where do you live? I'll drive you home."

"Can we get some coffee or something first?" Her teeth chattered on the last word.

He flipped the heat on high. "The Grind is still open." He drove to the opposite side of the courthouse and parked in front of a tiny coffee shop. "What do you want? I'll run in."

"Caramel latte." She folded her legs under her and rubbed her arms. "They have my purse. I'll pay you back."

"I got it. We'll worry about your purse later." He hurried into the coffee shop.

Thank God, there wasn't a line to order. His slacks were wet up to his knees and he was dripping on the floor. The few people who were there stared as he squished to the counter. He didn't care. He just wanted to get the drinks and get back to Ryan. *What the hell happened?* Her arms and face were raw. He needed to take her home so her parents could tend to her.

When he got back to the truck, he found her curled on the seat with one of his football jerseys draped over her. He handed her the drink and slipped off his loafers and socks.

She warmed her hands on the cup. “I found—your shirt in the—the back seat. I can’t get—warm.”

He took off his suit coat and handed it to her. “You need dry clothes.”

She set her cup in the drink holder and turned her back toward him. “Unzip me.”

“What?”

She looked over her shoulder. “I’m not g-going to strip in front of you.” She pulled the jersey over her head and he leaned across the console to reach her zipper. His hands trembled and his fingers were clumsy as he worked the zipper down. She pulled her arms from the straps of her dress and into the sleeves of his shirt and did a whole lot of wiggling until the dress lay crumpled on the floor-boards. She pulled her knees close, stretched the shirt over them, and blanketed his jacket across her lap. She sipped her coffee. “Thank you for saving me.”

Justin stared through the windshield to keep from gawking at her. “Are you ready to go home?”

“No. Not yet. I can’t.”

He looked at the scrapes on her face and arms. He should get her to her parents, but after what she’d endured, he was going to let her call the shots. “Okay. Where do you want to go?”

“Anywhere. I’m just not ready to face my parents.”

He drove through quiet neighborhoods and tried to think of something to say. But the girl on the other side of the cab didn’t seem in the mood for small talk. She was probably in shock or something. He thought about calling his dad, but that would just complicate things.

It didn’t take long to cover the streets of Hillside. He pulled up to a stop sign and looked at her. “Want to go to the park?”

She shivered and nodded.

He pulled into a spot in front of the playground. "Are you warm?" She nodded and he cut the engine. In the glow of the park lights, he could tell her face was beginning to swell. Blood beaded across her cheeks where the skin had been rubbed raw. "You need medical help."

"I—I just can't. Not yet." She pressed her finger to her upper lip and winced. "I'm sorry. You probably have somewhere to go…"

"No. I don't. It's okay. I'll stay with you as long as you want." He pulled a spirit towel from the back seat. "I'll be right back." He jumped out of the truck, ran to the water fountain near the playground, and soaked the towel.

He got back into the driver's seat and faced her. "Here." When he pressed the cloth to her right cheek, she flinched. "I'm sorry."

She took the rag and held it to her face. "It's okay. Actually, it feels pretty good."

Justin watched water trickle down her neck as she squeezed the cloth against her throat, and told himself he was a jerk for thinking it was sexy. "What happened back there?"

Her lower lip quivered and tears filled her eyes, but she didn't cry. She pressed the back of her head into the seat. "At first I thought it was an initiation." She moved the cloth to the left cheek. "Those girls are crazy."

He waited for her to finish the story, but was met with silence. Whatever happened, she wasn't going to talk about it.

Finally she let out a breath and said, "I saw you dancing. What happened to your date?"

He shook his head. "I didn't have a date. I—ah—was asked to leave."

"What'd you do?"

"Got in a fight."

"Austin McCoy?"

"Eric Perez."

She patted her arms with the cloth. "I know Eric. He's in the Purity Club. I thought you guys were friends."

"Yeah. Not so much." His body tensed as he thought about the note his sister had written. Eric had let him believe it was for Austin. When Justin figured out what Eric had done to his sister, the bastard had laughed. He'd effing laughed.

"Hey, are you okay? You look like you're about to explode."

He looked at the red marks on her arms and blew out a deep breath. "Yeah. I guess we both had our friends turn on us tonight."

"They were never my friends." She pulled Justin's suit coat up over her shoulders. "I have to get my stuff from Macey. I don't even have my cell phone."

"I'll help you." He started the truck.

"How?"

"Do you know her number?" He pulled his phone from the center console.

"Not a clue."

He scrolled through his contacts. "I don't think I know anybody who'd have her number." He tossed his phone back on the console. "We'll just go there. Give me directions."

"No. I can't. I don't want to see them."

"I'll get your stuff. You can stay in the truck." She was shaking her head before he finished his sentence. "You'll be safe. They won't even know you're in my truck."

"No—just no." Fear flashed in her eyes. He needed to back off.

"Okay." He looked at the clock on the dash. It was already after midnight. "What do you want to do?"

"Just be."

What the hell did that mean? "O... kay. So do you want to hang out here for awhile?"

She nodded and got out of the truck.

Shit. He followed her to the swings. "You okay?"

"Yeah." She sat and dug her painted toes in the dirt. He liked the little silver ring on her middle toe.

He rolled the bottoms of his trousers to midcalf and sat on the swing next to her. The dirt felt good on his bare feet. A breeze wafted through the air carrying a soapy scent. He smiled and looked at the girl with the clumpy hair.

"What?"

"You smell like Dawn dish soap."

"Didn't you know? It's all the rage." She smiled back and his gut clenched.

He'd sat at the table behind her in Shop for weeks and, other than her comment on her shirt, they'd never spoken. Not even a hello. He wasn't usually shy around girls, but most girls didn't look past him like he was invisible either. Now, here she was, next to him on a swing in the middle of the night. He twisted the swing toward her. "So, other than tonight, how do you like Hillside?"

"It's different from Chicago, that's for sure. My dad grew up here. When the economy went south, so did we. He bought the feed store from my uncle. I like working in the store."

He lifted his feet and let the swing rock back and forth. "What was life like in Chicago?"

She pushed off with her feet and gained altitude. "Life in Chicago was about as different as it gets."

"How so?"

"For starters, we didn't live in an ancient farmhouse. We actually had places to shop and I went to the Fine Arts Academy."

"That explains Shop class."

"Yes, and I paint. I love it all, but my favorite is woodworking. Something about the smell of the wood as it's being cut...." She leaned forward and looked at him. For the first time since he'd rescued her, she didn't look freaked out. "Crazy, huh?"

"No. Not crazy." He was tempted to tell her that he understood art because of Chelsea. But saying *I get it because my dead sister was an artist* just didn't sound right.

She leaned back and pumped the swing higher. He caught up to her. They swung in sync, the only noise the squeak of the chains. The wind felt good on his face. He looked at her to ask if it stung her raw skin. She wore a smile, but it looked forced and tears leaked from her closed eyes.

He wanted to wrap her in his arms and squeeze away all the shit that had happened to her. He needed to take her home where her parents could deal with what those bitches had done to her. He let his swing stop, and then with the softest voice he could manage, he called, "Ryan." She didn't answer, but she let her swing slow too. "Ryan, I'm going to take you home now."

She nodded and dragged her feet until the swing stopped. When they stood, he couldn't help himself. He pulled her into a hug. She didn't wrap her arms around him, but she relaxed against his chest. He held her tight and rested his chin on the top of her head. His heart warmed at the feel of her pressed against him. He wanted to be her protector, to keep her safe from anybody who'd make her cry.

As if she'd read his thoughts, she stiffened and pushed out of his embrace. "Well, that's enough of that." She took a deep breath and blew it out in a huff. "I'm good. Let's go."

And just like that, the vulnerability he'd seen disappeared. She stretched to her full height and walked to the truck.

He followed and started the engine. "Do you want to call your parents and warn them we're coming?"

Her stomach growled and she gave him a sideways look. "Is there anything open at three in the morning?"

"Only gas stations."

"Can you spot me a few bucks?"

"Yeah." He pulled from the parking lot and headed toward the Quick Stop.

2

Ryan's arms burned and her face felt like it had been scraped with a cheese grater. Justin was right; she needed to go home and let her mom care for her. The explanations, rehashing the shame she'd already brought her family—it was all just too much to think about now.

It didn't matter that her parents had said that what had happened to her in Chicago wasn't her fault. She knew in her heart that it was. She'd made the decision to go to the party. If she hadn't gone, if she hadn't gotten drunk and high… if… if… if. She was sick of *if*s. There had been no *if*s in the fallout after it happened. She'd get high at the drop of a hat. And the sex? Well, what was the use in saying no when she'd already said yes?

She'd wanted out of that life, though. Her therapist said that getting caught with her dad's boss's son was a "cry for help." She begged to differ. It was trusting an idiot who'd forgotten to lock the door.

The anger, pain, and tears in her dad's eyes when he found them naked on his office couch was something she couldn't erase from her brain—and neither was the way she'd laughed about it. Somehow that night, reason had penetrated her drugged-up brain and she'd made a decision to change. She didn't know how, but she was going to find the good girl she hoped was still inside her. But the damage had been done and things had unraveled for the Quinn family at warp speed.

She pressed the spirit towel to her face as Justin parked in front of the Quick Stop. He turned to her. "What do you want? I'll run in."

"Junk food. I'm starving." Her lips felt like they had a sudden outbreak of cold sores and the slightest movement of her mouth sent pinpricks of pain across her face. She spoke flatly—not quite opening her mouth enough to fully get the words out. She tried not to wince. Judging by the expression on Justin's face, she hadn't been successful.

"Jeez. Don't talk—just nod, or shake your head. Chips? Candy? Soda?"

She nodded at all of the choices.

He slipped his bare feet into his loafers and opened the truck door. "I'll be right back."

She watched him all the way into the store. It wasn't the first time she'd noticed Justin Hayes. He was the kind of guy who could get her into trouble, so she'd made an effort to look past him in Shop class. It wasn't just the football-player frame, or the twin dimples, or the way his dark brown hair seemed to fall over his Tootsie Roll eyes in just the right way. He had a player reputation with a bagful of issues. He hated her sister's *friend*, Austin McCoy. Kelsey had actually had to rescue Austin after Justin had attacked him in the parking lot of a coffee house.

Ryan had had enough crazy for one lifetime. So while tonight he was her rescuer, as soon as she mustered the courage to face her parents, she'd place him back in the People to Avoid category.

Justin came back carrying two plastic sacks full of crap, and flashed those twin dimples at her as he climbed into the truck. "Okay, so we have chips." He pulled out bags of Nacho Cheese tortilla chips, corn chips, and Cool Ranch potato chips. "We have coke." He handed her a can of Dr. Pepper, a Coke, and a Sprite. He opened the other bag. "Now in the candy section, we have M&M's—plain and peanut—Snickers, and to add variety, Pixy Stix."

"What? No dip?"

Those dimples deepened. "What do you want? I'll go back." He reached for the door.

She caught his arm. "Kidding. This is great."

He sat back. "So, are we gonna sit in front of the Quick Stop and pig out or do you want to go somewhere?"

"Let's drive."

"Where?"

She held the wet cloth against her mouth and found it easier to talk. "Anywhere. Show me *your* town." She opened the bag of potato chips. "Which drink do you want?"

"Either Coke or DP."

She handed him the Coke and opened the DP for herself. He started the truck and pulled from the parking space. "My town?"

She nodded. "What makes Hillside special to you?" She held out the bag and he took a few chips. "Drive me through your life."

He made a right at the light and snaked through the quiet streets of Hillside to the hospital. "This is where it all began."

"Okay, that's taking it way back. Fast forward a little." She bit into a Cool Ranch chip and discovered a new hell. She fanned her face. "Salt bad." With one hand she pressed the towel to her eyes to catch any wayward tears before the salt from *those* seared her cheeks. With the other hand she held the can against her sore, swollen lips. *Jesus. I look like a freak.*

When the burn eased, she lowered the drink and towel and cut her eyes to Justin.

He'd half turned in his seat and those cute little dimples weren't showing anymore. His face was too serious, his eyes too full of concern. "How about some ibuprofen? I can go back and get you some."

"What, are you sixty? Who calls it that?" *Do not smile. Don't smile. Ouch. You shouldn't have smiled.*

"My parents are nurses. So, drugs or no?"

"No. Drive." *And stop making me smile.*

He drove past the elementary school and pointed to a field just beyond the playground. "That's where I learned to play ball." He slowed to a stop and gazed across the empty field. "Back then we were all friends—Austin, Travis, Eric, and me. We used to squirrel hunt at Austin's place. His mom would let us camp out in the woods near their house—probably to keep us away from Austin's dad. He was freaking crazy. There's this clearing on top of a hill. You can see the valley below. It's amazing. At night the stars are so bright it feels like you could reach up and snatch them." He drove forward again. "I guess that's where I spent most of my days. What about you? You ever hunt squirrel?"

She shook her head. Hunting for her had been completely different. Magnificent Mile different.

"So there's not a lot to see in Hillside. But I have an idea of another place we can go. Ever been to the trestle?"

She pressed the cloth to her mouth. "No. But I thought football players were banned from there."

"We're banned from drinking at the trestle. Besides, at four in the morning, nobody will be there. But we don't have to go. Do you want me to take you home?"

"No. Let's go to the trestle."

As he guided the truck down the highway, the only sound was the radio and Justin crunching the rest of the chips. Ryan had opted for the M&M's. She sat sideways in her seat, watched Justin as he drove, and wished she had her sketchpad.

He had a nice profile, even with the little zit on his cheek. His hair had fallen across his forehead, almost covering his thick brows, and his lips were full and even. But as she studied him, she saw something else. It was slight, but there were almost invisible lines angling down from his cheekbones. Her art teacher in Chicago called them *courage lines*. He said they appeared when people had survived a great tragedy.

She knew Justin's sister had been killed in a car accident a few years earlier. Was that where he'd earned those lines?

He exited the freeway and smiled at her as he signaled a right turn. In a flash those lines disappeared, replaced by the boyish dimples. "Feeling better?"

She nodded. It was a lie. Her face, chest, and arms were raw and swelling. She did not feel better. But she was better than she would be when she got home. She hoped she could sneak into the house before they saw that she wore nothing over her undies but Justin Hayes's football jersey.

He exited onto a dirt road. A rusted, bullet-hole-riddled BRIDGE IS OUT sign was illuminated briefly by the headlights. "We're here." He pulled to a grassy area close to the bridge. The full moon lit the rusted metal of the trestle. "So what do you think of our river?"

"River? Where?" *Crap. Smiled again.*

"It's not the Chicago River. But it's a great place to hang out." He raised his brows as though he were waiting for her approval.

"It's cute."

He turned the engine off, but the radio played on. He crumpled the empty chip bag and stuffed it in one of the plastic sacks. He sat back and took a long swig of Coke. When he turned to her, she saw more than concern in his face. Repulsion? "Ryan, what happened to you tonight was horrible. I don't know why they did it and I don't really care. Anybody who'd do that to another human being is sick."

God, how bad was her face? What if they'd scarred her for life?

She flicked the visor down and checked her reflection in the mirror. She looked like a circular sander had attacked her. Most of the damage was around her mouth. Tears threatened again, followed by a wave of fear that her face might be permanently damaged.

She slung open the passenger door, jumped from the truck, and ran toward the water. Justin followed, hollering frantically, "Ryan! Wait!" As she reached the bank, he grabbed her and pulled her back. He held her against him. "Don't. You don't know what's down there."

She pushed him away. "I wasn't going to jump."

He took a step back and held up his hands. "I'm sorry. The way you took off, I thought..."

She shook her head. "No. I'm not that stupid. I just needed some air. Besides, I don't want them to get away with this." She hadn't realized it until she'd said the words, but she was pissed. She may not have qualified for the Purity Club, but nobody deserved what they'd done to her. A cool breeze kicked up, offering solace to her face and strength to her spirit.

She turned and faced the water with her arms outstretched in the wind. From that horrible night at Loren's party two years ago until tonight, she'd let people dictate her actions. "I will not be a victim."

"Good." He reached toward her and she stepped away.

"Tonight, the warrior is born." *Hell, yeah. If this were a movie, Katie Perry would be singing* Roar *in the background.*

"Damn right." This time he didn't try to touch her, but he looked totally at a loss for what to do. "Ah, hey, Ryan? Wanna take that warrior attitude back a few feet? You are real close to the edge of the cliff. You can't see it in the dark, but it's about a ten-foot drop to limestone."

She dug her toes in and a wisp of dirt fell away under them. She jumped back and fell on her bottom. "Why didn't you tell me sooner?"

He helped her up. "You were having a moment." He flashed those dimples. "Truck?"

"Yeah." She felt a little shaky as she walked back. She wasn't sure if it was from her newfound strength, nearly falling to her death, or those dimples. But holy crap, if it was the dimples, it'd destroy her.

So I won't let it be the dimples. After tonight, we'll be strangers again.

*

Justin shivered as he climbed behind the wheel. "Mind if I turn the heat on?" She shook her head and he started the engine. This had to be the weirdest night of his entire life. Who was this girl? She'd scared the crap out of him when she'd torn out toward the river. His heart pounded just thinking about what could have happened.

He wasn't sure if she was crazy or cool, but either way, he liked it. She curled up sideways on the passenger side again and he spread his suit coat over her. He watched her try not to open her mouth as a yawn escaped, and his gut tightened at the pain that crossed her face when she failed. He clenched the steering wheel to keep from reaching out to her. He had a feeling that would win him another view of the warrior.

It was after five and the sun was breaking on the horizon. He turned to her. "Ryan, I'm taking you home." It wasn't a question and she didn't argue. She nodded and tried to stifle another yawn.

She gave him directions and he backed up. The trestle was halfway between Hillside and Spring Creek. Her house was on the opposite side of Hillside—at least thirty minutes. She rested her head on the console between their seats and was asleep before he hit the town limit. He ignored the urge to stroke her soap-matted hair.

What the hell had happened tonight? He should thank Eric for being such a douche. If he hadn't been kicked out of the dance, he'd never have driven by the fountain at the exact moment when Warrior Ryan needed a rescue. He let out a sigh. She was amazing, incredible, extremely hot—and he couldn't wait to get to know her better.

3

"Ryan, wake up. We're almost at your house."

She'd been awake, but hadn't given in to opening her eyes. She sat up. The skin on her face felt two sizes too small. Her arms and chest burned. She reached for the spirit towel, but it was too dry now to offer comfort.

What was she going to say to her parents? It was bad enough that she was going to have to convince them that nothing had happened between her and Justin. They were going to freak when they saw her face. She looked at her sopping, soap-caked dress crumpled on the floor. No way was she going to wiggle into that thing. Her only hope was to sneak into the house and change clothes. But as they rambled down the long dirt road to her house, hope flew out the window and dread took its place.

"Your whole family is sitting on the front porch." His gaze volleyed between her and the house at the end of the drive. "If your dad has a shotgun across his lap, I'm gonna freak."

She couldn't tell if he was serious. "He won't."

"Is that Austin's truck? What is he doing here?" He white-knuckled the wheel.

"He works for Dad. He helps with the chores."

By the time he parked, both of her parents, Mackenzie, Kelsey, and Austin had all risen to their feet and were staring at them. "Stay here. Let me talk to them."

She got out and reached to the floorboards for her dress and shoes. The jersey hung to her knees, but it was obvious that she wore nothing but panties beneath it. She wadded the wet gown into her arms and plopped the shoes on top.

Her dad stood by Justin's door. "Son, we need to talk."

Crap. They've tried and convicted us already. She stood on the bottom step and looked up at her mom.

"Good Lord, what happened to your face?"

"It's not what you think."

Her mom put an arm around her. "Let's get you in the house."

Ryan nodded and let her mom lead her without looking back. She heard Justin's door open and held her breath. He didn't deserve this.

"What happened? Did that boy—"

"Mom, he saved me."

"Who did this to you?"

"Let me change and I'll explain everything."

Her mom helped her up the stairs, but when they reached the bathroom, Ryan stopped. "I've got this."

"Let me fix you something to eat."

The junk food she'd eaten had long gone, but she couldn't think about food now—especially with Justin left to fend for himself with her dad. "Just coffee."

Her mom nodded. "If you need anything, yell." She turned and jogged downstairs.

Ryan hung her dress on the towel rack on the back wall of the bathtub. She didn't let a tear fall until she turned and caught sight of her full reflection. She looked like something from a horror movie. Her lips were swollen and distorted. Her face didn't even look like her own. Her cheeks burned as the tears fell. She sat on the edge of the tub and gave in to the pain and humiliation of the night.

Kelsey appeared in the doorway. "What did he do to you?"

She looked at her sister, too tired to argue. "It was the Purity Club. They found out—" She couldn't finish.

Kelsey sucked the air from the bathroom. "How?"

It took most of her energy to raise her shoulders in a pitiful shrug. "I don't know. Macey said they were cleansing me of my sins. If Justin hadn't come…"

Kelsey sat next to her and hugged her around the waist. "Come on. Let's get you dressed. Dad's giving Justin the third degree." When they reached her room, Ryan fell on the bed. It would feel so good to just crawl under the covers and sleep away the pain of the night, but she couldn't leave Justin alone to deal with her dad. She pulled on pajama bottoms and a T-shirt and made her way to the den.

Justin sat in an armchair cradling a mug of coffee, her mom on the end of the sofa next to him. Mackenzie and Austin stood on the other side of the room. When Mackenzie saw her, she covered her mouth and ran to the kitchen.

I look too horrible for my own sister.

"Justin didn't do anything wrong." She blurted it out as though he was about to be punished or something.

Her mom rushed to her and pulled her into a tight hug. "We know. He told us about the fountain."

Ryan relaxed into her mom's embrace and blew out a slow breath, hoping to stave off the skin-searing tears that threatened. It didn't work. A few slid down her cheeks, leaving pain in their wake.

Her mom released her and studied her. "What did they do to your face?"

"They used scouring pads to scrub the sin out of me." She pulled up the sleeves of her T-shirt and held out her arms. "They got my legs too, but not so bad."

Her dad came into the den from the kitchen and handed Ryan a cup of coffee. "We're going to file assault charges."

She wanted those girls to pay for what they'd done, but not at the expense of revealing her past to the world. "No. Dad, please."

"Somebody needs to pay for this." His neck muscles bulged with every word he squeezed through taut lips.

Ryan cradled the mug between her hands. "I can't."

"Tom, let's take care of Ryan first. We need to get her to the ER."

"Those girls are sick." He paced in a circle. "They should pay for what they did."

Her mom stood in front of her dad and placed her hands on his biceps. "But we don't need to ruin their lives. Let's start with calling their parents."

"Dad, listen to Mom. Please."

He gave a single nod. "I want the names and numbers of the girls involved—starting with that bitch, Macey Brown."

"They have my phone. They have all of my stuff."

Kelsey piped up. "You're secretary. Don't you have the PC roster on your computer?" Ryan nodded and started to get up, but Kelsey put up her hand. "I'll get it."

Ryan settled back on the couch. Her face burned. The right side of her upper lip throbbed with pain. Her arms and legs were sore, but nothing like her face. She didn't get it. No matter how horrible her past was, it didn't affect them. How had they found out? Why not just kick her out of the club? That was the part that hurt the most. It was bad enough to be outed for her past and rejected, but they'd gone for full-on violence. The image she'd seen in the mirror appeared in her mind.

What if they'd destroyed her face?

*

Justin stepped onto the front porch to give Ryan some time with her parents. Austin McCoy followed him out and leaned on the rail with his arms folded across his chest. "What really happened to Ryan?"

"They went batshit crazy on her." He rubbed his hand across his face. "God, I thought they were going to kill her. They looked like piranhas going after prey."

"You didn't have anything to do with it?"

"Hell, no. Why would you even say that?"

Austin pushed off the rail. "I heard Eric talking smack to Caleb. He said he had evidence that she was—easy."

"Eric's a dick."

"He's your best friend."

"Not anymore." But why would Eric spread a rumor? Granted, he was a first-class bastard, but what would he gain by ruining Ryan?

The screen door squeaked open. Ryan and her two sisters, Kelsey and Mackenzie, stepped out onto the porch. Justin didn't know the Quinn girls, but he imagined they were about as different as they looked. Kelsey, the oldest, had big eyes like Ryan. But instead of short spiky hair, she had brown hair that danced on her shoulders when she walked. Mackenzie, the youngest, had an athlete's body. Her dark hair was pulled back, except for a fringe of bangs that almost covered her eyes. He passed her in the hall every day after Calculus. She always looked sad. Even when she smiled, there seemed to be despair in her face. But then, he was intimately familiar with that look—lived with it every day.

Mr. Quinn's shouting could be heard through the screen door. "You have two choices. You come here to speak with us, or you speak with the police. Believe me, they will be interested in talking to your daughter." Pause. "Two o'clock. And I expect your daughter to accompany you."

Ryan let out a shaky sigh. "This is going to be a long day."

Justin took a step toward her. But she wrapped her arms around her waist and took a seat on the porch swing. He got the message: *A little space, please.*

"As soon as Dad finishes yelling at everybody's parents, we're going to the emergency room." She flopped back in the swing and then winced. "I just want to wake up from this nightmare."

Justin's arms itched to pull her next to him, to surround her in the safety of his embrace. Instead, he sat in a wicker chair across from her. "My dad is a nurse practitioner in the ER. Mind if I follow you? I'll talk to my dad. He'll make sure you get what you need."

"Thanks. Don't you need sleep?"

"Later." And as if on cue, a huge yawn forced its way out.

Austin spoke up. "Dude. I'll drive you."

Ryan looked over Justin's shoulder, her eyebrows raised about an inch, and a distorted smile formed on her lips. "Go Kelsey. About time."

Justin turned to follow her gaze. Austin stood behind Kelsey, who stood with her back against his chest, his arms wrapped around her waist. Kelsey blushed at her sister's words, but Austin only tightened his hold. Justin wondered what it would be like to hold Ryan like that. Would he ever be able to wrap his arms around her in a casual way because that was where she wanted to be? Would she feel soft snuggled against him?

Patience, dude.

"Thanks. I can drive." Justin slumped in the chair and yawned again.

Ryan yawned too. She winced and pressed her fingertips against her lips. "You've been up all night. Don't be stupid."

She wasn't afraid to call it like it was. It made him smile. Besides, if he left his truck here, he'd have an excuse to come back. "Okay."

Ryan's parents joined them on the porch. Mr. Quinn dangled keys from his index finger. "We're going to meet with the parents and the girls at two. Justin, if you're up for it, I'd like you to be here. If your parents want to come, they're welcome to."

Shit. My parents? Mom would be a disaster. Dad? He'll be working. "I'll be here."

Ryan stood. "Are you sure I can't shower first?"

Mrs. Quinn put her arms around Ryan. "I'm sorry, sweetie. I think it's best if you don't. Let them do what they need to do."

She nodded. "Austin is going to bring Justin. His dad works in the ER. It might help."

Mrs. Quinn turned to him. "That's nice of you, but don't you think you need to sleep?"

"No, ma'am. I'm fine."

"Okay, we'll meet you there." She turned to Kelsey and Mackenzie. "Are you girls riding with us?"

Mackenzie jogged down the steps. "I am."

Kelsey grabbed Austin's hand. "We'll be right behind you."

Justin followed everybody down the porch steps. He watched the Quinns pile into the dusty Lexus SUV and wondered if it had ever seen that much dirt in Chicago. *Hard to keep it clean when you have a dirt driveway.* He looked at the weathered farmhouse and thought about the designer furniture that filled the den. There was a story there and he had a feeling it had something to do with Ryan. Whatever it was, he'd do his best to keep it from hurting her.

She'd already endured enough pain for a lifetime.

*

Justin jogged ahead of the Quinns to the ER receptionist, Connie, a middle-aged woman with a big smile and a calming voice, who stood as soon as she saw him. "Justin. Looking for your daddy?"

"Yes, ma'am."

"Go on back." The double doors to the department clicked and swung open.

He made his way past the rooms to the nurses' desk. His dad sat behind the desk reading a computer screen, and looked up as Justin approached. "Justin? What are you doing here?"

"Do you have a minute?"

"I'm a little busy. Is your mom okay?"

Justin shrugged. "I haven't been home. I need your help."

His dad stood and motioned for Justin to follow him. "What's up?"

"A friend is coming in with her parents."

"And?"

"She was attacked last night. I got her away but... Dad, they messed up her face pretty bad. I just thought you could make sure she got what she needed."

His dad nodded. "Why didn't you bring her in last night?"

"She didn't want to go home. I didn't know what to do."

"You were with her all night?"

"Yes, sir."

"I hope you weren't stupid."

"Jesus, Dad. What do you think of me?"

He shook his head. "I'm sorry. Reflex. I see a lot of stuff…"

Typical—his dad was always in work mode. "Whatever. Can you take care of her?"

"I'll see she gets the best care."

"Will she have to wait long?"

"We're not busy. She'll go right back."

"Thanks." He turned to head back to the waiting room, but his dad stopped him.

"Assault exams take a long time. We have to be thorough. Do you want to crash in the sleep room?"

Assault. The word hit him in the gut, lending gravity to an already horrible event. "I'm fine. I'm going to go see what's going on with Ryan."

He left his dad and went back to the waiting room. That had been the most civilized conversation he'd had with his dad in weeks. The comment about being stupid pissed him off, but at least he hadn't asked him if he'd kept it covered. Besides, he was too tired and too worried about Ryan to argue.

Ryan was called in to Triage as soon as he returned to the waiting room. He stopped her as she was entering the tiny exam room.

"I talked to my dad. He said they weren't very busy, so you shouldn't have to wait long."

Mrs. Quinn put a hand on his shoulder and gave it a little squeeze. "Thank you."

Ryan just nodded and headed into the room. He watched the door close and longed to be with her. But he didn't belong. He wasn't her boyfriend. He wasn't even a friend. He was just a guy who had pulled her from the fountain and stayed with her. It was time to step back and remember his place.

His stomach knotted. Was this it? Would he always just be the guy who had saved her from the fountain?

*

The nurse was young—probably fresh out of school. She studied Ryan and concern filled her face. "Honey, what happened to you?"

Ryan hated being called *honey* by someone who was almost the same age, but this was Texas and she was getting used to it. The pain around her mouth had grown with the swelling. She held her fingers to her lips as she spoke—as if that was going to help. "I was attacked."

The nurse grabbed the blood pressure cuff and wrapped it around her bicep. "Does this hurt too much?"

Ryan shook her head. "Can I have some water?"

"Let's get you examined first." The nurse asked a jillion questions. Thank God her mom was able to answer most of them.

Ryan expected to be sent back to the waiting room, but Justin must have worked his magic, because instead she was ushered to an exam room. She'd barely settled on the exam bed when a guy wearing navy-blue scrubs and a white coat entered the room.

He stuck out his hand. "Hi. I'm Alan Hayes."

"Justin's dad." Ryan had never seen the man, but felt relieved just knowing they had a common bond. He pulled latex gloves out of a box and moved close to her. "What happened?"

"Girls from school. They dumped dish soap on me in the courthouse fountain and scrubbed me with scouring pads." Ryan felt like a loser just saying the words. How low a dreg do you have to be to be tortured with a scouring pad?

He examined her face. "It looks like your mouth got the worse of it, but you have some nasty abrasions. How would you rate your pain on a one to five scale?"

Emotionally? A ten. "Five or six."

"Let's get you something for that, then." His gaze flicked between her and her parents. "Are you planning to press charges?"

"No." Ryan answered before her parents had a chance to speak. Her mom looked at her dad. Her dad bowed his head, but Ryan could see him working the muscles in his jaw. "I just want to get past this."

Mr. Hayes pulled the gloves off his hands. "We're going to treat this as an assault case. You might change your mind later. I'm going to have an advocate speak with you. Her name is Regina, and she's a specially trained RN. She's going to take pictures. She's also going to take some scrapings from under your nails." His forehead wrinkled with concern, but he spoke with a soothing tone.

"But I know the girls who did this."

"It's protocol. It's not painful, it just takes a while. If you decide to press charges, we want to make sure we've gathered evidence. I'll order some pain meds. Would you like some juice?"

"Grape would be nice."

Ryan's mom was at her side as soon as Mr. Hayes left the room. "Are you okay, sweetie?"

Ryan nodded. But the truth was, she didn't know if she was or not. This was all so surreal. She figured she'd get some cream for her face and be on her way. She hadn't expected them to go all *CSI* on her.

A nurse named Cayla brought her some grape juice and a couple of pain pills. She scanned her hospital bracelet and the pills. "These will probably make you a little sleepy and they could make you dizzy. Don't get up without help." The nurse watched Ryan swallow the pills. "It'll be a few minutes before Regina gets here. Is there anything I can get you?"

Ryan tried the fingers against the lips thing again to speak. "Can I have a wet cloth for my lips? And can my sisters and friends come in?"

"I'll ask Alan about the cloth. You can have visitors until Regina gets here."

Ryan looked at her mom. "Will you tell them to come back?"

"Sure." She followed the nurse out of the room.

Ryan's dad turned his back to her and placed his hands on the counter. His shoulders shook. At first she wasn't sure what was happening—until she heard a sob escape.

She jumped off the bed and put her arm around him. "Daddy, I'm okay."

Her dad sucked in a deep breath and turned to hug her. He didn't say anything, just held her. After a few seconds he released her. "This shouldn't have happened. This is supposed to be a safe place." He shook his head and squeezed her to him. "I'm going to make this right."

Good grief. She was the one who'd screwed up—literally—and he was still blaming himself and trying to protect her. She hadn't done a lot to make her family proud of her. In fact, she'd done nothing. But that was somehow, some way, going to change.

She pulled away. "No, Dad. *I'm* going to make it right." She was sure he didn't get that they were talking about two different things. It didn't matter. Talk was just that. Changing her reputation wasn't just about joining some stupid club. *She* was going to change.

She heard Kelsey's voice outside the room and was glad to have company to relieve the tension. The curtain whooshed back and Cayla entered the room carrying large and small IV bags.

Ryan's stomach knotted. "That's not for me."

Cayla smiled. "'fraid it is. Alan wants you to have some anti-biotics."

Ryan climbed back on the exam bed.

As if on cue, Mr. Hayes returned. "Sorry. I talked to our attending physician, Dr. Mays. You have quite a few abrasions. These things tend to get infected, so we'd like to nip it in the bud with some IV antibiotics. And it wouldn't hurt to give you a little fluid. We'll send you home on oral antibiotics." He turned to her dad. "I think it'd be a good idea for her to see a dermatologist. I can refer you to a good one in Dallas."

"Okay. Think we can get a fast pass to be seen?"

"I'll do my best. I'm a little worried about the skin around her mouth."

Ryan's heart sped up despite the pain pill that was making her woozy. "Will I scar?"

"We're going to try to avoid it." Mr. Hayes patted her shoulder. "I don't know who did this to you, but think seriously about whether you want them to get away with it."

Cayla opened a tub of gauze sponges and poured sterile water over the top. With gloved hands, she wrung out a gauze square and handed it to Ryan. "See how this feels on your skin."

Ryan placed the square on her mouth and sighed. She would have told her it was like heaven, but the pills were making her groggy. She lay back on the bed and tried to keep her eyes open. "Where are Kelsey and Kenzie?"

Kelsey stuck her head in the room. "We're just outside."

Cayla put on a fresh pair of gloves. "As soon as I get this IV started, they can come in."

Ryan nodded and closed her eyes. She felt the nurse clean her arm and then pain as she introduced the IV. But before she could register enough to open her eyes, the nurse said, "All done."

Instantly the room was filled with her parents, sisters, Austin, and Justin. She forced her eyes open and focused on Justin. The bottoms of his suit pants were still rolled to mid-calf and he was sockless in his loafers. His dress shirt was untucked and the sleeves rolled halfway up his forearms. He had deep circles under his eyes. But he still looked dang hot. She stretched her un-IV'd arm to him. He took her hand and moved close to her. She crooked her finger and he leaned in. "You look goofy."

He laughed. "Goofy? Hey, I'm a trendsetter."

She squeezed his hand. "Thanks for saving me. I'm gonna call you Sir Goofy cuz you're my knight in shining armor."

Kelsey leaned over her. "What did you say?"

Ryan looked at her sister and shrugged.

Justin held tight to her hand. "I think she's a little high."

Nervous laughter filtered through the room, soothing Ryan. She was safe, surrounded by her protectors. She let herself drift in and out of sleep until she heard the curtain scrape along the track. The room got eerily quiet and she opened her eyes.

Mr. Hayes entered with a large pale woman with a salt-and-pepper braid trailing down her back. "This is Regina."

"Hi. I'm sorry it took so long to get here. There was a train." She looked at everybody in the room before focusing her smile on Ryan. "How are you feeling? I understand you've had something for pain."

Ryan nodded. "Better."

Regina looked her over. "Good. Are these the clothes you had on?"

"No. I was in a Homecoming gown."

Regina turned to her mom. "Don't wash them. Put them a large zip-top bag and seal it." To Ryan she said, "Have you showered?"

"No."

"Good."

Mr. Hayes said, "While Regina gets her part ready, I've asked Dr. Cooper to consult. He's a plastic surgeon who is here on another case." He looked at Ryan's parents. "I'd just feel better if he took a look at her mouth."

Her dad said, "Whatever we need to do."

"Okay. It's going to take me a few minutes to get ready." Regina looked around the room. "I'll ask everybody to leave during the exam. As soon as we finish, you can all come back in."

Ryan's throat closed. "Can my mom stay?"

"I'll need to ask some questions first. Then she can come in."

Do they think my parents did this? Or that I was raped?

Regina left the room and Dr. Cooper came in. Justin tried to release her hand and move away, but she tightened her grip. He was able to stand to the side and out of the doctor's way.

Dr. Cooper gloved his hands and touched the places that hurt the most with pinpoint precision. With each poke, pull, and pat, Ryan squeezed Justin's hand tighter.

When Dr. Cooper was satisfied he'd tortured her enough, he stepped back and removed his gloves. He turned to her parents. "It's hard to tell the extent of the damage until the swelling goes down. The lip is a concern. I'm afraid some of these abrasions will leave scars." Then he spoke to Ryan. "The important thing is to protect that skin. No sun, no makeup. I'll write a prescription for some cream." To her parents he said, "I'm here once a week. I'd like to see her either here or in my Dallas office in about a week."

Anger burned in Ryan. *Those bitches left me with a mangled face.* Tears threatened, but she'd be damned if she'd cry. She would not let them win. That meant no tears, no pity, no hiding away.

Dr. Cooper shook Ryan's hand and pointed to Justin. "And who is this?"

Justin let go of her hand and stuck his out. "Justin Hayes."

Dr. Cooper shook his hand and smiled. "Kin to Alan?"

Justin nodded. "He's my dad."

"Ah. Then Ryan is in good hands." He shook Ryan's parents' hands and left the room.

Regina returned and shooed everybody to the waiting room. Ryan thought she'd be more nervous, but whether it was the pain pills, exhaustion, or Regina's calm demeanor, she wasn't sure. It wasn't as bad as she'd imagined. Almost the first question out of Regina's mouth was whether she'd been sexually assaulted.

Ryan almost laughed. She assured her there was nothing sexual about it. The second question was whether it had been Justin, the third about her family. When she had assured Regina that it was nothing as heinous as that, she allowed her mom back into the room. Regina took scrapings from beneath her nails, clipped them, and meticulously placed each item in a bag, labeled and sealed. When she'd finished gathering physical evidence, she held Ryan's hands. “This has been traumatic. You may not realize it now, but it’s bound to affect you. We have counseling available. Even if you decide not to press charges, you need to tell someone who did this to you.”

Ryan started to tell her that she’d already done that, but Regina was on a roll.

“I’m going to give you my card. It has my cell phone number on it. There are three of us who are certified Sexual Assault Nurse Examiners. I know you weren’t sexually assaulted, but you were assaulted. If at any time you need to talk, you call. There is one more thing.”

Ryan was ready for this to be over with.

“Even though you are not going to press charges now, a police officer would like to ask you a few questions. It’s important that she takes a statement in case you change your mind.”

Ryan nodded and Regina released her hands.

By the time everybody had asked their questions and examined her, Ryan was sure she was not going to press charges. She’d had enough. It was after lunch when they walked out of the hospital, and she hadn’t slept in over twenty-four hours. She just wanted to get home, shower, and crash.

She watched Justin walk to Austin’s truck. There was something about his casual gait that made her smile. She’d never thought about how anybody walked before and wasn’t sure why his counted—but it did. Or maybe she was just too crazy tired to make sense.

Austin and Kelsey were ahead of Justin. Kelsey opened the back door of the truck and called, “Come on, Sir Goofy.”

He smiled and jogged the rest of the way to the truck and Ryan wanted to hide forever. Had she really called him Sir Goofy? *Yes. And I held his hand like he was my boyfriend.* Surely he knew she was just drugged out. This whole boyfriend thing wasn't happening.

Because that was the last thing she needed. No way. No how.

4

When they got home, Ryan's mom convinced Justin to crash on the couch for a few hours. Ryan dragged her bones to bed. When her mom woke her up, she felt like she'd just lain down. It was time to get the two o'clock meeting over with so she could crash for a year or two.

She wasn't about to wait for the PC in the den like a sideshow freak. Instead, she sat halfway up the stairs. Justin sat next to her and Kelsey, Austin, and Mackenzie sat behind her. It was the perfect vantage point from which to see and hear everything happening in the den without being noticed.

Mr. and Mrs. Brown and Macey were the first to arrive. Mrs. Brown handed Ryan's backpack and purse to Ryan's mom. Macey stood between her parents looking all confused and innocent. Ryan wanted to take a pad to her face—that'd take care of that look. Carle Davis and Katie McDonald showed with their moms. Christy Kaufman's dad came with her. Jessica Stern didn't show at all. At least the other girls had the decency to look scared.

Jeez. Does Macey really think she's going to get away with what she did?

When her dad invited everybody to sit, Ryan's stomach tightened. Her mom sat in a high-backed wing chair looking like a woman who did not want to be messed with.

Her dad walked around the room and stopped in front of each of the girls. Even from where Ryan sat, she could feel his gaze bore into them as he asked one by one, "Do you know why you're here?"

They all said yes. Before he'd made it around the room, Katie McDonald spilled tears. After he asked each of the girls his question, he straightened and said, "We're clear that the girls all know why they are here." He paused and looked around the room again. "Your daughters assaulted Ryan and I'm here to tell you, something is going to be done about it or we will press charges."

Mrs. Brown smiled at Macey, sandwiched between her and her husband on the sofa. "Assault?"

Macey managed to maintain that lying smile, but her eyes told the truth. She was scared shitless. "We didn't mean anything. We were just having a little fun."

Heat rose in Ryan's cheeks. *A little fun? Is that what you call nearly killing someone?*

Her dad stepped closer to the sofa. "You didn't mean anything? Tell your parents what you did. Let them judge how much *fun* it was."

Carle sobbed. "She made us do it. It was all Macey's fault."

Mrs. Brown's lips twitched. "My daughter does not control anybody."

Mr. Kaufman leaned forward in his chair and steepled his fingers. "What exactly are you accusing the girls of doing?"

Ryan waited for her dad to tell them, but he paused. Tension built in the room. He looked at the floor and cleared his throat before looking Mr. Kaufman in the eyes. "They held her down in the courthouse fountain and scrubbed her skin raw with scouring pads."

Mrs. Brown stood and faced Ryan's dad. "Raw? Really, Tom, they were just having fun. We've all had club initiations. They didn't intend to hurt anyone." It was all Ryan could do to keep from running down the stairs. But her dad was handling it. Then Mrs. Brown turned toward her mom and worked her neck as though she were scolding her. "You should know that your daughter left the fountain with a boy. She left with Justin Hayes."

Ryan's mom barely acknowledged the comment. "We're hear to discuss the assault on my daughter."

Mrs. Brown huffed and looked down at Macey. "Did you assault Ryan?"

"It was an initiation."

Mrs. Brown turned dramatically around the room. "See. There was no assault. Macey wouldn't lie. Our family is built on God's word."

Anger flooded Ryan. "That's it." She bolted downstairs. As soon as she entered the room, everybody stood. She strode up to Mrs. Brown and pulled the sleeves of her shirt up. She tilted her face toward her and said, "This is what they did to me. Macey sat on top of me and did this to my face. The other girls held me down and went after my arms and legs."

She'd barely gotten the words out when Mr. Brown slapped Macey so hard it knocked her flat onto the sofa.

Mrs. Brown turned toward her daughter sprawled on the couch and covered her mouth. Tears filled her eyes.

The whole room stood still. Everybody was too shocked to breathe. Mr. Brown glared at his wife. "She's no better than you." He turned and walked out of the house.

Mrs. Brown lowered herself to the sofa and pulled a crying Macey into her arms while everybody just stared.

Kelsey jogged down the stairs into the room. "This isn't about Macey." She looked at the red mark on her face. "I'm sorry that happened to you, but look what you did to Ryan. Jesus, if Justin hadn't come along…"

Macey looked at Ryan's dad. "You don't understand. We were cleansing her of her sins. She needed to be purified. We were only trying to save her soul."

The room echoed with sniffles. All of the PC girls had broken down. Mrs. Brown was the only parent who looked like she had any sympathy for the girls.

Ryan's mom glared at Macey. "No. You were bullying her. There is no excuse for what you did." She stood and walked close to Macey. "The question is, who is going to cleanse you of *your* sins?"

Macey looked at Ryan. "Forgive me?"

"I saw pure evil in your eyes. You enjoyed the power you had over me. You need serious help."

Mrs. Brown put her arm around Macey. "How dare you?"

Ryan backed away and sat on the fireplace hearth. Justin took a seat on one side of her and Kelsey the other. Austin and Mackenzie stood at the bottom of the stairs. Ryan had never seen her mom like this—she was so angry her lips trembled. When she spoke, her voice was dry, the words staccato. "We… spent… half the morning… in the ED. This… is serious. Her face will be scarred. She might have to have plastic surgery."

Mrs. McDonald swiped tears from her eyes. "I'm sorry this happened. Thank you for not taking this to the police. I'm not sure I'd have been so generous."

Ryan's dad nodded toward her and said, "I'm not the one who's generous."

Ryan looked around the room. How could she have thought these girls were her friends?

Carle looked at her. "I'm sooo sorry, Ryan. Please forgive us."

Ryan couldn't answer. She wasn't ready to forgive.

Her dad spoke to the room again. "Monday, I will have a meeting with the principal. I'm expecting the club to be disbanded."

Mr. Kaufman rose. "I can't apologize enough for what happened. Christy will take full responsibility for her part in all of this. We will pay for whatever medical bills you incur. You do what you have to do, and if that includes pressing assault charges, she'll accept the consequences."

Mrs. McDonald stood too. "I feel the same way. Katie will accept whatever you decide and of course we'll help pay the medical bills."

Katie sobbed into her hands. "I'm sorry. I wish we could reset last night."

Mrs. Davis agreed with the other parents and everyone apologized to Ryan.

Everyone except Macey and her mom. They stood too. Mrs. Brown looked around the room. "We don't have a ride." She locked eyes on Carle's mom. "Will you give us a ride?"

Mrs. Davis looked down and ignored the question.

"Will anybody give us a ride?" The rest of the room remained quiet. "But how will we get home?"

The air grew thick. Until Ryan's mom said, "Walk. Think of it as a pilgrimage. A soul cleansing, if you will."

Mrs. Brown and Macey walked out the door with their heads bowed.

Mr. Kaufman handed Ryan's dad a card. "Keep me informed about the treatment for Ryan." He shook his head. "These are all good girls. I don't understand how they got it in their heads to do such a thing." He put his hand on Christy's shoulder. "Come on. We have some talking to do."

The girls and their parents filed out of the house like a funeral procession, but Ryan didn't feel as though anything had been put to rest. So their parents had offered to pay her medical bills. Their world would go on.

She was disfigured.

*

Two days ago, if anybody had told Justin he'd be accepting a ride home from Austin McCoy, he'd have said they were crazy—just being in the same room with the guy made him want to punch something. But two days ago, Ryan Quinn hadn't rocked his world.

As soon as they pulled onto the highway, Austin started in on him. "I don't know what's up with you and Ryan, but if you hurt her I'll bash your freaking brains in."

If Justin's head hadn't been doing that trying-to-stay-awake bob, he'd have had a decent comeback. As it was, Austin's words barely penetrated the brain fog. So he just gave a thumbs-up sign.

He wasn't conscious again until Austin pulled into his drive. "Thanks for the ride, man."

"I did it because Kelsey asked me to."

Justin got out of the truck and rubbed his hands over his face to wake up enough to make it into the house and to his bed. As he walked up the sidewalk to the door, his heart sank. The house was dark. It was after four in afternoon *and the house was dark.*

He opened the door and the weight of exhaustion tripled. *Shit.* He kicked off his loafers and padded down the hall to the bedrooms. But he didn't go into his room and fall into bed. He couldn't. He had to take care of her first.

"Mom?" He knocked on the door before pushing it open. The room was darker than the rest of the house. He knelt next to the bed. "Hey, are you okay?" *Of course she's not okay. Why else would she be in bed on a Saturday afternoon?*

The covers had been pulled over her head to shut out any light that might have seeped through the closed blinds and curtains. Her thin hand reached out from under the bedspread and touched his arm.

He uncovered her head and stroked her hair. "Can I get you anything?" Conflicted feelings churned in his gut. His mom couldn't help her depression. But he was exhausted. And just once, he wanted to come home and find his mom the way she'd been before the accident.

"No. I'm sorry, Justin. It's been a dark day." Tears ran down her cheeks and onto her pillow. "I haven't thought about dinner."

"It's okay, Mom, I'll do it." *Again.*

"I'm not much of a mom anymore." She dabbed her eyes with what was left of the wadded-up tissue she held.

"Don't say that." He handed her a fresh tissue. "Have you eaten anything today?"

She didn't answer.

"Come on. Let's get some food inside you." He helped her sit up and grabbed her robe off the end of the bed. "Have you talked to Dad?" She shook her head and allowed him to help her with her robe. "Let's move to the den." She leaned on him as he led her to the den and then plopped onto the sofa as if the walk down the hall had taken the last bit of her energy. He was tempted to join her. Just flop down on the couch, sit in the dark, and rest. But knew he couldn't. No matter how tired he was, he had to take care of her.

He pulled open the vertical blinds covering the sliding patio door. Light poured into the den and kitchen. His mom flinched.

"What do you want to eat?"

"Maybe some crackers. I'm not hungry."

He dug his keys and wallet out of his slacks and tossed them on the eating bar that separated the kitchen from the den. "How about a salad? You like salads." He riffled through the refrigerator and found an anemic-looking head of lettuce and a squishy tomato. She hadn't been to the store in a while, and he'd been so busy with school and football practice that he hadn't noticed.

He pulled his cell phone from his pocket and called his dad. "Hey, I just got home. Are you working late?"

"Dark day?"

"It's bad. I got her to the den. Dad, there's nothing to eat. Can you pick something up?"

"Sorry, son. I'm working until eleven."

"Don't worry about it." He hung up and tore the pale lettuce into a bowl. It felt good to shred the pieces, but not good enough. As tired as he was, he wished he had something to hit—hard. This was not supposed to be his life. He shouldn't be taking care of his mom. It wasn't like his dad was too dense to see that she was in a severe depression. Anger surged at his dad for not insisting she get help.

"Was that Dad?"

"Yes. He's working until eleven. Do you want me to bring your salad to you?"

"No. I'll come there." She got up and moved to the eating bar.

Good, maybe she was coming out of it. He chopped the tomato into her bowl, squirted some ranch dressing on top, and pushed it in front of her.

"Are you wearing your suit?"

"Yeah, I just got home from the dance."

She nodded and let out a long sigh. "Eric is a good kid—good family."

Yeah, a good kid. Except he screwed Chelsea and dumped her. He wanted to tell her about the fight, about rescuing Ryan from the fountain, and the drama at the Quinn house afterward. But the mother he could share those things with had died along with his sister.

Tears rolled down her cheeks. "I can't erase the image of her lying there, cold and all alone."

"Think of something else, Mom. I'll get some crackers for your salad." He placed a roll of crackers next to her plate and poured some ginger ale into a glass. There was no point trying to stop her—he'd been through this countless times. It was always this way when she was having a dark day. But he had to try.

"Eat some salad."

"I was house shift manager that day. I had to go to the ER. Careflight was on the way and they called in extra people to work. Both trauma bays were full and the third girl was taken to room eight."

He felt his chest tighten. He hated this part of the story. "Mom, it was horrible, but it's done. Please, eat some crackers."

"I saw her there, Justin. All alone."

"Mom, they didn't know who she was."

"It didn't matter—she shouldn't have been alone." His mother's tone turned angry.

"She was gone, Mom. They were trying to save the other two."

She shoved the bowl across the counter toward Justin. It dropped off the end and clattered into the sink below. "They should have tried to save her."

He rounded the counter and placed his hands on her shoulders. "She was gone by the time they got there. You know there was nothing anybody could do. You have to let it go. We can't fix this."

Her eyes filled with tears. "Don't you see, Justin? If I let it go, I'm abandoning her—just like they did."

He gave her shoulders a slight squeeze and looked into her eyes. "Chelsea's gone. But Dad, and you, and me—we're here. We have to keep going. You're stuck. She wouldn't want that. She'd never want you to stop living." He was wasting his breath. She didn't want to get better. He dropped his hands from her shoulders. "If you don't start eating, you won't be here either." He went back to the kitchen, fixed a peanut butter and jelly sandwich, and slapped it on the counter in front of her. "Here, you can eat this." He bit the words out. "We don't have much else to eat. I'll go to the store tomorrow."

He retreated to his room and flopped onto the bed. Tears came to his eyes and a few trickled down his cheeks before he was able to check his emotions. He wouldn't give in to it. He wouldn't allow himself to be sucked into the hurt and anger he felt in his chest.

He'd watched his mom go there too many times over the past two years. More than that, he'd watched his family fall apart. God, his family was a freaking hot mess. His dad was obsessed with work. He spent more time taking care of strangers than acknowledging the shit at home. His mom was frozen in her grief. All Justin wanted was to be a normal guy. Play football, kiss girls, have a little fun. Chelsea used to call him "little brother heartbreaker." He took a deep breath and let the pain settle deep.

He missed his sister.

He looked at the drawing that hung above his desk—a pen and ink of a football player diving through the air with his hands clasped around the ball and reaching toward the goal line. Chelsea had given it to him for Christmas the year she died. She'd drawn other football pictures, but this was his favorite. He liked the anonymity of it. It could be any player.

Guilt for leaving his mom to fend for herself seeped through his self-pity. He got up and headed back to the kitchen. She was sitting on the sofa with the remote in her hand, but she hadn't managed to turn on the TV.

"I'm sorry, Mom. I haven't slept." He sat next to her.

She patted his thigh. "It's okay. I needed something to snap my brain out of it." She tried a smile but it looked awkward on her face. "Did you boys play video games all night?"

He gave a sort of shrug nod.

She clicked on the TV. "Get some sleep. I'm okay now."

"Sure?"

She nodded. "Go."

He kissed her on the top of her head and went back to his room. He stripped off his trousers and dress shirt, fell into bed, and didn't open his eyes again until the next morning. When he awoke, the first thing on his mind was Ryan Quinn. He stretched and moved to his desk.

He clicked on his Facebook page and did a search for her. *Bingo!* He sent a friend request. He got an acceptance almost instantly.

Justin: Hey. How're you feeling?

Ryan: Eh. Better since I've slept.

Justin: Good.

He was trying to think of something to say when she sent the next message.

Ryan: Family time. Got to go.

He sat back. *Family time.* What a concept. He scrolled through her pictures. Most of them were of various sculptures… and no pictures of friends. On the sidebar he noticed that some chick named Kat Guilin had tagged her in a picture. He rolled the cursor over the entry to highlight it. Wow. Something about the lip and eyebrow rings told him this chick wasn't a member of the Purity Club. Or it could be the way her tongue hung out of the side of her mouth like she was looking for head. Ryan's face was smashed against the other cheek—though it hardly looked like Ryan. Her short hair was spiked and her eyes looked messed up—like high messed up. Next to her profile picture, Kat had written, *Epic party, better than Ryan Quinn's legendary bong-a-rama.*

What's this? The sins the PC scrubbed from her? How did they find out? Why pick on her? It wasn't like she was the only kid in school who'd smoked weed.

There was more to this story than bullying. They had targeted her and he was going to find out why.

5

Ryan slept for most of the rest of the weekend. She'd hoped by Monday that her face would look somewhat normal, but when she looked in the mirror, nausea rolled through her stomach. Some of the scrapes were weeping and had a yellowish crust. The right side of her mouth was swollen more than the left and it hurt to open her mouth.

She was a monster.

She dropped to the floor and leaned against the bathroom cabinet. Why? Was she so horrible that she deserved to have her face ripped up? She couldn't go to school—couldn't go anywhere.

Kelsey leaned into the bathroom. "Wow, it looks worse than yesterday."

Ryan nodded. "It hurts worse." She spoke without moving her mouth.

"I'll get Mom."

Ryan retreated to her room. She wanted to crawl into bed and forget the whole thing. She hurt everywhere—arms, legs, chest, neck, and face. Her face. She looked like something from a horror flick. She hugged her pillow.

Her parents came into her room and sat on the edge of her bed.

"Can I stay home? I don't think I can handle school today."

Her dad said, "Another day in bed would probably do you some good. Come for just the meeting. Mrs. Johnson needs to see what they did to you."

Ryan nodded and let a few tears trickle out of the corners of her eyes. He was right. Nobody would believe what had been done to her without seeing it.

Her mom hugged her. "You look like you hurt." Ryan nodded. "I'll get you a cold compress. Do you need pain meds?"

She'd love to take the meds the doctor had prescribed and be zapped into oblivion, but she wanted to be alert for the meeting. "Just ibuprofen."

Thank God, her parents waited until after school had started to escort her to the office. She didn't want to be gawked at by kids in the hall. The sweatshirt with the hood pulled over her head didn't hide much of her face, but she felt less exposed in it.

When they walked into the office the receptionist recoiled. "Honey, what happed to you?"

Her dad leaned on the counter. "We need to see the principal, please."

The receptionist picked up the phone and pushed a button. "Mrs. Johnson, Ryan Quinn and her parents are here to see you." She hung up the phone and stood. "Right this way." She guided them down a short hallway to the principal's office.

Mrs. Johnson greeted them and ushered them to a table in the corner. Once they were all seated, Mrs. Johnson's face creased with concern. "Ryan, what happened?"

Her mom answered, "She was attacked by Macey Brown and several other girls in the Purity Club. They held her down in the courthouse fountain and took scouring pads to her. They claimed they were cleansing her of her sins."

"What?" Mrs. Johnson pushed a button on her phone. "Mrs. Bettis, could you join us, please?"

Ryan zoned while her parents explained what had happened, including the meeting with the girls' parents, to Mrs. Johnson and Mrs. Bettis, the counselor. They agreed to disband the club.

Mrs. Johnson told Mrs. Bettis, "I want the girls involved in the fountain incident in my office, now."

Ryan looked at her dad. "I don't want to be here when they come in."

Mrs. Johnson's expression morphed from *in-charge principal* to *sad lab puppy*. "You don't have to face them, honey." At the word *face* she blushed, which created a weird contrast with the pity-eyes. To Ryan's parents, she said, "I'll make sure her assignments get to Kelsey. I'm assuming she'll be out at least a week."

So Mrs. Johnson didn't want the freak at school. Granted, Ryan didn't want to be there either, but somehow having someone else echo that feeling annoyed her.

Ryan's mom stood. "We're taking it a day at a time."

"Kids can be so cruel and I'd hate for Miss Ryan to endure any more trauma." Her tone oozed sap. Mrs. Johnson stood and clasped her hands in front. "Take care of yourself."

Ryan crawled into the backseat of the SUV and tried to put a name to the feeling in her chest. Sorrow? Anger? Despair? They all seemed to fit, yet none of them adequately described what was going on inside her.

She had been the one excited to move to Hillside, who couldn't wait to start a new life at a new school. It seemed like such a good plan. Leave her old life behind, reinvent herself, become who she wanted to be. How had it all gone so wrong? She leaned her head into the seat. She'd tried so hard to fit in, to be one of them. Now she was back to ground zero. No friends. And worse, she was left looking like a monster.

Was this the punishment for her past—her scarlet letter?

She took a deep breath and sighed it out. No. She refused to believe God worked like that. She'd been attacked by bullies hiding behind Christianity. Nothing more, nothing less.

Mrs. Johnson's words swirled in her mind. It would be so easy to hide away until her face healed. But then they'd win. She leaned forward. "I want to go back to school."

Her dad had just pulled from the parking lot. "What?" He did a U-turn and pulled back in. "Are you sure?"

"I'm not going to run. I have to face everybody sometime. I want to get it over with."

Her mom swallowed hard. "You constantly amaze me."

Her dad parked the car and opened his door, but Ryan stopped him. "I've got this, Dad."

He looked back at her. "Are you sure you don't want us to walk you in?"

"Yes. I'm good." She forced a smile. "I'll see you after school."

"Okay. If you change your mind, call." Her dad closed his door as Ryan grabbed her backpack and opened hers.

"I won't." She straightened the strap on her shoulder and walked back to the office.

I can do this. I can do this. I can do this.

The bell signaled the end of first period as she signed in. The halls were instantly filled with students and as soon as she exited the glass cocoon of the office, they would see her. *Maybe this wasn't such a great idea.* She choked back fear. *If I hide, they win.*

She forced her face into a smile and ignored the pain she felt—inside and out. When she turned from the desk, she saw her sisters waiting for her on the other side of the glass doors.

When she joined them Kelsey said, "Mom texted us."

"Thanks."

Mackenzie didn't say anything, but her eyes glistened with unshed tears.

"I'm okay, Kenzie."

She bit her lip, nodded, and looked away.

Kelsey said, "I saw the PC girls this morning. They acted like nothing happened. They're going to get away with it, aren't they?"

"I don't know. Mrs. Johnson called them into the office." They set off toward her locker. "I don't want to think about them now. I just want to get through today." She pretended she didn't see the winces and wide-eyed looks of pretty much everybody she passed. She would survive.

Erica, a girl from her Art class, approached her at her locker. "I heard what happened. I just want you to know I hope those bitches get what they deserve."

"Thanks." *So do I.* She grabbed her books and turned to her sisters. "I've got it from here." She hugged them. "Thanks."

Kelsey said, "Text if you need us."

"I will." She closed her locker and headed to Shop class, where she sat at her worktable. She'd been by herself since the term began. It'd never bothered her before, but today she felt isolated from the rest of the class and her confidence waned.

Then Justin slid onto the stool next to her. "Hey, you okay?"

She smiled the first non-fake smile of the day. “I’ll survive. Did you get some sleep?” He didn’t look like he’d rested since he’d left her house Saturday. Dark circles hung beneath his eyes.

“Some.” He rolled his shoulders like he’d dumped weight from them. “Hey, gimme your phone.”

“Why?”

“So I can enter my number.”

She handed over her cell and he typed in the number.

“If you need anything, you call. I mean it.” He flashed his dimples and her stupid, sore face went from smile to painful grin. She grabbed her mouth and squeezed her eyes shut until the pain eased.

Justin handed back her phone. “Ouch. I’m sorry.”

“It’s okay.”

The bell rang and he moved to his spot at the table behind her. Class seemed to drag on forever, but mostly because Mr. Hesby kept staring at her. After class, Justin put a protective arm across her shoulder and walked her toward the door. *What’s this all about?* She wasn’t sure how to handle it. Was he being a protective friend, or—more?

She wasn’t ready for more. She wasn’t sure she wanted a protective friend either. But since friends were in short supply, she chose to go with that.

When they stepped into the hall he pulled her closer. “Where’s your next class?”

“Art.”

“I’ll walk you.”

“You don’t have to do that. I’m good.” *And please drop your arm.*

“It’s on my way.”

She nodded. Okay, this was the guy who'd rescued her. The one who'd spent the night and next day with her. But the last thing she wanted was to be seen in the hall with his arm around her. Sure, he had dimples that made her stomach flip. And yeah, he'd made a horrible ordeal bearable. And that was the problem. If she'd learned one thing in Chicago, it was that no guy ever did anything nice without expecting something in return.

Her body tensed beneath his touch.

"You okay?"

"Your arm hurts my skin," she lied.

He dropped it like he'd been burned. "I'm so sorry." They walked side by side but she was able to put some space between them. He stopped a few feet from the door to the Art room. "This is where I peel off."

Not that Ryan minded, but it was weird that he'd stop in the middle of the hall ten feet from the room. "Thanks for walking me." She made it a point to ignore those dimples and the way his hair had flopped across his forehead. She couldn't help but notice that his face had an uncomfortable, almost panicked look. "Are you okay?"

"Yeah. It's the Art room. Long story." He ran a hand through his hair, making it look even sexier. "So, I'll see you after class." He turned and practically ran from the art department.

Mr. Smith stood outside, shaking his head when he saw her. "Ryan Quinn. They did a number on you."

They? "How'd you know what happened?"

"We got an email. It must hurt."

"I've felt better."

She relaxed as soon as she entered the room, where the smell of cheap manila paper, crayons, and paint was her aromatherapy. This was her place to just be. Mr. Smith always had some weird assignment that seemed completely pointless, but somehow in the end, she was always touched by it. It was like sitting in church and feeling like the homily was just for her.

Church. How could a group of supposed good girls have turned out to be so whacked?

When class started, Mr. Smith walked around the room with his right arm folded across his chest and left elbow propped on the arm. "The theme so far this year has been focused on unlocking your creativity and finding your voice. Open your sketchpads. I had planned to have you draw where you are now—in the moment. But sometimes, I think we need to see the future to get through the day. Your assignment today is to draw your future. Don't hold back. The only rule is that you must write an artist statement first."

Ryan raised her hand. "How can we write it first? I mean, our art is an expression of what we're feeling. So how can we be free to express that, if we are confined by thoughts that aren't gelled until the piece is set free?"

"I challenge you to look at it the other way around. Writing an artist statement first gives you direction and frees you to focus in that direction. But, I'll compromise. Write your statement. After you finish your drawing, if you want to edit your statement, you can write a new one. But, I must have both."

Ryan tried to focus on her future. What did she want? What were her dreams? She knew she wanted to go to college and major in art. That was a given. She didn't want to focus on life after that. She didn't want to focus on life next year. Her future was tomorrow, next week, next month. Would her face heal? What would happen when she saw the PC girls again?

On the corner of her sketch paper she wrote:

The future is... now.

She sketched a self-portrait with her hands covering her face, her fingertips just below her eyes. Each pinky nail had a heart in the center. The other nails spelled out SURVIVOR. The fountain was in the distance behind her, where five faceless girls stood in a cross formation, their hands poised in prayer position.

Mr. Smith called time on the assignment. They held their sketchpads up for the rest of the class to critique. One of the girls had drawn herself at the Eiffel Tower, while another had drawn a fighter jet. John, the lone guy in the class, drew himself as a superhero. Mr. Smith went around the entire room discussing each drawing before he got to her. "Ryan, tell us about your work, beginning with the artist statement."

She pointed to the sketchpad. "The future is now. Umm." Heat crawled up her neck and face. "I—ah—think it's self-explanatory." She held her breath. As a class, they critiqued each other's work. Today, she didn't want to hear what they had to say.

He nodded. "That it is."

She let out a breath and the bell rang. She watched her classmates shove their sketchpads in their backpacks and hurry out of the room, but her aching arms kept her moving in slow motion. Kristen, a curly blonde who sat in the back of the class, dropped a note on her desk as she walked by. Ryan slung her backpack over her shoulder and opened the note.

It was a cartoon face covered by two hands. Painted across the fingernails of the right hand was *Slut,* and across the left, *Whore*. The air froze in her lungs.

How did she know? How many others know?

She crumpled the paper and shoved it deep into her backpack.

She felt like she was wearing ten-pound shoes as she trudged from the room. How had this all gone so wrong? So the whole school must know who she'd been in Chicago. But how? She'd removed every bit of evidence on her Facebook page. She'd un-friended all of her Chicago friends.

Justin waited in the same spot where he'd left her. Great. All she needed was to be seen with a guy—especially a hot guy with a reputation.

He smiled when he saw her. "Hey. How was class?"

She told her stomach not to flip at those dimples and gave him a half-shrug. "Okay." He walked close to her as they headed down the hall. She didn't need this—didn't want this. Everybody in school thought she was a slut. She had to do what she could to change their minds and that meant not being seen with Justin Hayes. "You don't have to walk me to class. I'm a big girl, you know. Don't need protecting." She tried to sound lighthearted, but speaking through a barely open mouth had made it sound whiny.

He gave her a sympathetic look. "I don't mind. Where do you go next?"

"Lunch." She was about to tell him that she could *really* manage without his help, when one of the PC girls who hadn't been at the fountain bumped into her going in the opposite direction. It could have been an accident—the hall was packed—except that she'd swerved to collide with Ryan shoulder to shoulder.

Justin turned and yelled at the girl, "Hey, watch it." He moved closer to her, almost hovering. Ryan gritted her teeth. How could she tell him to leave her alone? He'd saved her and apparently was still in that savior and protector mode.

Her phone signaled a text.

Kelsey: Just heard that the PC got sent to alternative school.

Ryan showed the text to Justin.

"I heard." He bent his nearly six-foot frame close to her. "Listen, Ryan—it doesn't make sense, but some people are pissed at you for this."

"Screw them." She said it with more grit than she felt. She shoved her phone in her pocket and turned away from him toward the cafeteria.

What kind of crazy place is this?

*

She'd tried to sound tough, but Justin hadn't missed the color draining from her face. Word had spread fast that the PC girls had been sent to an alternative school. He'd heard talk in the halls and it wasn't going to get any easier for Ryan. Pretty much everybody was horrified by what the girls had done to her, but there was a small group that blamed her for the PC girls' exile. A small but vicious group.

"Ryan, wait up." He caught up with her. "There are more people who think what happened was horrible."

She looked up at him and squeaked through her swollen mouth, "Well, give them a freaking gold star."

Ouch. "Just trying to help here. I'm not the enemy."

"Why do I have to have an enemy?" She opened her mouth wider when she spoke and flinched, swallowing and looking up at him with those deep blue eyes that made him want to wrap his arms around her and keep her safe from the world. "I'm sorry."

"Come on, I have to walk by the cafeteria on my way to class anyway."

They walked the rest of the way without speaking and she maintained a two-foot gap between them. He tried not to let it bug him, but it did. What happened to the girl who'd had a death grip on his hand in the emergency room?

As they neared the cafeteria, he saw Kelsey waiting for her. Standing with his arm around Kelsey was Austin McCoy. They'd had a momentary truce at the hospital, but he still couldn't stand the guy. If he hadn't texted his sister…

Two years and the anger just wouldn't go away.

Kelsey gave Justin a look that said *I've got this, so go away.* To Ryan she said, "Come on. We'll sit together."

Justin adjusted his backpack on his shoulders and turned to Ryan. "I'll see you later. Text if you need anything."

She nodded, but was already walking away with her sister and Austin. He turned toward his next class and almost ran smack into Ashley Boyd, who wrapped her hands around his arm. "Hey, cutie. Where have you been? We missed you at the afterparty Saturday night."

"Oh, yeah." He smiled down at her in full flirt mode. She was one of those girls who always wore boob-revealing shirts and liked to touch him—a lot. It was hard not to flirt, and yeah, he'd hooked up with her last summer after a party at the trestle. But that was all it had been—a summer hook-up. They'd both dated other people since, but flirting between them was like an automatic reflex.

Flirting in general was an uncontrollable response for him—except with Ryan. He sucked at flirting with her.

And then it hit him.

Was she distancing herself from him because of his reputation? He'd never given his player rep much thought. Hell, most of the guys on the football team were players. He thought of the words he'd heard thrown around in connection with Ryan. *Slut. Whore.*

Raunchy Ryan. The last thing she needed was to hang around with someone like him.

"Hey. Are you in there?" Ashley tugged on his arm. "I'm speaking to you."

"What?" He peeled Ashley off him. "Yeah, just tired."

He took a deep breath. *Okay. So I don't give up. I work to earn Ryan's trust.*

And if he was really lucky, her respect.

6

Ryan exited the food line and followed Kelsey and Austin to their table. She sat next to Kelsey, but couldn't keep her gaze from drifting a few tables away. Seeing the empty chairs where she used to sit with the Macey Brown and the other Purity Club girls made her chest tighten.

Kelsey bumped her with her elbow. "Hey, are you okay?"

"Yeah. It's just seeing all those empty seats. It's my fault those girls are gone."

"Whoa. It is not your fault. You didn't ask for what they did to you."

Ryan nodded. "I know. It's just weird to think that five girls got kicked out of school."

Kelsey's friend Shelby Cox shook her red curls. "They should be wearing orange after what they did to you. I never did like that hypocritical bunch. How can you call yourself Christians when you go around judging everybody?"

Hannah Ellis said, "My cousin is in a club kind of like the PC, but it is nothing like this one. I think they take a pledge, but they focus on more than just that. They talk to other schools about dating violence."

Kelsey wrinkled her forehead. "Is that a problem here?"

Hannah nodded. "According to her, it's a problem everywhere. They talk about dating respect, date rape, stuff like that."

Ryan had almost managed to slip a bite of the pasta through her barely open mouth when she heard the words *date rape.* The words still made her jump. Her fork clattered on her plate loudly enough for everyone to look at her. Even Austin stopped talking football with the guy across from him. "Oops." She managed a half-smile and tried to will away the heat crawling up her face.

She stabbed another piece of corkscrew pasta, focused on her food, and shut the rest of the conversation out of her brain.

Mrs. Bettis, the counselor, spoke to two girls who sat at the PC table. Whatever she said to them had them talking with their heads close together when she left. She spoke to a few other people whom Ryan had seen at the PC meetings, but weren't hard-core enough to isolate themselves from the rest of the students.

Mrs. Bettis made her way to their table and bent low next to Ryan. "We're having a PC meeting after school to discuss the situation. It's mandatory for all members, but if you'd rather not come, I'll excuse you."

"Thank you."

Mrs. Bettis straightened and patted her shoulder as she walked away.

Kelsey turned to Ryan. "Is she freaking crazy? Why would she think you'd want to come?"

Ryan sat back. "I guess she figured I had to know, since I am a member."

When they left the cafeteria, Ryan tried not to look for Justin. She wanted to be relieved that he wasn't there, but the truth was, she felt a little let down.

Kelsey walked on one side of her and Austin on the other.

"You don't have to escort me."

"It's no big deal."

Not that she didn't appreciate the support, it was just that it was... smothering. "No, seriously. You don't. I don't need babysitting. *I* need to deal with this."

"You don't have to deal with it alone."

Ryan stopped and faced her sister. "I appreciate the support. Really. Right now, I need some space."

Worry wrinkled Kelsey's forehead. "Okay. You know I'm here if you need me."

"I know. Thanks." Ryan peeled away, turned down the hall where her locker was located, and stopped. Her locker seemed to be the topic of discussion as people passed it. They would point and some even giggled.

What now? Two steps in, she figured out why. *Can't this nightmare end?*

She took a deep breath, forced an *I don't give a shit* look to her face, and marched past the gawkers to the door. Her hand trembled as she dialed the combination. She could smell the red lipstick that had formed the letters across her locker: SLUT. She pulled her Physics book from the shelf and closed it as if she hadn't noticed the word.

When she turned around the group was gone. Almost.

Justin stepped up and had smeared part of the *T* before she caught his arm. "Don't." He withdrew his hand and gave her a *why the hell not* look. "It's just a word."

She turned and wasn't sure if she wanted him to follow her or not. He did.

"That's some sick shit. At least tell the office and let them clean it up." He was behind her, so close she could almost feel his shirt.

It would be so easy to let him protect her, but it wasn't going to happen. She had to be strong. She stopped and faced him. "I can't care—if I do, it gives them power over me." Then he flashed that smile with those dimples that made her want to forget about being strong and fall into his arms.

"You're pretty amazing, Ryan Quinn."

She wasn't sure how that made her amazing or even how to respond to the compliment. So she just gave an awkward shoulder shrug. "You're obviously the only one in school with that opinion."

"I hope my opinion counts." He looked at her with those dark eyes, as though she mattered to him. That made her more nervous than opening her locker in front of onlookers. "I know you can take care of yourself. I'm here if you need me."

She couldn't respond. It was too much, too big.

She pointed down the hall with her head. "Come on." They walked side by side to her Physics class in comfortable silence.

When they got to her class, he shifted his backpack and snuck a half-hug. "I have football practice after class. I won't be able to meet you."

"It's okay. I'm good." *And I didn't ask you to.*

"I know. I—I'm an idiot. You don't need me watching over you." He played with the straps of his pack. "So you still have my number."

She nodded. "Didn't delete it."

He ducked his head. “Good.” He stood there for a couple of breaths. “I guess I’ll see you tomorrow.” He turned and headed down the hall.

God. He went from protector to awkward guy in a heartbeat. Something about that shift totally endeared him to her. “Hey, Justin.”

He turned and walked backward. “Yeah?”

“I’m glad you were there.”

He smiled as though she’d called him a hero. “Thanks.” He turned and jogged away.

*

“I’m going to the meeting.” Ryan heaved her backpack on her shoulders.

Kelsey shook her head. “Why put yourself through that? I’ll go.”

“We’ll tell you everything they say.” Mackenzie looked at her sister through bangs that almost covered her eyes. Mackenzie, the invisible girl. So quiet she tended to blend into the background. Ryan was touched that her little sister was willing to go to a meeting with a bunch of strangers on her behalf.

“It’s really sweet of you, but I have to show them that they may have knocked me down, but I’m still here.”

“I think coming to school today pretty much did that,” Kelsey said.

“Did you see my locker? Somebody is pissed that I’m here.”

Mackenzie stared at the ground. “I don’t understand how you became the bad guy in all of this.”

Ryan nodded. "Me either, which is why I'm going to that meeting. If they say something about me, I want to be there to defend myself."

Kelsey said, "Okay, we'll all go together."

Ryan was grateful for her sisters, but part of her wanted to go by herself. Having them with her made her look weaker. She slid into the classroom a few minutes later with her sisters trailing behind. Mrs. Bettis made eye contact, but didn't acknowledge her to the group. The Purity Club had about thirty members. Today, only about half that attended. As she entered, every head in the room turned toward her. So much for the stealth entry she'd planned.

But, instead of the hatred she'd expected, she saw compassion in their eyes. As she scooted past the desks, a girl with dark blonde hair touched her arm. "I'm sorry for what they did to you. That's not who we are."

"Thanks." Ryan continued to the back of the room.

Mrs. Bettis began, "Thank you all for coming on short notice. As I'm sure you've all heard, some of our members were involved in a horrible incident after the Homecoming dance Saturday night. Those girls acted on their own, not as any part of the Purity Club. Their thoughts and actions were in no way supported by this group. However, what they did was a serious event."

Kelsey whispered, "*Event?* She called it an *event*."

"Shhh," Ryan hissed.

Mrs. Bettis continued, "We have decided, at least for the rest of this year, to disband the club."

The same girl that had reached out to Ryan said, "What about our community service credits?"

"You'll get partial credit. There are plenty of other opportunities to earn what you need."

Another girl raised her hand. "Why are we being punished for what they did? It's not fair."

Pretty much everyone in the room agreed.

Mrs. Bettis held up her hands. "I understand how you feel. But we want to send a clear message that this behavior is not tolerated. It doesn't mean you can't abide by the intent of the club."

A boy who had super curly hair and wore glasses stood. Ryan knew him from Calculus class—Braden McGuire. He wasn't Mr. Football or Mr. Sports anything. But he was smart and kind and everybody liked him. "Mrs. Bettis, this club is more than just making a promise. It's a place to socialize with people who have the same values. Those girls got carried away and went totally rogue, but that was them. Not us." The group applauded. He looked back at Ryan. "I don't know your story. I don't know why they picked on you. What they did was awful, but we're all being punished."

He made a good argument. It wasn't the club. Somehow the message of the club had become twisted, but still, the disbanding wasn't Ryan's fault.

When she didn't respond to his statement, he turned back to Mrs. Bettis. "Can we work on refocusing the club?"

Most of the room nodded.

Mrs. Bettis said, "I'll discuss your suggestion with the principal. But for now, there will be no meetings." She dismissed the group.

Ryan waited for everyone to file out of the classroom before moving away from the back wall.

Braden McGuire made his way to where she stood with her sisters. "I really am sorry for what they did to you. I don't blame you for the club being disbanded." He spoke to Ryan, but his gaze kept darting to Mackenzie.

"Thanks. I understand what you meant about the club."

"The girls that did this aren't here any more. Why punish those who didn't have anything to do with it?"

According to the word scrawled across her locker, there were still Ryan-haters in school. Besides, the girls hadn't been kicked out forever. But maybe there was a way to keep the club together—just not as the Purity Club. "Have you ever heard of a high school group that teaches about dating violence?"

He dragged his gaze from Mackenzie to her. "No. Why?"

"Hannah Ellis mentioned it at lunch. Maybe that could be the new focus."

"We don't have that problem here."

Kelsey jumped in. "I bet there is more of a problem than any of us realize. You don't have to be beat up to be a victim." For half a second, Ryan wondered if Austin might have done something. But before she could completely form the question, Kelsey continued, "My ex never did a thing to me physically. But he played a lot of mind games—and that's a kind of abuse."

Ryan could have hugged her. It was obvious that Kelsey was deliriously happy with Austin, but Ryan had wondered how much crap Drew had done to her before she'd opened her eyes. To Braden she said, "I'll find out more about the group. Who knows—maybe it's what this school needs."

"Sure." His focus went back to Mackenzie. "Hi. I'm Braden McGuire."

Ryan saw Mackenzie's eyes widen beneath her bangs. She nodded. "Mackenzie Quinn."

"What year are you?"

"Freshman." Mackenzie backed up half a step.

Braden smiled. "Cool." To Ryan he said, "Let me know what you find out." He left and Mackenzie let out a breath.

Ryan smiled at her little sister. “He was flirting with you—or trying to.”

“No, he wasn’t.” Mackenzie shook her head. “Guys don’t notice me.”

Kelsey put a hand on Mackenzie’s shoulder. “Yeah, they do. You just can’t see them while you’re hiding behind those bangs.”

“That’s crazy.” Mackenzie headed for the door as though the classroom was the last place she wanted to be.

Ryan smiled. It was nice to see something positive happen for her sister.

*

The girls climbed into the beat-up blue truck that Kelsey drove. After school, Ryan and Mackenzie worked at their dad’s feed store and Kelsey either worked a shift at the Early Bird Café or at the store. Today they were all working at the store.

Ryan was exhausted and her face hurt. Some of the sores had crusted with a yellowish scab, others oozed watery yuck. She looked like something from a bad zombie movie. Her brain was fried and she was tired of acting like none of it bothered her. The last thing she wanted to do was smile in front of customers.

“Do you think Mom would let you take me home before you go to the store?”

Kelsey started the engine. “Text her.”

Ryan pulled her phone from her purse and tapped out the question. Across the parking lot, the guys were heading from the field house to the practice field. Most of them walked in groups. Justin didn’t. He lagged behind the others. Did he have friends on the team? She’d always figured that if you were on the football team or the basketball team or the whatever team, you were automatically part of a group. But not one guy spoke to Justin as they passed him. She'd seen him hang out with Eric Perez, but the fight at the dance had ended that friendship. That could explain why he was so interested in hanging out with her. But if he wanted friends, he could pick someone whose face didn't look like it'd been run through a vegetable peeler.

Her phone dinged a reply. She read it and turned to Kelsey. "She said we could all go home. The store's been slow all day."

Mackenzie squealed from the back seat. "Yay! I'm going for a long run."

Ryan turned to her sister. "You know there's something wrong with you, right? Nobody in their right mind says that."

Mackenzie brushed her hair from her eyes. "You should try it. It's a great way to just think."

"So is feeding the animals." Kelsey pulled from the parking lot.

"Those chickens are the spawn of the devil."

Ryan twisted in her seat to look back at her sister. "Kenzie, we've been here for months. How can you still be so afraid of the chickens?"

"They peck at things—like feet."

"All you have to do is shoo them away."

"You and Kelsey can have fun with the chickens, the horses, and that pig. Not me. I'd rather clean toilets every day than risk my life with those critters."

Kelsey hadn't liked feeding chickens at first, either, or she said she hadn't. But Ryan had watched her talking to them when she fed them or cleaned the coop. And Ryan was pretty sure her sister had bonded with Winifred, the pig. Ryan could take or leave the chickens and the pig. She thought the two horses were pretty cool, though. She liked to watch Austin ride. Someday, she'd like to learn, but Austin should probably teach Kelsey first, since he was her boyfriend and all.

Ryan's escape was art. Whether it was to express the turmoil churning inside her or to escape it, drawing gave her peace. It centered her.

Kelsey stopped at the gate that crossed the dirt drive that led to their house. "Who's the gate bitch?"

Mackenzie opened her door. "I've got it."

Wow. A few months ago we didn't even know what a gate bitch was. She looked at the peeling paint on the old farmhouse. It was hard to believe they used to ride the "L" home or that they'd hang out at Millennium Park.

Wasn't this supposed to be the simple life? She rubbed her arms. She'd been excited to get away from that old life, but had she really traded it for a better one? At least one sister was happier. She wasn't sure about Mackenzie, who'd had to give up gymnastics. It had to be a huge adjustment to fill all those hours she'd spent in the gym. She never complained, though. She wouldn't—she was too busy trying to be the perfect kid.

Was it better for Ryan? She'd exchanged one pain for another. She touched her cheek. This one she couldn't hide.

Kelsey parked and the girls didn't waste time getting out of the truck. Mackenzie ran up the porch steps and into the house, but Kelsey waited for Ryan. "Are you okay? Really? Today had to be rough for you."

Ryan nodded. "I got it over with. Not everybody hates me. Justin waits for me after most of my classes."

"Yeah, what's up with that? You know he's crazy."

Ryan gazed at her sister. "He saved me."

Kelsey rolled her eyes as she opened the front door. "Okay. I'll give him that. But you know he jumped Austin in the parking lot. I was there. It was totally unprovoked."

Ryan scooted through the doorway and let the screen bang shut behind her. "There had to be a reason. No normal person would just randomly jump someone."

"We were walking to Austin's truck, when out of the blue, Justin tackled him. That is not normal."

Ryan had to admit that the whole incident was bizarre. But the Justin who'd rescued her was not the same guy who'd attacked Austin. "There had to be a reason," she repeated stubbornly.

"Yeah. He's insane." She dropped her backpack at the bottom of the stairs.

Ryan slung her backpack next to Kelsey's. "He's not. He's sweet and caring."

"Pu-leeze, Ryan. He got kicked out of the Homecoming dance for fighting with Eric Perez."

"Again, he had to have a good reason. Look, all I know is how he treats me. And he treats *me* really nice."

Kelsey shook her head. "He's got a lot of baggage. You can do better."

"God, Kel. We're friends. End of story." Ryan grabbed her pack and ran upstairs to her room. Just when she thought they were getting close, Kelsey had to go all judgy on her. She wasn't sure she wanted to hang out with Justin, but she sure didn't want her sister telling her she shouldn't. Besides, the Justin she knew wasn't crazy. That Justin was kind and gentle. But that Justin was also hot and made her want be more than friends.

She dropped onto her bed and grabbed the throw folded at the end, pulled it over her, and closed her eyes. She didn't want to think about it. Any of it. But Justin's face kept popping into her mind.

Damn it. He was trouble. Big trouble.

7

After a grueling football practice, all Justin wanted was to see Ryan or at least talk to her. Yeah, he was freaking crazy. They weren't a thing. But she was amazing. After the hell she'd gone through, she'd faced everybody with a *bring it on* attitude.

Still, he worried. As strong and freaking mind-blowing as she was, she was not invincible. Maybe it was just a feeling he had, but for a second, he'd seen a look in her eyes that frightened him. The look he saw in his mom every day.

Helplessness. Hopelessness. Drowning.

He shook the thought away. Ryan needed to fight. It would keep her from going to that bad place. He'd stand by and let her. And if she stumbled, he wanted to be the one who pulled her to her feet and let her enter the ring again. Would she let him? She had his cell number, but she hadn't offered hers.

Patience. Right now, it was about earning her trust.

He parked in front of his house and hope flickered. The blinds in the front window were open. Was Mom having a good day?

He pushed through the front door and called, "Mom! I'm home." When she didn't answer, he headed toward the bedroom. "Mom?" She wasn't curled up in bed. His heart began to beat a little faster as he made his way through the house. Things didn't feel right. He headed toward his sister's room. God, he hoped she wasn't in there. He'd found her there once before wrapped in Chelsea's bathrobe and hugging her stuffed bear. He knocked on the door. "Mom?" He listened for sounds of despair coming from behind the door. Nothing.

He cracked the door and peeked into the room. Empty. He opened the door wide and stepped inside. He hadn't been in her room in months. His mom didn't do much with the rest of the house, but she kept Chelsea's room clean. An extra-large Taco Bell cup stuffed with various sizes and shapes of paintbrushes sat on the corner of her desk next to a plastic storage box bulging with twisted tubes of paint. Her portfolio case leaned against the side of the desk. It was all so surreal, as if she might walk into the room any second and start a new project.

He slid the portfolio case from the side of the desk, laid it on the carpet in the center of the room, and carefully opened the cover. Sketches of high school life filled the case. The first drawing was of a football game viewed from the stands. Cheerleaders were stacked in a pyramid while players fought to move the ball forward in the background. There was a drawing of girls huddled around a locker, giggling. The looks on their faces made him want to know their secret. His muscles tensed as he turned to the next sketch. He hated this one.

Austin McCoy stared back at him with a shit-eating grin on his face.

Justin closed the case and propped it against the desk, trying to replicate its exact position. Otherwise, his mom would freak.

He turned to leave and froze. She stood in the doorway with her fingertips pressed to her mouth. She was dressed and her hair was fixed. She seemed to be having a good day—maybe this wouldn't spin her out of control.

"Mom, I'm sorry. I was just looking…"

"It's okay… it's just seeing that boy." Justin hoped to lead her out of the bedroom, but instead, she sat on the bed.

"I know. Let me take the picture out of the case. I won't mess it up, I'll just put it where you don't have to see it."

"No. I mean I saw him at the cemetery."

"What?"

"He was there, at her grave, and there was a girl with him. I've seen him there before, but this time he had a girl with him."

"When was this, Mom?"

"A few weeks ago, before school started. Why would he bring a girl there?"

Justin took a deep breath to calm his nerves. Not exactly a hot spot for a date. But now the important thing was to keep his mom from unraveling. He sat next to her, put an arm across her shoulders, and guided her to stand. "Come on, Mom. Don't worry about him. Let's go to the den and I'll fix you something to eat. You look nice—did you go out today?"

She nodded. "I went to the store. I could use some help unloading."

Relief spread through him. *She went to the store! This is a good day.* "I'll unload and you can make sure I put things where you want them."

She looked at each of the paintings that hung on the walls, the bookshelf, the desk, and the dresser. Justin could see the war that raged inside her. She was on the verge of slipping back into the depression that held her captive. "Mom?"

Slowly, she smiled. "Don't worry. I'm okay today."

She needed help. Why couldn't his dad see it? He followed her out of the room. As soon as they were in the hallway, he closed the door. "Have you eaten today?"

"I had lunch with some of the girls from the hospital. They want me to come back."

"It might be good for you to go back to work. I'll be leaving in a couple of years..." *And who will take care of you then?*

"It's something to think about." Her words were vacant—space fillers. Say anything to keep from talking. Avoid emotion, avoid affection, and above all, avoid living.

He was sick of living in the house of gloom. He'd coaxed his mom through almost every waking hour to keep her from retreating to the darkness. His dad ignored the situation at home by working extra shifts at the hospital. Frustration tensed Justin's muscles. This was not supposed to be his freaking life.

"I'll get the groceries." He pushed through the screen door onto the porch. *Chelsea may be dead, but I'm still here and I'm tired of being your freaking parent.* He pulled the bags from the back of her SUV and slammed the lid.

His mom held the screen open for him as he lugged his load through the door. As soon as he dropped the bags on the counter, she began to unpack them. Guilt at being angry with her settled in.

"I've got this, Justin. Go do your homework and I'll call you when dinner is ready."

"You're cooking?" She was good today. He should hold on to that.

"I know it's hot, but I thought spaghetti."

"It's never too hot for your spaghetti. Are you sure you don't want help?"

"I'm good, really." She flashed a weak smile and even though there was a little quiver in the corner, he'd take it.

He retreated to his room and settled in to kill some zombies before starting his Calculus homework. He couldn't get the vision of Austin McCoy bringing a girl to Chelsea's grave out of his mind. What kind of game was he playing? Three girls had lost their lives because of him. Leave it to Austin to figure out how to take advantage of that. He pretended each zombie was Austin, but it didn't make him feel any better. He would never get his family back no matter how many zombies he destroyed.

He set the controller aside and picked up his Calc book, but he couldn't focus.

Later. He tossed his homework aside and made his way to the kitchen. His mom looked almost back to normal, stirring the sauce with a wooden spoon. Salad fixings were laid out on the counter next to a bowl and a cutting board.

Justin washed his hands and began to chop mushrooms. "Is Dad going to be home for dinner?"

"If he gets off on time." She'd barely spoken the words when his dad came in through the garage door.

"Umm, I thought I smelled spaghetti." He tossed his keys on the counter and took a seat at the bar.

Before the family had been torn apart, his dad would have kissed his mom when he came in. But at least they were all in the same room, speaking. Usually they moved around the house like three strangers trying to stay out of each other's way.

His dad reached across the counter and stole a carrot from the salad. "I heard you went to lunch with the girls."

Justin saw a smile form on his mom's lips, but it looked awkward, as though she didn't want it there. "Yes. We went to Lady May's Tea Room."

"How was it?"

"Nice. They want me to come back to work. There's an opening in Day Surgery."

Justin saw hope in his dad's eyes. "And?"

She turned away from her sauce and bit her lip. "I don't know, Alan."

His dad rubbed his eyes. "I'm going to change before dinner." He slid from the bar stool and headed down the hall to the bedroom.

Justin's mom turned toward the stove, but he didn't miss that she swiped tears from her eyes. He set the knife down and went to his parents' room.

His dad had changed into shorts and was pulling a polo shirt over his head.

"Really, Dad?"

"What?"

"She's trying. She's thinking about going back and instead of encouraging her, you just walk out."

"We've been down this road before."

"So, keep going down it. When Chelsea and I were little you taught us never to give up. You said if it's important to us, we had to keep trying."

"I'm not the one who's given up."

"Dad, she's trying. Can't you see her struggle? *Help* her."

His dad slid his feet into flip-flops and shuffled out of the room without saying a word. Justin had to get out of the house before he exploded. Screw dinner, he needed space from his parents. He grabbed his keys.

As he neared the kitchen, he saw that his mom had taken his place chopping vegetables for the salad. His dad stood next to her and said, "Sandy, I'm sorry. Let's talk about it."

His mom nodded and his dad pulled her close to his side—it was an awkward movement, but it was a start. Justin returned his keys and finished helping with dinner. And for the first time in too long, they sat at the table as a family.

His dad pulled a piece of garlic bread from the loaf and asked, "How was practice?"

"McCoy hit all of his passes in practice."

At the name McCoy, Justin's mom set her fork on her plate. The air grew tense and Justin could see that she was on the verge of unraveling. *Shit. He had to go and say the name.* He willed her to hold it together. But he knew the meltdown had begun.

"That boy, McCoy, has been at the cemetery. I saw him with a girl…"

Justin's dad put his hand over hers. "It's okay, Sandy."

"Why would he bring a girl there?" Tears filled her eyes.

Justin waited for his dad to leave the table. That was his MO—run from conflict.

But this time he didn't. He looked at Justin and said, "I've got this."

Part of Justin wanted to take care of his mom—after all, he wasn't sure his dad knew how to handle her. The other part of him felt relief. It was about time Dad manned up.

Justin set his plate on the kitchen counter and retreated to his bedroom.

He tried to concentrate on his homework, but his mind lingered on Ryan Quinn. Before the attack, he'd thought she had one of the most beautiful faces he'd ever seen. It was perfect. A petite nose with freckles sprinkled across the top. A mouth with a full lower lip that gave her a sexy-pouty look… and her eyes. God, he could get lost in those cobalt eyes. They were wide and full of fire.

His stomach burned when he thought about what those bitches had done to her. It was beyond cruel. What if her face scarred? How would he feel about her? He'd like to think it wouldn't matter, that it was the girl on the inside he was attracted to. The shameful truth was that he wasn't sure if he'd feel the same. He didn't really know Ryan well enough to know what was on the inside. He smiled when he thought of how she'd handled the message on her locker. She was brave—probably the bravest person he knew. What if her face was messed up for life and he couldn't handle it? He felt like a jerk just asking himself that question.

His dad knocked on his open door. "Hey, your mom and I are going for a drive."

"Is she okay?"

"Yeah. We're just going to get out of the house for a few—maybe get some ice cream."

"Cool." Justin refused to let hope burn in his chest. Things could fall apart in the next breath.

"Do you want to go?"

"Naw. I have homework to do." *And Ryan to get off my mind.* "Hey, Dad?"

"Yeah?"

"Do you think Ryan's face will scar?"

His dad stepped into the room and sat on the edge of the bed. "Some of the abrasions are pretty deep."

"English."

"The scrapes on her face. The deep ones might scar." He steepled his fingers. "I'm more worried about her lip. How is she doing?"

"She was at school today. Somebody wrote the word *slut* on her locker."

"Christ. What did she do to get on the wrong side of the mean girls?"

Justin shook his head. "I don't know. Macey Brown got it in her head that she was evil. You should have seen her, Dad. When I carried Ryan out of the fountain, Macey looked at me like she was possessed."

"Her dad is a real head case."

"He hit her." Justin rubbed the back of his neck. "When we were at the Quinns'. Macey confessed to what she did and he hit her so hard it knocked her down." He told his dad about how Mr. Brown left Macey and her mom and nobody would give them a ride home.

"So did anybody report Brown for hitting Macey?"

Justin shrugged. "We were all in shock when it happened and then we focused on Ryan."

"Jesus. Did they really walk all the way home?"

"I heard that one of the moms picked them up." He looked at his dad. "Macey has a screwed-up home life, no doubt. But she didn't have to rip up Ryan's face."

"That was just heinous." His dad stood. "Are you sure you don't want to come?"

Justin nodded. "Yeah." When his parents had gone, he clicked on his Facebook page. Ryan was on too.

Justin: How're you feeling?

Ryan: Tired. Sore.

Justin: Anything I can do?

Ryan: Got a TARDIS?

Justin: A what?

Ryan: It's a Dr. Who thing. A time machine.

Justin: Who is Dr. Who?

Ryan: That's the question. LOL It's a British TV show full of awesomeness.

Justin: I'll have to check it out.

Ryan: If you're cool, you will.

Justin: :) Oh, I'm cool.

Ryan: Don't make me laugh, it hurts.

Justin: Okay, I'm totally uncool.

It was great to hear her so lighthearted and he hoped like hell that if scars were left on her face, they wouldn't take that away from her.

Justin: How's the lip?

Ryan: Messed up. I'm going to the doctor tomorrow morning. I won't be in school until after lunch.

Justin: Want to go to the art gallery with me after I get out of practice tomorrow?

Ryan: We have an art gallery?

Justin: Spring Creek does. It's only twenty minutes from here.

Ryan: You're not embarrassed to be seen with me?

Justin: I should ask you that question.

Ryan: Yes, I'm horribly embarrassed for people to see my messed-up self with you.

Justin: That's not what I meant.

Ryan: I know. Yes. I'll go with you to the art gallery.

Justin: Great. I'm out by five.

Ryan: Pick me up at the feed store. I gotta go.

Justin: Bye.

He closed Facebook and sighed. Yes! He had a date with Ryan Quinn. And no, he wasn't embarrassed to be seen with her.

Besides, hardly anybody he knew ever went to the tiny gallery in Spring Creek.

8

Ryan tried not to pace while she waited for Justin. Why had she agreed to go the gallery with him? It had been a horrible day, her face hurt almost as bad as it had the first day, and now it had gooey ointment smeared all over it. If she didn't scare him off at the door, it would be a small miracle.

She looked toward the back of the store. Her parents discussed rearranging the horse section while Mackenzie and Kelsey unloaded feed sacks onto the racks. She manned the cash register—which meant she'd rung up exactly two transactions since school ended.

Justin's black truck pulled into the parking lot and she called to her mom, "My ride is here. I'll see you later."

She almost made it to the door before she was stopped. "Wait a minute," Mom called. "Let me give you some money."

"That's okay. I have some." Ryan moved closer to the door.

"Who are you going with again?"

"I told you, a friend from schoo—" Which was as far as she got before Justin came through the door. *Crap.*

Her parents moved to the front of the store together, and her dad spoke. “Hello, Justin.”

“Mr. Quinn.” He stuck out his hand.

Her dad shook his hand, but it was obvious he was not happy. He turned to Ryan and said, “Can I see you in the back room?”

She nodded and followed her parents to the makeshift kitchen in the back of the store. Her dad leaned against the counter. “I’m not opposed to you going to a gallery with a date…”

“He’s not a date.” *Please don’t make this a big deal.*

Her dad straightened. “Whatever it is, I don’t like that you didn’t tell your mother or me.”

“It’s not like I lied. I said I was going with a friend. Justin is a friend who happens to be a boy.” *And the only friend I have, by the way.*

Her mom looked at her dad. “Let it go, Tom. She needs an evening away from all that’s happened.”

Her dad pulled a twenty from his billfold and handed it to her. “Home by ten, not one minute later.”

“Yes, sir.” She took the twenty and hurried out, but as soon as she stepped from the back room, she could feel the tension in the air.

Kelsey stood close to Justin by the cash register. Her arms were crossed and whatever she was saying to him, her expression told Ryan it wasn’t nice.

Ryan glared at her sister. “What’s going on?”

Kelsey turned to Ryan. “I was just giving Justin a little advice.” The tone of her sister’s voice pegged the pissed-off meter.

“You’re unbelievable.” She grabbed Justin’s hand and blew out a breath. “FYI, Kels—next time you want to get all sanctimonious, you might want to hide that big honking hickey first.”

Her sister pressed her collar against her neck and flushed.

Ryan didn't stick around to see her recovery. She dragged Justin out the door and down the rickety wooden steps. "God, I can't stand it when she gets like that. What did she say, anyway?"

"That if I hurt you, she'd clip my balls with a butter knife."

Ryan slid to a stop in the gravel driveway and dropped his hand. "She *what?*"

He put his palms up. "Honest to God. That's what she said."

Ryan couldn't help the slow smile that crossed her face or the heat that accompanied it. "That's awkward."

"Tell me about it." He put his hand on the back of her neck and walked her the rest of the way to his truck.

Once they were on the road to Spring Creek, he asked the question she'd been expecting. "How'd the doctor's appointment go?"

"Well, I guess you probably noticed my new look." She flashed him a fake grin. "He cleansed my face, and by *cleansed* I mean *scrubbed.* It was brutal. Then they spread this gross antibiotic gel all over. On the upside, it doesn't hurt my mouth to talk now. He looked at my lip. When every thing else heals, he wants to see it again." She studied her hands and refused to give in to the tears that struggled for release. "I might have to have cosmetic repair done to my mouth. I'll have scars, but he won't know how bad until I heal."

She watched Justin squeeze the steering wheel until his knuckles were almost white. "I wish I'd gotten there sooner."

"I wish I'd never met them. But I did and what happened, happened." She shrugged with more indifference than she felt. "So now I learn to live with a new face."

"You have a perfect face." He smiled and it even looked real. Her dad had said those exact words, but the sadness in his eyes betrayed his true feelings.

"I think the goo gives it an extra special glow." She flashed one cheek and then the other at him.

"Definitely."

*

This girl is amazing. After all she's been through, she jokes. And she holds my hand.

Justin felt stupid over getting excited about that, but he was. She was unlike anybody he'd ever met and he didn't want to screw it up.

Silence grew in the truck and even Eric Church singing about his hometown couldn't dissipate the awkwardness. When they finally neared the gallery, he gave her a wink. "Are you ready for Spring Creek's big gallery?"

"So, how did a town as small as Spring Creek end up with an art gallery?"

"It's not exactly the Tate."

"The Tate? You know it?"

Score one for small-town boy. "Well, I've never been to London, so I've never seen it. But I know it's supposed to be pretty cool."

"We went during spring break a couple of years ago. My parents don't get modern art, but I thought it was fantastic. The first room we entered had this huge canvas, the size of a wall. The beauty was in the strokes, the color changes, and the texture. It was so deep, and rich, and big that it pulled you into it." She closed her eyes for a couple of seconds and gave a deep sigh. "It was one of those pieces that you could just feel. Then Dad turned to Mom and said, 'We can throw red paint on a wall and call it art.' I was so embarrassed."

"Yeah, don't expect anything that spectacular here." He parked against the curb in front of the gallery. Next to the door was a cat sculpted from car parts.

The gallery was narrow, maybe twenty feet across. Pottery was displayed on a three-tiered wooden shelf that stretched the length of the space. "These are cool." She pointed to a row of jugs that had faces on them.

"Those are by an artist named Block. He's a local guy."

Some of the jug faces grimaced like gargoyles, while others grinned with an I've got a secret expression. The colors were bold, matching the attitude of the pieces. At the end of the row was a squat green-glazed pitcher covered in eyes. "This is awesome. The piece is studying the viewer. We become a part of the exhibit. I'd like to read his artist statement."

A thin, gray-haired woman appeared from behind a curtain in the back of the gallery. "Hi, I thought I heard somebody come in." Her eyes grew slightly larger when she saw Ryan, but she seemed more interested in Justin. She patted him on the shoulder. "It's been too long, Justin."

Ryan gave him a questioning look and he knew he'd have to explain his knowledge of art. But that would come later. He nodded. "Yes, ma'am."

She turned to Ryan. "The artist once said he allowed the jugs to decide what to become. Welcome to our little gallery. Let me know if I can help with anything—I'm wrestling with a frame in the back." She turned to Justin again, her face drawn, her eyes heavy with sorrow. "It's good to see you."

Justin mumbled, "Thanks." The woman retreated to the room behind the curtain.

The atmosphere turned heavy. “So, who is this guy who frequents small-town galleries, knows about a gallery on the other side of the pond, yet won’t walk all the way to the art room?”

“It’s a long story.” And time to change the subject. “What do you think so far?”

“It’s interesting. I never expected to see these face jugs.” She turned toward the pictures hanging on the walls. Most of them were old renderings of the courthouse or the shops around the square. As she studied them, he watched. Her expression said they were good, but not unique. Then, she noticed a soft light illuminating a picture in a dark corner at the back of the gallery. As she moved toward it, dread built in him.

In that moment, he knew bringing her here had been a colossal mistake.

*

Ryan was mesmerized by the painting.

It was of three football players from the perspective of inside the huddle. They held hands with their heads bowed, and their pained expressions could be seen behind the facemasks. Mud and grass stains smeared their uniforms. The sky above them was dark and angry and the scoreboard behind them indicated the final score was seven to zero. Ryan waited for the rest of the story to unfold. Were the players the winners? The pain in their eyes seemed much deeper than anything caused by a losing score. Had they suffered injuries?

She turned to speak to Justin, but he’d walked to the other end of the gallery. The gray-haired woman came out of the back room and stood next to her. “It’s fascinating, isn’t it? I moved it back here after the accident. It sort of keeps her with me.”

Accident? “Who’s the artist?”

“Oh, I assumed you knew. See here.” She pointed to the signature: *C. Hayes*. “Chelsea. Justin’s sister.”

“Sister?” She heard the door rattle and watched him step outside. Her heart beat a little faster. “The one who was killed in the car wreck?”

“Oh, it was terrible. Our precious Chelsea was the driver.”

The appreciation he had for art—the emotion she’d seen in his eyes when he talked about it—all came from his sister. Why hadn’t he told her? She was bound to find out somehow. If he hadn’t wanted her to know, why had he brought her to the gallery?

The woman wrung her hands and looked at Ryan. “The family hasn’t been the same since. Poor Justin. He and Chelsea were thick as thieves. He’s been a little lost without his sister, full of anger… but he’s a good kid.”

Why are you telling me this? I’m just a friend. I don’t need to know these things. I don’t need to know his secrets.

Ryan looked toward the door. “I’d better go…”

The woman followed her. “I hope you come back. It would be nice if you could bring Justin.”

“Thanks. I’ll try.” She had to get outside. Had to find him.

She didn’t have to look far. He sat on a metal bench that had been bolted to the sidewalk halfway between the gallery and the store next to it. He leaned forward, his elbows on his knees.

So, now what? God, this is so awkward.

She practically tiptoed to the bench. He didn’t move a muscle—even his eyes seemed fixed. She took a shaky breath and sat next to him. She hugged her purse to her, swallowed, and waited for him to speak.

Nothing. He didn't move.

She should say something. What? She released the hold she had on her purse and rested her hand on the seat of the bench. She practiced in her head what she could say.

I'm sorry about your sister. Do you want to talk about it? No. If he had wanted to talk about it, he would've. *I'm sorry about your sister. She was such a good artist—and now she's dead.* No! You idiot. How about: *Would you freaking talk to me? You're the one who suggested we come. You're the one who brought me here.*

She looked at him and looked away. She tried to form words in her throat, but it felt a little like it was collapsing.

He broke the silence with a deep sigh and leaned back. He rubbed the palms of his hands on his jeans and then grabbed Ryan's hand. He curled his fingers around hers, drew it across his lap, and cupped it with his other hand. It didn't feel like a flirty move, or a prelude to a kiss.

He was holding on for dear life.

At first, her muscles tensed, numbing her to the feel of his skin next to hers. But then, something crazy happened.

Warmth from his hand beckoned her to relax. And as it radiated into hers, she let go. Her fingers and palm melted into his. Her chest filled with grief, sorrow, anger, and all the horrible unspoken emotions that a human can endure. But they weren't his emotions.

They were all hers.

Shame for the embarrassment and hurt she'd caused her family. Self-loathing for what she'd done. Anger at the girls who'd attacked her. They poured from her heart, and it was okay, because she had a lifeline too.

They sat on the bench, not speaking, hanging on to the world, their souls connecting through clasped hands until the sky slowly turned pink.

Finally, he looked at her and said, "Are you ready?"

She nodded and together they stood, their hands still clasped. He didn't acknowledge her tears, nor she his.

He hesitated before he opened the passenger door of his truck, and looked into her eyes. Any other time, she would have expected a kiss. But he wouldn't kiss her. Not now, maybe never. But what had passed between them was way bigger than a kiss. They were lost and broken, neither really knowing the other's story. Where that left their friendship was bound to be as bizarre as what had blossomed there on the bench.

*

He wiped the remnants of his tears away with his forearm and pretended not to notice her fish a Kleenex out of her purse to wipe her eyes. If Mrs. Walters hadn't walked up, he'd have probably been okay. But as soon as she started telling Ryan about that painting, he'd had to get out of there.

Just leaving the gallery wasn't enough. The pain and sorrow threatened to pull him into that dark place that held his mom. He needed to feel something alive to remind him not to go there. So he'd done the only thing he could—he'd held Ryan's hand and fought his way back. He hadn't expected the emotions that passed between them. She had hung on to him, too. Her tears weren't for him; she carried her own set of mental luggage.

He watched her dab hopelessly at the mascara under her eyes. "Do you want to talk about it?"

"No. Do you?"

"No." Thank God she didn't want to talk. Whatever the hell that had been, it was way bigger than saving her from the fountain.

The last thing he wanted to do was analyze it. "Wanna get a coke?"

"Yeah."

He started the engine and pulled away from the curb. Neither spoke as he made his way to the drive-in. He angled into a slot and shifted into Park. "What do you want to drink?"

"Cherry vanilla Dr. Pepper."

He pushed the red button below the sign and turned to her. "Do you want to share chili cheese fries?"

"Sure."

He gave the order and the mood in the truck began to lighten. A Beatles tune played over the drive-in's speakers. Ryan lowered her window and sang along. If anyone could take a sad song and make it better, it was Ryan. She didn't have a great voice or anything, but he liked it.

While they waited for their order, they didn't talk, didn't really look at each other, but it was okay. His chest felt lighter than it had in a long time and he was happy. Not the fake smile he forced on his face to get through the day, but genuine, from-the-gut happy. When the two dozen repetitions of the chorus began, he joined in.

As they progressed, they got louder. They didn't look at each other or do any crazy music swaying. They sat in their places with their heads pressed against the back of the seat and sang. Their food arrived just before Paul McCartney broke into the final riff.

Justin sat the boat of fries on the console between them and passed Ryan her drink. The moment he made the handoff was the first time their eyes actually met. They held and he felt an enormous geeky grin form on his face. It was okay, though, because she had the same goofy grin. Then, they both started laughing like somebody had just told the most awesome joke ever. And it felt so good, like the first bite into a cold watermelon on a long, hot summer day.

Ryan looked at him again and shook her head. "Your sister's art—wow."

"Yeah. She volunteered at the gallery after school. They have a studio in the back room where she worked on her paintings." He didn't talk about Chelsea, ever. So why did it feel safe with Ryan now?

"I'm sorry. What happened—it just sucks."

"That it does." He crammed a couple of cheesy fries in his mouth and watched her pick one up and take two bites to eat it. He thought about the emotion pouring from her as they'd sat on the bench. Had it been connected to the attack? Somehow it felt bigger. He wanted to reach out to her and convince her she could trust him. "What happened back there—it was more than... Did you lose somebody?"

She snapped her gaze to him. "What?"

"I felt it..."

She looked through the windshield and shifted in the seat. He shouldn't have asked. A tear slipped from the corner of her eye and his heart began to pound in his chest. He should have left it alone.

She tilted her head up and sniffed. "Yeah. Me."

"What?" Crap. He didn't mean to say that. He didn't want to know, if it was going to make her cry. Where was the edit button?

Her gaze darted to him and back to the view in front. Her chest rose and fell as though she couldn't get enough air. "I lost me." She closed her eyes and slowed her breathing. "If you ask me to talk about it, I *will* throw my drink at you."

"Well, shit. Do you like football?"

She opened her eyes, perplexed. “What? What kind of question is that?”

“I don’t know. You scared the shit out of me.” He took a drink from his coke and twisted in his seat toward her. “Do you?”

She sat cross-legged in the seat with her back against the door. “I’ve only been to two games.”

He threw his head back and stared at the headliner of his truck. “Seriously!” He dropped his gaze then, grateful they were on a lighter topic. “How can you be in high school and only have been to two games?”

“I went to an art magnet school, remember?”

He shook his head. “Crazy. So what’d you think?”

“Actually, I liked it.” Ryan pointed to the dash clock. “Is that the right time? Because if it is, I have twenty-five minutes to make my ten o’clock curfew.”

“We’ll make it.”

Justin gathered the trash and started the engine. “So, the Purity Club.”

“Yeah?”

“Can you explain it to me? Why a *virgin* club?”

“It wasn’t a bad idea. We made a promise to stay chaste. It just all went horribly wrong.”

Justin turned onto the main drag and headed south out of town. “But what are meetings all about? It’s one thing to make a promise, but do you discuss near misses at the meetings?”

She shook her head. “Yeah, that’s it.” She looked at him with those big blue eyes. “Of course not. Besides, a near miss is a hit.”

He laughed at her joke but he wanted to get lost in her gaze, to hold her against him—and not in an I’m-coming-unwound kind of way. “But what do you *do* at those meetings?”

“I’ve only been to a couple. Mrs. Bettis gives an incredibly long blessing and then we eat disgusting pizza. I guess the purpose is to encourage each other. Not everybody knows it’s okay to say no.”

“Most of the girls in the PC don’t have to worry about it.”

“That’s cold. Don’t be a jerk.”

He held his hands up in defense. “Just sayin’.”

“Yeah, but some girls get crazy when it comes to guys. Everybody says *just say no*, but if a girl is desperate to be liked, things happen.” She slammed the back of her head against the seat. “I can’t believe I am discussing this with a guy.”

His gut clenched. He had a reputation in school, but in reality, he’d gone all the way with a grand total of one girl. Had she wanted to say no? No way. When things started happening, she couldn’t wait to go all the way. “Not every girl is like that. Some girls go after it—they want it as bad as guys do.”

“I’m not so sure. I mean, maybe for some couples it’s right. But what girl wants to be known as the school slut?”

“Every school has a girl who doesn’t say no.”

“Maybe she doesn’t know she can.”

He’d never thought about it like that. A guy’s MO was to keep trying until the girl gave in. Sneak a hand on the side of the boob, it gets pushed away, try again. Until the girl actually says no, it’s fair game. His shoulders felt heavy. He’d gotten to various bases with different girls. Had they wanted to say no? He remembered the note he’d found in Chelsea’s room. How many times had Eric tried before she gave in?

“You okay?”

“Yeah, just wrapping my brain around what you said. Guys are dogs.”

“Pretty much.” She nodded.

"Did you hear what the fight with Eric was about?" He squeezed the steering wheel.

"No."

"I found a note in my sister's room a couple of days before the dance. It was to Eric. She was begging him to talk to her. He'd had sex with her at the trestle and then dumped her. My best friend effed my sister." He shook his head. "When I confronted him, he laughed. He said, 'Dude, we were sophomores back then. I was going to score with someone. She won the ticket.' Can you believe that guy?" He shook his head. "The note was dated the day before she died."

"I'm sorry, Justin."

He gave a fake shiver. "Let's change the subject. I'm starting to feel guilty for holding your hand."

"I didn't say no."

"You could've."

"No. I couldn't have."

She reached across the console and his hand met hers halfway. The emotion of what had passed between them squeezed his heart. They held onto each other with a white-knuckled grip. Something scary was building between them. A bond composed of secrets and sorrow.

He hated that it was time to go. He wanted to know her better. He wanted her to know that part of him that was still a nice guy. He liked her sarcasm. He liked her strength. She hadn't shrunk into the corner when he'd asked her who she'd lost. She was a fighter and he had no doubt that if he'd pressed her for more, she really would have thrown her coke at him.

He gave her hand a squeeze and she squeezed back. The air in the truck grew heavy, but not with the unspoken sorrow it had held before. It was a good kind of heavy. The kind that came from two people who were waiting for that moment when they could kiss.

When he turned down the dirt drive leading to the house, she let go of his hand, and his heart sank a little. He parked in front of the house and his heart sank a little more. Her parents sat on the porch.

He opened his door and Ryan gave him a panicked look. "What are you doing?"

"Walking you to the door."

"You don't have to do that." Before he had a chance to get out of the truck, she beelined up the porch steps and past her parents. She tossed a "'Night, Justin," over her shoulder and ran into the house.

He gave her parents a little wave and backed away, inhaling the flowery smell of her perfume that still hung in the air.

Shit. No hug, no kiss, not even a freaking handshake. He smiled. *But she held my hand.*

9

Ryan didn't wait for her parents to come in before running upstairs. If they wanted to ask questions, they could come to her room. Nothing had happened. At least, nothing physical. On an emotional level, her world had been officially rocked. Justin was the most confusing, complex, amazing guy she'd ever met.

She had already changed into her sleep shorts when she heard her parents come in downstairs. There would be questions, no doubt. She took her time washing her face, applying fresh gel, and making sure every tooth was flossed and brushed. She slid under the covers thinking she'd avoided Twenty Questions.

But before she could turn off her bedside lamp, her mom entered her room and sat on the end of her bed. "How was your date?"

Crap. Here it comes. "It wasn't a date. We're just friends."

Her mom arched her brows. "Okay. How was the gallery?"

"Small, but there was some cool stuff." *Can we drop it now?*

"Did you get something to eat?"

"Yeah. We went to Sonic. We were in public the whole time and nothing happened."

Her mom sighed, but it seemed more out of frustration than relief. "Look, Ryan, we know you're going to want to date…"

"Seriously, Mom. It wasn't a date."

"Okay, hear me out. You're going to want to date some guy. It's okay. What happened in Chicago is a lifetime away. We trust you. You need to understand that. If you want to go out with a guy, even on a non-date, don't be afraid to tell us."

"What about Dad? He didn't look too thrilled when he saw Justin."

She shook her head. "He doesn't trust any guy with you girls. That's just the way it is. But you know he's all bark."

"Mom?"

"Yes?"

"We are just friends, but Justin is different from any guy I've ever met. When we talk, it's real. Does that make sense?"

"Sure it does. That's the way it's supposed to be." She stood, tucked the duvet cover under Ryan's chin, and kissed her on the forehead. "'Night, sweetie."

"Thanks, Mom." Her parents trusted her. They had a right to—she'd been with über hot Justin Hayes and nothing had happened. No shame. Instead of dreading seeing him again, she was excited to see him at school. She snuggled a little deeper under the covers and realized she was grinning. Her plan to put Justin in the People to Avoid category had been deftly foiled by those stupid twin dimples.

She touched her lip and sighed. It didn't matter that her face had been shredded. Justin Hayes liked her. Life was good.

*

Justin's phone buzzed in the cup holder, so he stopped at the end of Ryan's drive and fished it out. His throat tightened at the sight of the number. His dad never called. "Hello?"

"Where are you?"

"On my way home. Why?"

"I have to stay late at work. I can't get ahold of Mom."

"She was fine when I left. Did something happen?"

"No. I just—I'm sure everything is fine. Call me when you get home, okay?"

"Sure." Justin ended the call and tossed his phone back in the cup holder. *That was weird.* His dad was not the worrying type. Justin pulled onto the highway and floored it into town.

Everything looked completely normal when he pulled into the drive. He unlocked the front door and looked around. Nothing seemed out of the ordinary, but at the same time, he didn't want to yell for his mom in case she was asleep. He padded down the hall toward the bedrooms. His was on the left, his parents' on the right. He was reaching for the knob to check on his mom when he saw the light peeking from under the door at the end of the hall.

His heart sank. He pulled his phone from his pocket as he opened the door to Chelsea's room.

But nothing in his wildest imagination could have prepared him for what he found.

10

His mom sat on the floor, slumped against the bed, her eyes closed. Chelsea's clothes were strewn across the bed and her paintings were scattered on the floor. The one of Austin McCoy lay in her lap.

He stepped into the room. "Mom."

Her head lolled toward him and she opened her eyes. The movement seemed to take all of her energy. She blinked a couple of times, but her eyes closed anyway. "Jus—sin."

"Mom? Are you okay?" His heart pounded in his chest. Something was different. He'd never seen her this bad before.

"Nooo." She raised her eyebrows and her eyes fluttered open. Her hands moved beneath the painting of McCoy and that's when his heart stopped.

In her right hand, she held his dad's .38. Her hand was wrapped around the grip and her index finger rested on the trigger.

"Mom, put the gun down." He felt the cell in his hand and with trembling fingers called his dad.

"Don't wor-ry. I couldn' do it?" She picked up the picture of Austin. "I want to shoo' a big hole in it. But I can't. Is' too pretty." She broke into sobs. But the gun was still in her hand.

"Mom, set the gun down." He heard his dad's voice on his cell. "Dad, she has a gun. I—I've never seen her like this. Her speech is slurred. I think she's drunk." His mom may have been locked in the pit of depression for the past two years, but alcohol had never been a part of it.

But then, neither were guns.

"Get out of the room, Justin. I'm dispatching the police now." His dad fired the words at him.

His mom's shoulders shook as she sobbed. "I can't do this. So tired of sad."

"I'm on my way, son. Stay on the line." Justin ignored his dad and focused on the gun. His heart pounded in his chest. "Put the gun down and we'll talk, okay?" He inched closer to her.

She looked up at him with tears streaming down her face. "I sor-ry, Justin."

"Mom, let go of the gun."

His dad yelled, "Get out, Justin! Now!"

"I miss her. I wanna be with her." Her hand rested in her lap, but it was still wrapped around the grip and her finger was still on the trigger.

"I miss her too." He squatted next to her and hoped like hell that she wouldn't accidentally pull the trigger. "She's here in our memories, in these paintings."

His mom shook her head. "No, no, no. I'll go to her…" She rolled her gaze to his face. "You're so good to me. You need a life."

His throat had closed but he forced words from his lips. “Then hand me the gun, cuz you’re scaring me, Mom.” *Where are the freaking police?*

“You need to be happy. Dad needs to be happy.”

“We can all be happy, but only if you let go of the gun.” He heard sirens in the distance and silently prayed she wouldn’t freak out. “Mom, the police are coming.”

Confusion crossed her face. “Poli…?” She closed her eyes and opened them but couldn’t seem to get them open all the way.

“They’re afraid you’re going to hurt yourself. I’m going to take the gun and put it away. Will you let me do that?”

She didn’t answer, but her grip relaxed a little. Slowly he reached for the pistol.

Her fingers tightened again. “No.” She lifted it out of her lap and pointed it toward her head. “I’m so tire… I don’ wanna hurt.”

“No. Mom!” Justin lunged across her chest and knocked her arm down, sending the pistol spinning across the floor in one direction and his phone in the other. He dove for the gun and caught it just before it slammed into the baseboard across the room. His hands trembled as he felt for the safety.

It was on.

She hadn’t taken the safety off.

He crawled back to her. She lay in a heap on her right side. He tried to shake her awake, but she was out.

Pounding sounded at the front door. He ran toward the sound. “Coming.” He opened the door and dangled the pistol, barrel down, from his index finger and thumb. “I got the gun from her. Take it from me, please.”

The officer took the gun and stepped into the house. “What’s going on?”

Justin opened his mouth to speak but he trembled so hard he couldn't form coherent words. He pointed toward Chelsea's room. "Mom."

"What about your mom?"

"She had the gun. I got it from her, but I think she's unconscious."

The officer started down the hall with his hand on his sidearm and his back at a forty-five degree angle to the wall. Justin started to follow, but the officer put up his hand. "Step outside, please."

Justin did as he was told and leaned against the brick wall on the porch. The trembling started again. Every muscle in his body seemed to be on the verge of losing control. His dad parked in front of the house and ran across the yard, and in a moment Justin felt his arms wrap around him in a tight embrace. He fell against his dad and let the tears come.

The front door opened and Justin pulled away and rubbed his eyes. The officer said to him, "Is this your dad?"

"Yes, sir. He's a trauma nurse."

The officer motioned to Justin's dad. "Sir, come with me."

Dad followed the officer back into the house. Justin slid down the wall to the concrete. An ambulance pulled up in front of the house, followed by a second police car. Justin watched the scene unfold as if he were watching a movie. He focused on the red bag centered in the stretcher as the paramedics rushed into the house. The second officer escorted him into the kitchen. There, he finally saw the empty fifth of vodka and the pill bottle on the counter. He sat at the table and somebody wrapped a blanket across his back. He told the the cop what had happened, but he was completely detached—as though it had happened to someone else.

He didn't see the paramedics carry his mom out of the house, but somehow, he wound up in the passenger seat of his dad's car.

A whisper from somewhere in his consciousness told him he should reconnect with what was happening around him. But he wasn't ready—instead, he focused on the blinking lights of the ambulance ahead of them.

They pulled into the employee lot and parked across from the ambulance bay. His dad sighed deeply and said, "She's going to be okay. She'll be in the hospital until she's stable—after that, she'll be transferred to a psych unit. Do you understand?"

He understood. He understood that she shouldn't have had to completely unravel before getting the help she needed. He understood that his dad should have taken care of her. But he didn't say anything. He couldn't. He was still watching the movie unfold. The paramedics opened the double doors of the ambulance, pulled the stretcher out, and rolled the gurney into the hospital.

His dad reached across the seat and squeezed his shoulder. "Son, are you okay?"

Justin turned his head and said, "Don't. Fucking. Touch me." He squeezed the words through his lips. He wanted to say more, but judging by the look on his dad's face, he'd gotten his point across.

His dad pulled the keys from the ignition. "The police will probably want to talk to you again. I'll be there with you."

Now you decide to be a dad? "Can we check on Mom first?"

"Of course." His dad scanned his badge to gain access to the staff entrance of the emergency department. Jeannie, a willowy nurse, met them at the door. "She's in T-one." She put her arm around Justin's dad. "Alan, they're intubating her."

Justin wasn't sure what that meant, but knew it couldn't be good. He looked at his dad's colorless face for an explanation.

"They're putting her on a vent—a machine that will breathe for her."

Justin's chest grew heavy and the world seemed to be shrinking away from him. His dad slipped his arm under his shoulders. "Come on." He led him to the staff break room and sat him at a table. "Breathe."

Jeannie handed him a miniature can of some off-brand coke. His hands shook when he took it from her, but he managed to gulp it anyway. Slowly, as they sat there not talking, he reconnected. He wasn't a spectator—this was his life. Sadness weighed his body down. His sister was dead, and now this.

While they waited, a couple of nurses came in and offered solace before leaving in that awkward helpless way people do in these situations. Justin watched the clock tick off thirty minutes and tried not to think about what might be going wrong.

"Alan." A middle-aged, squat nurse stood in the doorway. "Dr. Shulkin said you could see her. He's with her now." Her voice was matter-of-fact, but her eyes held concern.

Justin stood with his dad. "I'm coming too."

His dad reached out, but stopped short of placing a hand on Justin's shoulder. "She'll have a couple of IV lines, and she'll be on the vent."

Justin nodded, but the lump in his throat and the burn of unshed tears kept him from speaking. He followed his dad into the room that held his mom.

She lay on the stretcher with the machine fastened over her mouth, breathing for her, and Justin was struck by how peaceful she looked. No worries. For the first time in years, she was free from the pain—she didn't have to try anymore. Hell, she didn't even have to breathe for herself.

Fear raced through him. What if she never woke up? What if she died? He stepped back from the bed and looked at his dad. He wanted to hear that she was going to open her eyes any second.

Dr. Shulkin pulled away from the computer he was typing into and introduced himself to Justin. He folded his arms across his chest and leaned against the counter. "She's stable. We're going to transfer her to the unit as soon as a bed is available." He shook his head. "Vodka and Ambien. Bad combination. I understand there was a gun."

Justin blinked away the burning in his eyes. "She had Dad's thirty-eight. She wanted to shoot one of my sister's paintings." It sounded ridiculous when Justin said it out loud. Of course she wasn't just going to shoot the painting. She'd covered all her bases—booze, pills, and a gun. He moved close to his mom again and covered her hand with his. It felt cold and lifeless. He squeezed, hoping that some part of her consciousness would reach out and squeeze back.

Nothing. The only sign that there was life in her body was the steady beeping of the heart monitor and the rhythmic swooshing of the ventilator.

Dr. Shulkin left the room and his dad proceeded to inspect all the gadgets and lines hooked up to her. He hadn't come close to actually looking at her. But that was his MO. It was all about the mechanics of a functioning family and a total disregard for the emotional side.

"You're unbelievable."

"What?"

"This isn't some stranger from the street. This is Mom."

His dad released the IV bag he was inspecting. "Justin…"

Jeannie and the squat nurse came into the room. "We're moving her to the unit." To his dad, she said, "Why don't y'all get a bite to eat or a cup of coffee. We'll let you see her briefly when she's settled."

His dad rubbed the back of his neck. “I’ll take Justin home and come back.”

“No, you won’t.” Justin faced his dad. “I’m not leaving.”

“You won’t really be able to see her until morning. ICU has strict visiting hours.”

“So? There’s a waiting room. Somebody has to be here when she wakes up.”

The squat nurse volleyed her gaze between them. “You can discuss this in the family room, but right now we need to move Sandy.”

His dad nodded. “Right. Come on.”

Jeannie began preparing the equipment for transfer. “I’ll call when she’s settled.”

Justin followed his dad to the family room. Chairs and end tables lined the walls. Tissue boxes were stacked like blocks on the tables, all set up for the delivery of bad news. The last time he had been ushered in here, his world crumbled. When the door clicked closed behind him, his emotions went back to that horrible day. Sweat prickled his skin and it took a couple of seconds for his breathing to kick back in.

His dad pointed to a chair. “Sit.”

Justin dropped into a chair and tried to hide the anxiety gripping him. “I’m not leaving.”

“Mom might be on a vent for a couple of days. They’ve given her meds to keep her from fighting the machine. She won’t know you’re there.”

But I’ll know I’m there. The shakes were getting worse. “The image of her lifting that gun to her head keeps replaying in my mind. She wanted to blow her brains out.” He gripped the arms of the chair in a failed attempt to stop the trembling. “I can’t go back. Not yet.”

His dad sat on the coffee table across from him and leaned forward. "I get it. We'll go together, after she's settled. She is very sick right now. Dr. Shulkin feels she'll pull through this, but it's going to be a slow process."

Justin glared at his dad. "How'd it get to this? I begged you to get her help."

"It's not that easy. I tried."

"Bullshit." Justin squeezed the arms of the chair and pressed his body against the back of it in an effort to control the rage that consumed him. "You didn't even take care of her. *I'm* the one who's helped her get through the dark days."

"You're not the only one who's had to handle her."

"*Handle* her?" Justin's grip tightened even more. "Is that what she is to you? Something to handle?"

His dad rubbed his forehead. "Bad choice of words. The thing is, there is no way to force her into treatment unless she's a danger to herself or others. Unfortunately, it takes an event like this."

"So, you were waiting for this to happen?"

"Good God, no." He stared at the floor and shook his head. "I've tried to get her help. I've begged her. I've asked friends to talk to her." He ran a hand through his hair. "That lunch with the girls from work? I arranged it."

"You did everything but take care of her." Justin couldn't keep the sarcasm out of his voice.

His dad stood and paced the room with his hands on his hips, shoulders back, and chest forward. He was pissed. Justin propped his feet on the coffee table where he'd been sitting and watched his dad try to regain control.

Finally he faced him. "I was wrong to expect you to take care of her while I worked. I should have found another way."

Justin let his feet drop to the floor. "Dad, you don't get it. It's not that *I* had to care for her, it's that *you* never did."

"You don't know what you're talking about. I checked on her while I was at work. I had friends drop in on her. Who do you think is with her at night?"

The door opened and Jeannie stuck her head in. "You can see her now."

Justin's dad nodded. "Thanks."

They snaked through back halls to the secure door. His dad swiped his badge and the doors popped open, ushering them into the Intensive Care Unit. Justin was taken aback by the contrast between the dimly lit halls and the urgent sounds of alarms beeping. The rooms had glass walls and he heard the rhythmic swooshing of the breathing machines from several of them. He followed his dad to the nurse's desk in the center of the department. A computer screen displaying rows of heart tracings beeped. One of the lines flashed red. A guy looked up from the desk and turned to another nurse. "Check the leads in four."

The nurse got up and headed out of the station, but she didn't seem to be in a super big hurry. *Shouldn't she be in a super big hurry? This is the intensive care unit, after all.*

The same guy studying the monitor looked away from the screen. "Hi, Alan. She's in six. Patty is with her now."

His dad muttered his thanks and Justin followed him to glass room number six. He saw his dad scan the equipment as soon as they entered the room. But he went to the bedside and brushed his wife's hair away from her face, leaned close, and whispered something in her ear. When he straightened, a tear fell down his cheek and for the first time in two years, Justin saw his dad's resolve crumble.

Justin crumbled too as tears rose to the surface. Dad wrapped him in a tight embrace. This time he didn't fight it. He needed to be held, and he needed to hang on to his dad.

11

Ryan arrived in Shop class before Justin. She thought of the way his hand had felt in hers and the emotions they'd shared. She couldn't wait to see him, and tried not to grin as she perched on the stool at her table.

Students filtered into the room. A few even said hello to her, but Justin wasn't among them. She was about to text him when the bell rang. The zero tolerance cell-phone policy made her slip her phone back into her purse. Mr. Hesby called roll and disappointment began to settle inside her. As the last name was called, the door to the room opened and excitement surged—until she saw him.

Justin closed the door and made his way to the table behind her. Every movement seemed to take extraordinary effort. His hair was still damp and he hadn't bothered to brush it. He wore a blue and silver Dallas Cowboys T-shirt, but it was wrinkled as though it had been wadded up before he put it on. His eyes were puffy and held a sleep-deprived daze.

He didn't smile at her, or say hello. He just dropped onto the stool as though she were a stranger. She spun around to face him. "Hey."

He nodded but he didn't speak, didn't look at her. What had happened between last night and this morning? Worry gnawed at her. Had she done something wrong?

Mr. Hesby instructed them to work on their projects, but as soon as he was done, Ryan stood and turned to Justin. "Are you okay?"

"Long night." He looked her in the eyes and away. It was a quick look, but Ryan thought she saw a plea for help there.

"Wanna talk?"

"No."

Ryan sighed in an exaggerated way and said, "Thank God."

A tiny smile formed on Justin's lips and he nodded. But the circles beneath his eyes told her it had been more than just a long night. Apparently Mr. Hesby noticed too.

He walked close to Justin and bent down. "Are you okay?"

"Tired."

"Well, I think you can be tired somewhere else—principal's office. Go."

He got up and shuffled out of class, his head hanging low, his eyes shimmering with tears. *What happened?* Ryan wished she could talk to him, somehow comfort him. But if the situation were reversed, she'd hate that. So, she turned and faced the front.

*

Mrs. Johnson leaned against the desk. "I talked to your dad."

Shit. Here it comes. He didn't want her sympathy. He was too tired. His emotions were too raw. All it would take was a couple of nice words and he'd cry. He couldn't go there. He had to be strong—like Ryan.

Mrs. Johnson continued, "I'm sorry about—your mom. Your dad said you were up all night. You should go home and get some rest."

"I can't go home."

"You can't sleep through your classes."

"Please. Don't make me leave. I'll be okay." He closed his eyes and pressed his fingers against the lids. The whole school would know by lunchtime, and the whole town by the end of the day.

He felt a hand on his shoulder and opened his eyes to Mrs. Johnson's concerned look. "Let me walk you to the nurse. Maybe a catnap will get you through the day."

Get through the day. That's where he was now—on autopilot—one giant struggle to get through the day. He didn't say anything. He just stood and followed her out of the office.

He awoke to the sound of the bell. It took him a second to realize where he was. He heard hushed voices on the other side of the blue curtain that divided the two beds in the nurse's office.

Coach Peterson's voice carried, even though he whispered. "Any news on his mom?"

"Not that I've heard. I can't imagine why Alan Hayes sent him to school. He should've stayed home."

Because I can't go home. Not yet.

Coach Peterson said, "All right if I talk to him?"

"Yes—he's been asleep since second period. Slept right through lunch."

He heard Coach's heavy footsteps coming toward him and sat up. *Crap, he's going to go all nice on me.* People were always super nice after a tragedy. It was so fake. Why couldn't they just be their same asshole selves?

Coach pulled the curtain back. "Feeling better?"

Justin nodded.

"You coming to practice today?"

Justin looked up. "Yes, sir."

Coach worked his jaw as though he were chewing on his next words. "If you want to check on things at home, I'm good with that."

"No, sir."

Coach gave a quick nod. "Don't be late." He closed the curtain and left.

The nurse caught him outside. "You're making him practice?"

"I'm not making him. But, I'll tell you, working out is probably the best thing for him right now. That boy is bound to have a lot of anger inside him."

The nurse didn't respond. Justin smiled, picturing Coach Peterson leaving the office and the nurse's mouth hanging open in stunned silence. Leave it to Coach to understand him.

His phone buzzed in his pocket. "Hello."

"Justin, I've called a dozen times."

His heart raced at his dad's voice. "How's Mom?"

"Same."

Justin stood and stretched. "What's the big emergency, then?"

"No emergency. I wanted to let you know that I'm picking up a shift tonight."

"Mom is fighting for her life and you're picking up a shift?"

"It's where I'm needed. Besides, I'll be close."

I need you, Dad. The words begged to be said, but he couldn't. It wouldn't matter anyway. "I'm staying up there tonight." He waited for his dad to reply, but he was talking to someone in the background. He didn't wait for him to come back to the phone before tapping End. Why bother? His dad's life was the emergency room. Family was an afterthought.

Mrs. West, the nurse, pushed the curtain aside and handed him a bottle of water and a package of peanut-butter crackers. "Here, you can probably use this."

"Thanks." He twisted off the top and took a long drink. "I don't suppose they'd give me a pass to grab something to eat."

"No, but I have a frozen dinner in the teacher's lounge. It's a pasta thing. Let me zap it for you."

"Nah. I'm good." He looked at his phone. "Wow, I slept pretty much all day."

The nurse sat in a chair across from the bed. "I heard you on the phone. Any news?"

"No." He sat too, since it didn't look like he was going anywhere.

"Justin, I need to ask some questions. I'd like for you to be as open as you can."

She looked at him as though she was waiting for an answer, but he just half shrugged. *Here it comes, probing into my home life.*

"Does your dad live with you and your mom?"

"Yes." *Not that it's any of your business.*

She nodded and he could almost see her making a mental check beside the question.

"Do you fear for your safety while at home?"

He smiled at that one. "No." Relief crossed her face and Justin shook his head. "You know the police covered all of those bases, and then some."

An awkward smile crossed her face. "I'm obliged to make an assessment in these situations." She sat back in the chair and cleared her throat. "One more question. Why did you come to school today? You obviously hadn't slept. Why didn't you stay home?"

He started to point out that she'd asked two questions, but he wanted to end this interrogation and get to class. "I didn't want to miss school." She looked disappointed with his answer. If she was fishing for juicy stuff to put in her *assessment,* she wasn't going to get it from him. "Can I have a pass back to class?"

She stood too. "Yes. But if you're going to football practice, I'd like to see you eat something more than crackers. If you don't want a frozen dinner, how about a peanut butter and jelly sandwich?"

"Okay."

She smiled like she'd won a big negotiation. "Hang out here. I'll be back in a minute."

He flopped back on the bed and checked his Facebook page from his phone. Ashley Boyd had posted, "I'm SOO sorry to hear about your mom. If there is ANYTHING I can do, you know I'm there. XOXOXO." Beneath the post were a dozen "me too" comments. He hid the post.

His phone dinged.

Ryan: Where are you?

Justin: Nurse.

His text had barely swooshed into cyberspace when he heard someone come into the nurse's office. His stomach growled in anticipation of food. He stood, but the person barreling down the short hall to the beds wasn't Mrs. West.

Like ray of sunshine, a breath of fresh air, and all the other corny things he could think of, Ryan appeared with a smile on her face. Not concern or sympathy—a smile. And without hesitation or thought, he pulled her against his chest, wrapped his arms around her, and held on. She hugged him back and it felt so good. All of the horror of the past twenty-four hours dissipated like the wisps of a bad dream. He pressed his lips against her hair. She pulled away and their eyes met. He'd never wanted to kiss someone so bad in his life.

But he didn't. Instead, he pulled her tightly against him, again luxuriating in the feel of her. He ran his hands up and down her spine.

"Justin Hayes!"

They jumped apart.

Mrs. West stood next to the blue curtain holding a paper plate with the sandwich in one hand and a bag of chips dangling from the other. "Not in my office, you don't."

Justin tried to speak, but all that came out was a sort of contorted, "We weren't..." Ryan stared at the floor as though she were waiting for it to open up and swallow her. He put a protective arm across her shoulder.

"Young lady, I believe you have class to attend."

Ryan nodded, but her gaze never left the floor.

Justin rubbed the back of her neck with his thumb. "I'll walk you."

They followed Mrs. West to her desk at the end of the hall. She dropped the plate and chips on top of a sign-in ledger. Then she yanked a hall pass from a pile, signed it, and thrust it toward Justin. "You'll need this."

"Thank you." He kept his hand on Ryan's shoulder. "Nothing happ—"

"Class." She picked up the plate. "Take this."

He grabbed the sandwich off the plate and nodded. "Thanks."

The sound of a curtain sliding across the track made him stop. He turned and Brittany Boyd smiled. "I'm feeling *much* better, Mrs. West. I think I can go back to class." She looked Justin up and down. "I guess you got what you wanted too."

*

By the end of school all anybody could talk about was Justin's mom and Ryan and Justin in the nurse's office. That rumor had gone from *Ryan got caught kissing Justin in the nurse's office* to *Ryan got caught screwing Justin in the nurse's office*.

SLUT had been cleaned off her locker the day after it happened. But whoever had done it was relentless. Now, SCARFACE BITCH was written in pink lipstick down her locker. Ryan grabbed the books she needed, replaced the ones she didn't, and slammed the door.

Mackenzie and Kelsey waited a few feet away. Mackenzie shook her head. "Again?"

"Yeah. What a waste of lipstick." Ryan pulled her backpack up on her shoulders.

Kelsey said, "You need to find out who's doing it."

"No. I don't. I don't care. If there's one thing I've learned, it's that people are gonna believe what they want to believe. I don't know why they hate me. But that's their problem, not mine."

Kelsey faced her. “Have you heard the rumor about you and Justin?”

“What do *you* think? Of course I have.”

“Ryan, he’s bad news. Stay away from him.”

Anger flashed through Ryan. “Really? You’re as bad as the rest of them.” She slammed through the door to the parking lot.

Kelsey was right on her heels. “Listen to me.”

Ryan stopped and turned toward Kelsey. “No. You listen to me. You don’t know what you’re talking about. He was there for me, has been there for me, and I’m going to be there for him. He’s my friend. I’m not going to abandon him because some stupid, jealous girl wasted her lipstick on my locker.” She headed toward the truck. She expected Kelsey to yell at her, but she didn’t.

Usually Ryan sat shotgun and Mackenzie took the backseat. But today Ryan couldn’t stomach being that close to Kelsey, so she piled in the back.

Kelsey looked in the rearview mirror and put the truck in gear. “I know nothing happened. Those girls are ridiculous. It’s just…” She took a deep breath and let it out. “I don’t want it to be Chicago all over again.”

“It already is.” Ryan said the words without emotion. The truth was, just thinking about those words scrawled across her locker made her chest hurt. But those feelings were for her alone. Weakness was not an option.

She sank back in the seat and stared out the window. What was wrong with her? She didn’t even *want* to fit in anymore. Survival would be nice. Get through school and go to college.

Mackenzie twisted in her seat. “Is it true about Justin’s mom?”

“I guess. He looked awful, but I only saw him for a few minutes.” Was it weird that she hadn’t asked about his mom? They would talk about it eventually. All she knew was that he needed her.

Mackenzie looked at her as though she carried the weight of the world in her eyes. "It's so sad. I can't imagine if something happened to one of you."

Ryan gave her sister a weak smile. "Nothing is going to happen to us. Are you okay? You look like you lost your best friend."

"People can be so horrible. It's hard to know who your friends are." She turned and faced the front.

Ryan leaned forward and touched Mackenzie's shoulder. "Hey, what's going on?"

"It's just this whole thing…"

Kelsey said, "I heard Justin found her."

Ryan had heard the rumor too. Supposedly, somebody's dad was one of the cops who had answered the call.

Mackenzie cupped her face with her hands. "Can we just change the subject?"

"Okay." Kelsey glanced at Mackenzie. "Are you sure you're okay?"

"I just don't want to hear anything else that's sad."

Silence filled the truck all the way to the feed store. Ryan had never seen Mackenzie so upset. Even when she was told she had to quit gymnastics, she hadn't said a word. She'd just nodded and gone for a run. Was this town changing her too? Something was up with her little sister and she wasn't sure she liked it. The hopelessness Ryan saw in her face worried her.

Speaking of faces, Ryan's itched like mad. The doctor had said it would, but she was not to scratch because it could cause an infection. Why did her body tell her to if it was bad for her?

She pulled a compact mirror from her purse. The right side of her upper lip stuck out, giving her a permanent snarl. It felt lumpy.

The doctor said that was scar tissue. She couldn't imagine how he was going to be able to fix her face. The abrasions on her cheeks no longer oozed, but the circular pattern made her look as though she'd been attacked by a sander. The scabs on her forehead itched the most. She rubbed them, just enough to relieve some of the itching. But it felt so good, she couldn't stop. She rubbed harder—across her forehead and down her cheeks. Scabs fell away.

Ah, sweet relief. And blood. Crap.

"Mackenzie, hand me a napkin out of the glove box."

Mackenzie turned toward her as she held out the napkin. "Your face!"

Ryan dabbed at her face. Okay, it was bleeding more than she thought.

Mackenzie handed her another napkin. "What happened?"

"I scratched." It wasn't like she was bleeding to death or anything. But pretty much her whole face bled.

Kelsey looked at her through the rearview. "Ryan, you weren't supposed to scratch."

"Well, I did. Just get me to Mom."

By the time they pulled into the feed store's parking lot, Ryan had gone through several napkins. Most of the bleeding had stopped, but her face had blood all over it.

The mostly full parking lot sent panic through Ryan. "Pull around to the back. I'm not going to walk through the front door." Kelsey parked close to the loading dock, and Ryan practically sprinted from the truck to the store.

Her dad was at the dock loading sacks of shavings into the back of a pickup truck. When he saw her, he stopped with a sack poised for the next toss. "Ryan, what happened?"

"I need Mom."

He released the sack and followed her to the makeshift kitchen in the back of the store. "You sit at the table. I'll get her."

Mackenzie sprinted past them to the front of the store. "I'll get her."

Her dad wetted a paper towel and handed it to her. "Here. This should help."

She pressed it to her face. It felt cool against her skin and relieved some of the itching.

Her mom rushed toward the kitchen table. When Ryan removed the paper towel from her face, her mom sighed. "You scratched."

"I couldn't help it. Is it bad?"

Her mom inspected her face. "Well, the bleeding has mostly stopped. We'd better goo you up." She moved to the sink and washed her hands. "Why didn't you take the antihistamine he gave you?"

"I don't know. I didn't mean to scratch it like that." She tilted her face so her mom could apply the antibiotic gel the doctor had prescribed. "Did I just make it scar worse?"

"I don't know. You did a pretty good job of pulling those scabs off."

Ryan's phone rang. She pulled away from her mom to answer it. It was Justin.

"Hey. I got out of practice early. I'm heading over to the hospital now."

"How's your mom?" She turned her back on her mother.

"Still in a coma, on a ventilator." His voice cracked and Ryan's heart squeezed a little in her chest.

"I'm so sorry." She cringed. Those words were so inadequate.

"I'm sorry about today. People are stupid. "

"Yeah." She tried to think of something else to say to fill the awkward silence between them.

He sighed deeply and seconds ticked by before he spoke again. "Well, hey, I'd better go."

She nodded as if he could see her. "If there's anything…"

"Yeah. Thanks."

She tapped End.

Her mom inspected her face. "Everything okay?"

"Did you hear about Justin's mom?"

Her mom placed the cap on the tube of ointment. "Mrs. Miller told us that she took pills. How is she?"

"Bad. She's on a ventilator. I can't imagine what Justin is going through. I feel so helpless."

Ryan watched emotions play across her mom's face—anger, sympathy, frustration? "It's so irresponsible."

"What?"

"She has a child." She put her hand up as if to stop Ryan from speaking. "I know she's ill. I just don't get how you do that when you have a kid. That's a burden no kid should have to shoulder."

Ryan didn't get it either, but right now her concern was Justin. "Mom, what do I say to him?"

"All you can say is that you're sorry it happened."

"It sounds so insufficient."

Her mom stood. "It does. But there is nothing else you can say." She stuffed the tube of medicine in her purse. "Justin is dealing with issues that are way bigger than you need to be involved in."

Ryan's stomach tightened. "What does that mean?" She had a feeling she knew where this was going, and she didn't like it.

"I don't think you should get yourself too involved with this boy. He's still grieving for his sister and now this. He already has anger issues—I just think he needs a wide berth."

"Anger issues? You sound like Kelsey. He doesn't have anger issues. He's one of the kindest, gentlest people I know. He's my friend. My *only* friend."

"I'm not saying you can't be friends at school. Just be careful—he's got some heavy stuff to deal with." Her mom started toward the front of the store and Ryan followed.

"*I* have heavy stuff to deal with. Look at what's left of my face."

Her mom spoke over her shoulder. "Your face is beautiful. It's going to heal just fine."

"Mom, look at me." She waited for her mom to turn toward her. "It's a mess. It's gross. The ointment makes it look worse. Talk about a wide berth—even my teachers don't want to look at me."

Kelsey appeared from the short hall leading from the store to the back room. "And then there's the profanity written on her locker."

"Shut up, Kelsey."

Too late. Worry had already settled on her mom's face. "What?"

"It's not a big deal." Ryan shot Kelsey on of those help-me-out-here looks but her sister kept talking.

"Twice. The first time it was *slut.* Today they wrote *scarface bitch.*"

Her mom covered her mouth with her hand and tears came to her eyes.

Ryan looked at Kelsey. "You have a big mouth." To her mom she said, "It's just somebody trying to get attention. It doesn't matter."

"Did you report it to the principal?"

"No. It just doesn't matter. If I make a big deal out of it, they get what they want. Whoever is doing it can waste all of their lipstick on my locker for all I care."

Her mom folded her arms across her chest and tightened her jaw. "It does matter. You should report this."

"Mom, I went through this in Chicago. Believe me, it will make things worse. Just let me handle it. It'll go away." She glared at Kelsey. "Why did you say anything?"

"Because she needs to know." Kelsey looked at her mom. "That's not all."

"Don't." Ryan wanted to plaster duct tape over her sister's mouth. "Please, Kelsey, don't go there."

Of course Kelsey ignored Ryan's plea. "She and Justin are the rumor *du jour*."

Heat filled Ryan's face and her muscles tensed all the way to her toes. "You are such a bitch." She spat the words at Kelsey and stalked to the front of the store.

Kelsey called after her. "Wait, Ryan."

She braced for her sister to come after her until she heard her mom say, "Give her some space." *Thank God.*

Mackenzie stood at the register preparing to check someone out. Ryan sidled in next to her. "I've got this."

"Thanks."

Ryan knew her little sister hated waiting on people. She'd rather unload bags of feed than actually have to talk to people. But she'd stepped up to the plate since Ryan's face looked so bad. Ryan no longer cared whether customers stared at her. They could freaking gawk for all she cared—it was better than having to be around Kelsey.

She checked out the customer and moved to straighten the clothes racks. The bell jingled as new customers entered the store. She looked up and her heart stopped.

How dare they come in here?

She wasn't sure if she wanted to retreat to the back room or tackle the girl standing next to her father. But in the end, it didn't matter what she wanted to do, because her feet were not moving. She was frozen. She couldn't breathe, couldn't think, couldn't do anything but stare at the girl. It was like her senses had clicked off.

Jessica Stern stood less than ten feet away. She was practically glued to her dad's side, but her gaze was fixed on Ryan.

Ryan was vaguely aware that her own father had entered the room. She saw him walk up to Mr. Stern and heard him speak, but couldn't make out the words. Her body was on fire, her pulse pounded in her head, and she was totally helpless to stop it.

Jessica walked toward her, while Ryan watched through eyes that seemed to no longer belong to her. "Your face. Ryan, I'm so sorry."

"You're sorry?" Ryan felt her dad's hands on her shoulders and slowly, her senses kicked back in. "I don't have anything to say to you."

"I tried to stop it. I didn't know it would get so out of hand." Tears dripped from Jessica's eyes.

Ryan nodded. "I remember you telling Macey to stop. Once." She folded her arms across her chest. "My question is, why did you let it start?"

Jessica opened and closed her mouth, but didn't say anything.

Ryan's dad gave her shoulders a gentle squeeze before releasing her. "Was there something you needed, Bill?"

Mr. Stern shook his head. "This thing has been tearing Jessica up. She's not allowed at school, so I figured I'd bring her here. The girls need to make peace."

Jessica found her voice and said to Ryan, "Can you forgive me?"

She fixed a nonchalant expression on her face. "I can forgive you. The question is, will you be able to forgive yourself? Think of my face every time you're tempted."

Mr. Stern took a step toward Ryan. "Now, that was just uncalled for. Jessica is real sorry."

Ryan's dad stepped forward too. "You can leave now."

Mr. Stern put a hand on his daughter's shoulder. "Come on. You done your best."

Ryan didn't breathe normally until the door had closed behind them. "Well, that just about caps the crappy day I've had."

12

"Justin?" He opened his eyes and stared at the florescent lights above him. It took him a few seconds to return to the horror of his life. His dad stood above him dressed in navy-blue scrubs. Dark circles hung beneath his eyes. "Hey. Why don't you go home? It's nearly eight."

He leaned forward and the waiting room recliner popped to chair position. "Man, I didn't mean to fall asleep. How is she?"

His dad attempted a smile, but it was overshadowed by the sadness in his eyes. "She's tracking movement with her eyes and she's over-breathing the vent."

"English?" Justin rubbed his eyes and stood.

"Sorry. She's breathing on her own more than the vent. They'll probably remove it tomorrow."

Relief rushed through Justin, causing his knees to buckle. His dad caught him under the arms. "Whoa. When was the last time you had something to eat?" He eased him back to the chair.

What, you're worrying about that stuff now? "Does that mean she's going to be okay?"

"Physically, yes." He sat in a chair across from Justin and rested his forearms on his knees. Sadness rippled across his face as he sucked in his breath. His head dropped and his shoulders shook. Tears dripped from his eyes and down his face. "I'm sorry."

Justin's heart raced. "Dad. What do you mean *physically?* Is she brain damaged? Dad?"

His dad shook his head and wiped his eyes with his hands. "No, not that we can see. She'll go to a psychiatric hospital for a few days."

Justin let out a long sigh. "You scared the crap out of me."

"I tried to get her help. The more I insisted, the more she refused." He got that *I'm about to cry* look again and took a deep breath. "I admit I gave up. I couldn't understand why she didn't want to feel better. I shouldn't have given up."

Seeing his dad so vulnerable eased some of the anger Justin had been harboring. "She told me she was afraid she'd forget. It was like she felt that if she moved on, she'd be betraying Chelsea."

His dad sat up and cleared his throat. "Justin, we're all going to counseling. We should have done it two years ago."

Justin stood. "I don't need some shrink to tell me what to think."

His dad stood too. "First, they don't tell you what to think. More important, we're doing it for Mom. It's going to be part of her recovery. Will you do it for her?"

The teary-eye-chin-quiver feeling surged in Justin, but he managed to stuff it down. He nodded and said, "I'll go for her. But if they try to pull their shrink crap on me, I'm out of there."

His dad gave a weak smile. "We all need shrink crap."

"I'm fine, Dad. I've dealt with it. I've taken care of Mom, myself, the house. I've pretty much been the adult around the place."

"I think you'll be surprised if you just open yourself up to it."

Justin struggled to keep the growing frustration under control. He'd go for his mom and that would be enough. While his parents ran from the reality, he'd grieved his sister. It was time to move forward with his life. He gave a heavy sigh. He was too freaking tired to argue. "Can we see Mom now?"

The glass door to her room was open and from the hall, Justin could hear the soft swooshing of the breathing machine. He and his dad walked to opposite sides of the bed. The TV that hung above the door blared some talk show, but his mom seemed asleep. "Do they think she wants to watch TV?"

"They're stimulating her brain. We don't want to make it too cozy to stay asleep. Talk to her."

"Mom?" She opened her eyes and reached toward him. He took her hand in his and she squeezed. He squeezed back. "Dad's here too."

Her brow wrinkled and Justin pointed. She turned her head toward his dad and tears filled her eyes. His dad wrapped his fingers around her other hand. "Sandy, we're here."

She pulled her hand from his dad's and pointed to the tube that had been crammed down her throat and was now anchored to her mouth. His dad eased her hand away from the tube. "Sorry, sweetie. That has to stay a little longer."

An ancient nurse pushed a computer on wheels into the room. The bold letters on her badge said her name was Dorothy. She scanned the bracelet on his mom's wrist and the code on a bag of IV fluid. "Hi, Alan. She's doing much better today. We're just waiting on an order to extubate her." She switched an almost empty bag of fluid for the new one and backed out with the computer cart.

Justin gave his dad a questioning look.

"Take her off the ventilator. She's breathing on her own."

Justin squeezed his mom's hand and looked into her eyes. "Did you hear that? You're breathing on your own."

His mom kept her gaze on him. Tears slipped from the corners of her eyes.

His dad brushed them away and cupped her cheek with his hand. "Sandy, we're going to get better. We're going to make this work." He leaned in and kissed her forehead.

Justin couldn't remember the last time he'd seen his dad show that much affection to his mom. So maybe he was serious about them becoming a family again.

Dorothy came back in, smiling. "Good news. I just spoke to Dr. Shulkin and we're going to DC the vent. If ya'll will go to the waiting room, I'll come get you when we're done."

Justin followed his dad to the waiting room and sat in a chair across from him. The atmosphere was awkward, as if they were both trying to think of something to say.

"I thought you were pulling a double?" That was the best Justin could come up with.

"No. I found someone to cover it." His dad looked around the waiting room, rubbed the back of his neck, crossed his legs, uncrossed them, and finally stood. "How's football?"

"Good. Coach let me leave practice early today."

"Are you playing Friday?"

"Yeah."

His dad sat again and leaned back in the chair. "I'm off Friday. I thought I'd come to the game."

"That'd be cool." He refused to acknowledge the excitement fluttering in his chest. Dad always intended to come to a game, but got called in to work. Last year he'd made it to exactly zero games.

"I'm making some changes at work."

"Yeah?" *Why is he telling me this? I don't really care about hospital politics.*

"I'm not going to take more than my required call time, and I'm not going to sign up for extra shifts. It'll be less money, but we can handle it. It's time I lived my life outside the hospital."

Justin nodded. He should say something, but figured *Yay, you're going to be a dad* wasn't appropriate.

The double doors leading to the ICU swung open and Dorothy waved them back. She walked between them and said, "She did great."

Justin's heart soared when he saw his mom sitting up in bed eating ice chips. When she saw them, she set the pink plastic cup on the over-bed table and reached toward them with both arms. Justin hugged her first.

She held him tight. "I'm sorry, baby. I'm so ashamed to have put you through this."

"It's okay, Mom. We're going to be okay." He gave her an extra squeeze before releasing her. He straightened and his dad swooped in for his turn.

He cupped her face in his hands and placed a kiss on her lips, and then pressed his face next to hers and cried.

It was weird to see his dad like this. He was always so in control—so detached from his emotions. To see his parents hugging and crying bordered on surreal. Tears fell from Justin's eyes too, and he prayed that all these feelings, hopes, and promises would last.

After the hugging and crying, a *what next* feeling invaded the room. It probably only lasted a few seconds, but to Justin it felt like they shifted gazes from one to another for hours.

His dad finally broke the silence. "Sandy, it'll be a while before you get to come home."

His mom pressed her lips together and nodded. Tears dripped down her cheeks.

Justin leaned close. "It's okay, Mom." He wanted to tell her how good it was that she was going to get help for her depression, but he wasn't sure how much she knew or needed to know just yet. He had to follow his dad's lead on this one.

"I'm making some changes too." Dad laced his fingers with his wife's. "I'm going to be home more. We're all going to family therapy." He kissed her hand and held it against his cheek.

"I guess they're going to send me to a psych hospital." She let out a deep sigh. "It's okay. I have to find a way to feel better—because if I don't, I don't want to be here."

Pain squeezed Justin's heart. "Mom, don't say that. I need you."

Her gaze met his and she reached toward him. "I'm going to work hard to get better. I promise."

Nurse Dorothy toddled back into the room. "Visiting hours are over, but I'll let you stay a few more minutes."

"Thanks." Justin's dad gave a half smile.

Justin looked at his dad. "I hate these visiting hours. Fifteen minutes every hour? It's ridiculous."

"It's so patients can rest." His mom gave him a weak smile. "They'll probably move me to a room tomorrow, and then you can stay as long as you like." She shifted her gaze to Justin's dad. "Y'all go home and get some rest. I'm tired anyway."

He kissed her and said, "I'll be back early in the morning. Call me for any reason." He straightened and took in a shaky breath. "I love you, Sandy."

As they said their good-byes and left the hospital, weariness filled Justin. He wanted so bad to believe they were on the road to being a family, but couldn't see how what had happened would erase the years of dysfunction.

Justin pulled into the drive behind his dad and his chest tightened. The image of the paramedics wheeling his mom to the ambulance was burned into his mind. He dragged in a deep breath and pushed it away.

His heart thudded in his chest as he entered the house. He didn't want to see the pills and alcohol that were in the kitchen. Sweat prickled his forehead and he couldn't catch his breath. His dad grabbed him around the waist and guided him to the kitchen table.

"Breathe into your hands. You're okay."

Justin cupped his hands around his nose and mouth and concentrated on slowing his breaths.

His dad sat across from him. "You've been through a lot in the past twenty-four hours. How much sleep have you had?"

Justin dropped his hands and took a deep breath. "A few hours here and there. You?"

"Not enough for either of us." His stomach let out a loud, angry growl. "I'm going to order a couple of pizzas."

Justin nodded and shifted his gaze to the eating bar. The vodka and the pill bottle were gone.

His dad saw it. "I cleaned up this morning—Chelsea's room too."

"Thanks." Justin moved to the sofa in the den, clicked on the TV, and let his mind drift to the hug in the nurse's office. He wished he'd kissed Ryan, but he hadn't wanted to hurt that beautiful mouth. Every day her face healed a little more. It was just a matter of time until he got that kiss.

*

When Justin walked into Shop, he felt all eyes on him. *This is going to be a long effing day.* Thank God Ryan was already there. Her smile made him care a little less that the whole freaking school knew he had a screwed-up family. He gave her a half-hug before taking his seat.

She moved to sit next to him. "How's things?"

"Better. Mom is breathing on her own." He tried to make his tone sound positive, but it came out sort of flat.

"So she'll be coming home soon. That's good."

"Not exactly home. She has to go to a psych hospital for a while." He waited to see which look would settle on her face. Horror? Pity? Not pity—he hated that one the most. She skipped right past those expressions and did the unthinkable. She placed her hand on his forearm, looked into his eyes with her sparkly blues, and said, "How are you?"

It was bad enough that the spot beneath her hand radiated little tingles throughout his body, but her gaze sucked him in. He wanted to cup her face and kiss the crap out of her. His hand was on its way to her cheek when he remembered they were in class. He leaned back and said, "Better. Finally got some sleep. How about you?"

"Me? Well, nobody walked up and said, *'Hey, I heard you got caught with Justin in the nurse's office.'*"

"The rumor was ridiculous. Anybody with half a brain would know it was a bunch of crap." She nodded, but the wariness in her eyes told him she wasn't convinced. "Ryan, I promise you, I will keep that rumor from affecting you. I'll make it go away."

She smiled, but the corners of her eyes drooped just a bit. "The thing is, you can't take words away. You can't make people un-hear them. But it wasn't your fault any more than it was mine. It was just some stupid girl."

The conversation they'd had in the car two nights ago came rushing back to him. *Some girls don't know they can say no.* He couldn't tell her that he'd done nothing to stop the rumor that had spread about him and Brittney last year. If anybody had a reason, it was Brittney Boyd. "It wasn't you. You just got in the way of somebody getting back at me." The thing he didn't get was, why now? They'd moved on since their one date last spring.

"Jesus, what did you do?"

"Let's just say it was the date from hell." He hoped that would be enough. He didn't want to think about that night. He'd been that nightmare date that Ryan had talked about. All hands, no brains. Shit. He was an ass. He wasn't worthy of Ryan Quinn.

Thank God she let it drop. He looked into her eyes and thought about that future kiss. "Your face looks better."

She let out an almost laugh. "Do you realize how awful that sounds out of context?"

Heat flushed through him. "You're beautiful even with the scratches."

Her smile made him feel warm inside. He wished he could grab Ryan's hand and escape to a place where the two of them could be alone. Not rumor-producing alone, just spending time together alone. The bell rang and Ryan moved back to her table.

Ryan had a doctor's appointment, so he went the rest of the day without seeing her. He made it through football practice and drove to the hospital.

He arrived at the ICU at the beginning of the fifteen-minute visiting time. He tapped the metal plate on the side of the wall and passed through the doors when they swung open. As he neared his mother's room, his heart pounded a slow cadence in his chest. His feet turned to lead as he trudged closer to the door of the glass-walled room. The curtain was closed across the glass, but the room was lit up like a late-night construction site. He heard the familiar whooshing of the ventilator and the beeping of the heart monitor. A nurse quick-stepped into the room carrying an IV bag and a couple of syringes. He heard orders being given and repeated. Tension emanated from the room.

As he approached the doorway, his lungs could barely drag in air. *What happened? Where's Dad?* He reached to push back the curtain covering three-quarters of the doorway, but a hand clamped on his shoulder.

"Whoa. Where are you going?"

Justin turned to face a linebacker-sized nurse. "I'm here to see my mom."

"What's her name?"

"Sandy Hayes."

"She's been moved to telly—telemetry." He pointed to a girl sitting behind a computer at the nurse's station. "Betty can help you find her."

"Thanks." The post adrenaline rush zapped his energy. His muscles seemed almost too weak to hold up his bones. He concentrated on walking the three feet to Betty without looking like a drunk. Fortunately, by the time she gave him the room number, he was back to his normal after-football-practice tired.

He made his way out of the ICU and wished the best for the person who now occupied his mom's room.

It didn't take him long to find her. When he walked in, his heart sank. She looked up at him with a fake smile and swollen red eyes. She pulled a tissue from a half empty tissue box on the over-bed table and dabbed her eyes. "Hi, sweetie."

"Hey, mom." He bent down and kissed her cheek. "Where's Dad?"

"He's in the ED."

So much for his promise to be around more. "Can I get you anything?"

She shook her head and stared at the wadded tissue in her hands.

Justin sat in the chair next to the bed. Silence stretched between them. *Shit. I should say something.*

His mom let out a ragged sigh. "I'm so ashamed." Tears rolled down her face and Justin covered her hand with his. She looked at him and blinked tears down her cheeks. "Can you forgive me?"

He sucked in a breath. *This is not how it's supposed to be. My whole freaking life is not how it's supposed to be.* "Mom, there's nothing to forgive. Just get better."

She nodded and pulled her hand away to wipe her face.

They sat there for a freaking eternity not saying anything. The silence in the room amplified the awkwardness between them until he thought he'd lose his mind. "Mind if I turn on the TV?"

"Okay." One word, but saying it seemed to take all of her energy.

He clicked on the news and let the frustration that simmered beneath the surface curdle him. Same scene, different location. Mom depressed, crying, not speaking. Dad working. Justin full of resentment and a heavy dose of guilt.

His mom's dinner tray arrived and he helped her sugar her tea and butter her roll. His stomach reminded him he'd neglected to feed it. Even the pale Salisbury steak and rubber noodles smelled good.

"Go get something to eat, Justin."

"I'm good. I'll get something later." *After Dad shows up—if he shows up.*

His mom pushed food around on her plate but didn't take a bite. "At least run down to the cafeteria and bring something back."

"I'm okay. Eat." He could get something. His mom was safe here. But it was easier to fill himself with anger at his dad's absence. He stared at the news reporter and let bitterness build until he tasted bile in his throat. The news ended and one of those Hollywood entertainment shows came on. His dad's shift was about to end. Depending on whether he chose to work late or not, he should be coming to the room soon.

It wasn't long before his dad arrived wearing jeans and a polo. He carried an envelope and a vase full of daisy-looking flowers. *What, no scrubs? That doesn't make sense.*

His dad leaned across the bed and kissed his mom. "Sorry it took me so long. The gang in the ED sent these. They want to know if they can visit."

Justin studied his dad's face. *Does he even notice her tear-swollen eyes?*

His mom studied the congealed gravy on the plastic plate and shook her head. "I don't want to see anybody."

"It's okay." He bent down and kissed her on the cheek. "One day at a time." He sat in a chair on the other side of the bed. "I set everything up. You should be discharged tomorrow and I'll drive you to Garden Oaks. Are you still good with that?"

His mom nodded, but didn't speak.

Justin looked at his dad. "I want to go too."

"You'll miss part of school."

"Really, Dad? You're worried about that shit now? It's just one day."

"Drop the attitude, Justin."

Justin gripped the arms of the chair and imagined the wood crumbling beneath his hands. "It might kill *you* to miss a day of work for Mom, but I want to be there. Jesus, Dad, you couldn't even take today off."

"Stop it. Don't fight. Don't hate each other because of me."

Nausea swept through Justin as he reached for his mom's hand. "I shouldn't have said that."

His dad locked eyes with him. "I didn't work today. I was taking care of getting Mom help. I'll pick you up from school on the way to the hospital. We'll take Mom to Garden Oaks as a family."

So, I jumped to conclusions. I'm a prick. "Okay." He turned to his mom. "I'm sorry. Maybe I do need to get something to eat." He looked at his dad. "Can I bring you something?"

His dad pulled a twenty from his billfold and handed it to him. "Yeah, the hamburgers are pretty good. How 'bout it, Sandy—will you try something from the cafeteria? You know it's better than this."

His mom nodded. "Maybe a tuna salad." Her voice was so weak she sounded like an old lady. She looked old too. Her body was frail and thin, with dull eyes, and pale skin. Who was this woman? Would he ever again see the mom who sang while she cooked dinner? The one whose eyes sparkled when she laughed? That mom had been missing for two years. Could Garden Oaks bring her back? He missed that mom so much his chest ached. He stood. He had to get out of the room.

"Do you want me to come with you?"

"No, I've got it. Stay with Mom." It was all he could do to keep from bolting from the room. He didn't want to think about the dysfunctional family that had replaced the happy one he used to know. That family was gone forever. He pulled his phone from his pocket and sent Ryan a happy face.

She responded with a blushing face and he felt ridiculously better. It was good to do something normal—like texting.

13

Ryan floated across the water. The silver lining to living in the old house her dad had bought from her uncle was the pool. It was their refuge on hot summer days—or in this case, hot fall days. She stared at the gray wood peeking from beneath the white flecks of peeling paint. A fresh coat might revitalize the place, but Ryan liked seeing the strength in the weathered wood. Oddly, it made her think of her mom.

From the time Ryan had been caught in bed with Will Blankenship, her mom had supported her. She was angry, no doubt. But she never made Ryan feel unloved. It would have been easier if she had. It was the sheer disappointment that she'd seen in her parents' faces that dug at her. Then her dad had lost his job and it all turned into a hot mess. When weeks of no work turned into months, it became a supernova-hot mess. Her mom, her hero, never blamed, never withdrew her love.

Her mom was like the wood beneath the peeling paint. Her life was crumbling around her and yet she stayed strong and held the family together. But Ryan's room was next to that of her parents.

She heard her mom's midnight sobs beneath her dad's seesaw snoring. Just thinking about it shoved the guilt blade into her heart.

As the weeks passed, she no longer heard her mom cry. She laughed more and things seemed to be good. And then the fountain thing happened. Last night she'd heard her mom again. If only Kelsey had kept her mouth shut, Mom wouldn't have known about the rumor or the stuff written on her locker. Ryan could take some stupid kids bullying her. But seeing her mom hurt over it ate her up.

She rolled off the float and sank into the water. The cool water refreshed her face. But tightness born of guilt sliced her heart. If she stayed down here forever, she'd be free of the guilt. The blade couldn't filet her soul. The pain would end.

She opened her eyes and blew air out of her lungs. Bubbles floated to the top while her body sank to the bottom and she felt peace. Could a person drown herself?

Her lungs burned. And she tried to ignore their signal for oxygen.

She felt her heart beat a little faster as a sense of urgency swept over her. Her lungs were no longer asking politely. They'd sent the *breathe now* signal. She fought it, for about a millisecond.

She pushed off the bottom of the pool and prayed she would make it the twelve feet to the surface.

When she surfaced, she used what strength she had left in her muscles to tread water while she took deep gulps of air.

Mackenzie grabbed her by the arm and pulled her to the side. "What were you trying to do, drown yourself?"

"No" she lied. "I was just seeing how long I could stay under."

"You scared the crap out of me. Don't do that again without warning me."

"Don't worry, I won't. I scared me too."

Stupid. Stupid. Stupid. What the hell was I thinking? I, Ryan Quinn, will never try to escape my life again. Besides, I want to kiss the breath out of Justin before I die.

Admitting that thought took her by surprise. When had had he gone from *Person to Avoid* to *boy I want to kiss*? She didn't know, but for the rest of the evening all she could think about was the stupid emoticon on her phone and kissing Justin.

Just as she crawled under her covers, her phone dinged and her heart soared.

Justin: Hey.

Ryan: Hey.

Justin: Can I call?

Yes! Yes! Yes!

Ryan: Sure.

The phone had barely rung before she pushed Answer. "Hey."

"Hi. Uh, Ryan, I'm going to miss most of school tomorrow."

"Everything okay?"

"Yeah." He paused and Ryan sensed there was more.

"Do you want me to do something?" *That was lame!*

"No. It's just—see, my mom is better…"

"That's good." *Slow down, girl. He barely got the last word out.*

"Yeah. She's better physically. But she has to spend time in a psych hospital. I'm going with my dad to take her."

Crap! What do I say to that? Have fun? "Oh?"

"So the deal is, we have to do this family therapy thing."

"That's good." *Family therapy didn't do a lot for my family. But I won't go there.*

"I don't really want to go. I'm not the touchy-feely talk about shit kind. I'm going for Mom. And..." He struggled again, but this time Ryan kept her mouth shut and let the silence on the phone get heavier. He coughed and started again. "The thing is—Ryan, you inspire me."

"Me?"

"You're the strongest person I know."

Yeah, so strong I nearly drowned myself. "Justin, I..."

"It's true. With all that's happened to you, you just keep going. I'm going to therapy. I'm going to be the kind of friend you deserve. And if something grows from our friendship, then that's like, *really cool.*"

Ryan's heart pounded. Nobody—no—boy had ever said those things to her before. "You are better than I deserve."

"No. Not yet. But I will be. I promise. I will be."

What do I say to that? I love you? Because right now, my heart is beating about a thousand miles an hour and that's exactly how I feel.

"Ryan, are you there?"

"Yeah, I'm here. I'm just taking it all in."

"Please don't freak out on me. I didn't tell you to screw up our friendship."

"You didn't. I'm just... Just don't be too hard on yourself."

"I'm not sure when I'll be back tomorrow, but can I call you?"

"Yes. Yes. Absolutely."

They hung up and she snuggled deeper under her covers, wishing he was going to be at school tomorrow. She hadn't seen him at all after Shop. She'd spent most of the day in the doctor's office. Thank God they didn't have to cleanse—aka torture—her face. It looked better every day. Her lip was still lopsided but it didn't hurt. When she was ready, Dr. Cooper could repair the knot that had formed in her lip. He assured her they could take care of any scars left on her face.

She'd looked at countless before and after pictures. The nurse explained that victims of abuse had an easier time healing when they didn't have a constant reminder. It took Ryan a couple of beats to realize she was suggesting that Ryan had been a victim of abuse.

Duh. Of course she had. She'd thought of it as bullying, as though the two things were completely separate.

She wanted to erase the evidence of what had happened to her. She wanted to move forward with her life. But the words scrawled across her locker told her that others didn't give a rat's ass that her face had been shredded. Until the culture of the school changed, fixing her lip wasn't going to remove the reminder of what they'd done to her.

She ran her hands across her skin. It was smooth where the abrasions had healed—a sharp contrast to the scabs that remained. A tear dripped down her cheek. She wanted her face back.

She climbed out of bed and pulled the appointment card from her purse. Only, it wasn't an appointment card. Across the top it read: TEEN VIOLENCE HOTLINE. Below was a number and a website.

She clicked on the website and as soon as the page opened, her eyes did a little opening of their own. She knew what she had to do. If ever there was a reason she'd ended up in Hillside, Texas, this was it.

*

He'd done it. He'd told her he was going to a shrink and then all but told her he loved her. He was an idiot.

Justin fell back on his bed and thought of the way she pulled at her hair when she was nervous. He closed his eyes and tried to remember the feel of her hand in his, her body pressed against his…

He sat up. Shit. He needed to run, shower, anything to keep him from thinking of the feel of her. He pulled on his jogging shorts and running shoes and headed toward the front door.

His dad was watching TV in the den. "Hey, where you heading?"

"Going for a run."

"Wait up. I'll come with you."

"Okay." *He's trying. I can do this. It's just a run. We don't even have to talk.*

They'd run about half a block when his dad started talking. "How's school going?"

"Okay."

"How are you handling all of this?"

Now he's going all shrinky on me? "Okay, I guess. Why?"

"It's been a traumatic experience. You were the one who found your mom. You fought for the gun. It's a lot for anybody to handle, much less a kid."

"I haven't been a kid since you buried yourself at the hospital." Justin caught a twitch in his dad's jaw muscle. He probably shouldn't have gone there. But his dad was the one who wanted to talk. All Justin wanted to do was run.

"You're right. I work a lot and I take extra shifts. Things are changing. I've been asked to be the director of the ED."

"Really. Congratulations." Justin's voice was flat. *How could a promotion possibly equal fewer hours?*

"I'm not sure I'm going to do it. I haven't talked to Mom. It's a Monday through Friday, eight to five job, though."

Justin remembered the days before the accident, when his dad always had at least a couple of days off during the week. Sometimes he'd pick up Justin and Chelsea from school and they'd get ice cream and go to the park. If it was cold, they'd hunker down at the house with a mug of hot chocolate. On the occasions when his mom was off too, they'd play games. Or his mom would take Chelsea to the mall in Spring Creek and he and his dad would watch ESPN or toss the ball around the yard. But those days were gone forever, so it didn't really matter to Justin if his dad took the job.

"It would make it easier to pay for your college."

Don't put this on me. "Do what you have to do, Dad. I'll figure out college."

"*We'll* figure out college. Theoretically, there won't be as much overtime. But, when all hell breaks loose, the director has to be there. "

"They call you in anyway." He wasn't being mean this time. It was a fact.

"Yeah." They turned the block to head home. "Enough work talk. How's Ryan getting along?"

"She's amazing." He hadn't meant to say that, but the words just tumbled out. "I mean, she's put up with a lot of crap. She doesn't let it get to her."

"Uh-huh. So, is she aware of how awesome you are?"

"We're just friends."

"And you want to take it up a notch?"

Or two. "Yeah. But she's like my best friend. I don't want to mess that up."

"It's nearly impossible to stay just friends with someone you have feelings for. Eventually, you have to go forward or say good-bye."

"That's harsh."

"But true. The going forward part should be awesome. If it's not, it wasn't meant to be and it's better to say good-bye anyway. Just be smart about what you do if you take this to the next level."

"Jeez, Dad. She's not like that. She was in the Purity Club."

His dad shrugged. "Yeah, well, the Purity Club ain't going to be in the backseat when the blood runs south. Be sure you're thinking with the right head."

"Got it." *Shut up already.*

Great. Now the image of Ryan hugging him in the nurse's office was playing in his mind. His dad was right. He couldn't just stay friends. He was sunk. He was crazy about Ryan Quinn.

Now he had to find the right time, the right place, and the right way to convince her that she was crazy about him too.

14

On the way to school, Ryan thought about her plan. She couldn't tell her sisters yet—they were too close to the situation—but the first thing she wanted to do was run it past Braden McGuire. He'd spoken so passionately at the last Purity Club meeting, she figured he'd be her litmus test. If he thought the idea sucked, then she'd drop back and regroup.

It didn't take her long to find him. He was on the yearbook committee and she figured he might be hanging around the journalism department before school. She was right.

He was leaning on the wall close to the door talking to a couple of guys she didn't know. "Hi, Braden. Do you have a minute?"

"Sure." He pushed off the wall with his shoulder and made his way to her. "What's up?"

"I found information on the group that teaches about dating. It's called Dating Respect. The focus is on healthy dating relationships and helping people who are caught in abusive relationships." She could tell he was turning the idea over in his mind. "I thought we could take it to Mrs. Bettis." She pulled some paper from her backpack. "I printed this stuff from their website. Check it out and let me know what you think." He took the papers. "If we form this group, we could get community service credits."

He gave a shrug. "Do you think there's *that* much dating violence in this tiny school?"

"It's not just violence. It's everything from a slightly unhealthy relationship to the violent." The five-minute bell rang and students began moving into the classrooms. "Take a look and I'll meet you after class."

"Okay." He took a step back. "Why are you doing this?"

"Because it's important." She turned and headed to her Calculus class. *Very important.* If she could save one girl from what had happened to her in Chicago, then everything that had happened to her since would have had a purpose.

*

Justin's heart pounded as they neared Garden Oaks. His mom sat in the front seat next to his dad. She hadn't cried since they'd picked her up from the hospital, or even spoken. She looked too tired to do either. She just sat in the passenger seat twisting her hands together.

His dad had brushed her hair while they waited for the discharge papers. It reminded Justin of when he and Chelsea were little. On the days his mom worked and his dad was off, his dad would struggle to brush Chelsea's long, curly hair. He usually managed to get it into a ponytail, but it never looked as good as when Mom did it.

His mom's hair didn't look quite right either. But then, nothing about her looked normal. Her face was pale, with deep circles under her eyes and wrinkles at the corners. Her eyelids looked as if they were too heavy for her to hold open. She was frail. Bones covered by skin.

His dad parked in front of the single-story building and Mom let out a long sigh.

"Are you okay, Mom?"

She gave a slow nod.

Justin and his dad helped her out of the car and together, as a family, they walked through the doors of Garden Oaks Psychiatric Hospital.

She signed a billion papers before they were escorted to her room, which looked more like a hotel than a hospital room. There was a regular bed and a bedside table. A dresser stood against a wall across from the bed. Two chairs and a small table were nestled in the corner and a love seat was centered under a window.

"This is nice, Sandy." Dad helped her to the love seat.

She nodded.

The girl who had brought them to the room smiled. "Dr. O'Malley will be down to talk to y'all in a few minutes. But you have time to put your things away first. We don't want our residents to live out of suitcases." She pointed to a closed door across from the bed, next to a chest of drawers. "That's the closet. The bathroom is on the other side of the dresser."

Justin sat next to his mom and took her hand. "You're going to be okay."

She patted his hand and leaned her head on his shoulder. "For you, son."

"No, Mom. For you."

His dad paced around the room. "How about I get your bags from the car?"

It was obvious that he was anxious to get out of this place, and that pissed Justin off. "I'll get them. You can have a few minutes with Mom."

His dad jangled his keys. "I've got it." He practically bolted from the room.

The muscles in Justin's neck and shoulders tensed and his mom lifted her head from where it rested. "I've made a promise to get better. Now I need you to make a promise too." His mom's voice was gravelly and weak. It sounded like it had been transplanted from an old person.

"Anything."

"Go easy on your dad."

His gut contracted, along with every muscle in his body. It was all he could do to keep from jumping up and pacing around the room.

His mom sighed deeply. "I can't stand the anger between you two."

Then Dad needs to man up and be around. "I promise I'll try." *Will he?*

She patted his thigh. "You know, you're just like him."

"I'm nothing like him." He blurted it out before he caught himself.

"When you set your mind to something, you're like a freight train racing down a track until you get it. I see your dad's mannerisms in you. The way you stand and the expressions on your face. The way you're struggling not to pace. It's not a bad thing. He used to be your hero."

Justin nodded. "That was before he decided work was more important than we were."

His mom didn't say anything, but gave a weary sigh.

I shouldn't have said that—even if it is true.

His dad returned with a bag. "I didn't know what to pack. I tried to pick some comfortable clothes."

"It's fine."

Justin helped his dad put her clothes away. *See, Mom? I'm playing nice.*

They'd barely finished when Dr. O'Malley entered the room. He looked a little older than Justin's parents, but he was thin and as tall as Justin's six-one frame. His thinning dark hair was cut short, but not military short. He smiled and shook everyone's hand. "I don't believe in wasting time. I'd like to get started right away. I want to spend a few minutes with everybody individually first. If you'll follow me, I'll show you my office."

Justin wasn't sure what he'd expected, but this wasn't it. There were a few people milling around, but the only one with a white coat was Dr. O'Malley. Everybody else was dressed in regular clothes. They passed a lounge, where several people watched *The Price Is Right* on a flat-screen TV.

Dr. O'Malley punched buttons on a keypad next to a door. A click sounded, a green light came on, and he led them through into his office. It looked like any other office waiting room. Chairs lined the walls and a coffee table sat in the center. "Have a seat. Sandy, I'd like to start with you. Is that okay?"

She nodded and he led her through a second door.

Justin sat next to his dad and stared at the floor. *Wow, this is real. Mom is in the nut hut, the loony bin.* He squeezed his eyes shut and repeated silently, *please get better, please get better, please get better...*

*

Ryan sat next to Braden McGuire and tried not to focus on Mrs. Bettis's expressions as she perused the Dating Respect information Ryan had printed. She hadn't had to talk Braden into being on board. She practically ran into him after first period.

Her idea was to get a group together to talk about the organization. But he'd expanded beyond that. He leaned forward when Mrs. Bettis lowered the papers. "We could run a series in the school paper leading up to February—it's Teen Dating Violence Awareness Month. We could even have a Dating Respect Valentine's dance."

Mrs. Bettis put a hand up. "Slow down. Great ideas, but I'll have to run them by Mrs. Johnson." She stood. "I'll be honest—it might be a hard sell after what happened to the Purity Club. But it's a great idea."

Ryan stood too. "Should we get a petition going or something?"

Mrs. Bettis smiled. "Let me see what I can do first."

With that, they were dismissed. As they left the office, Ryan looked at Braden. "Thanks for coming with me."

"It *is* a great idea. And if Mrs. Johnson doesn't listen, we'll make her listen."

They walked together until they reached the intersection where the junior lockers and the fine arts hall met. Braden smiled at her. "This is where I split."

"Thanks again for your help." Ryan was anxious to get her stuff and check her phone for a message from Justin, but Braden wasn't leaving.

His face flushed. "No worries." He slow-blinked and shifted his weight nervously.

"Is there something else?"

"Um. I was just wondering… is Mackenzie dating anybody?"

Ryan grinned. *Go, Kenzie!* "Nope. Not at the moment." She walked backward down the junior hall. "But you'd better hurry." She didn't wait for him to answer before she turned toward her locker. She pulled her phone from her pocket. No text from Justin. She tried not to let herself be disappointed, but she missed seeing him.

She met up with her sisters in the parking lot and together they walked to the truck. She nudged Mackenzie. "So, Braden McGuire."

"Who?" Mackenzie munched on a Twizzler.

"You know, the guy who couldn't keep his eyes off you at the Purity Club meeting?"

"What about him?"

Ryan bumped shoulders with her. "He asked me if you were dating anybody."

Mackenzie stopped and pulled the red licorice from her mouth. "Why would he ask that? I don't even know him."

Kelsey waggled her eyebrows at Mackenzie. "Maybe you should."

"No. I shouldn't. He's not even my type."

Ryan starting walking and Mackenzie and Kelsey fell in step. "What's your type?"

"Not him."

Ryan shrugged. "Okay. It's nice to know somebody is interested, though, isn't it?"

Mackenzie stuck the licorice back in her mouth. "I guess. What made him tell you, anyway?"

Ryan told her sisters about the Dating Respect program, and by the time she finished, they'd reached the truck. Kelsey climbed behind the wheel. "It's a great idea. I'll help in any way I can."

Mackenzie climbed behind Kelsey. “Me too. That’s so much better than PC.”

Ryan sat shotgun and closed the door. “I hope so.” She checked her phone again. Still nothing.

Kelsey pulled out of the parking lot. “Justin wasn’t in school today. Everything okay?”

Ryan shrugged. “As good as it can be. They’re moving his mom to the psych hospital today.”

“Wow, that’s major.” Mackenzie spoke up from the back.

Ryan twisted sideways in her seat. “Yeah. I can’t imagine what he’s going through.”

Kelsey didn’t say anything, but she gave Ryan a look that said she wanted to.

Ryan looked back. “What?”

“Nothing.”

“Obviously, you have something you’re struggling not to say. So say it.”

Kelsey put a death grip on the steering wheel and gazed straight out the windshield.

Ryan flipped her cell in her hand and waited.

Finally, Kelsey took a deep breath and said, “I know you think he’s different with you, but he’s still crazy. He might hide it better with you, but he has anger issues. It’s just a matter of time before it’s aimed at you.”

At that moment, Ryan had so many *anger issues* it was all she could do to keep from chucking the phone at her sister. “He doesn’t have anger issues. He doesn’t like Austin, but can you blame him?”

“You weren’t there when he jumped Austin in the parking lot. He was crazy.”

"Look, Kelsey, I know Justin. And if he tackled Austin, there was a reason."

"Yeah, so you've said. I'm telling you, he's screwed up in the head." She glanced at Ryan and sighed. "You've been through so much. I just don't want to see you with a guy who doesn't treat you right."

Ryan's face burned with anger. Kelsey just couldn't look past that one moment in the parking lot. "You're judging him on a narrow view. He's so much more than that."

Kelsey bit her lip. "Just be careful. Sometimes it's hard to see past the nice things they do. When I was with Drew, I couldn't see how controlling he was. It took getting away from him to open my eyes."

"Justin is not Drew and I'm not you." God, she wanted to scream. How dared Kelsey compare Justin to Drew? Kelsey had dated Drew when they lived in Chicago. He'd had everything in life handed to him, from the A4 he drove to a summer in Europe. Yeah, nothing like Justin.

She didn't speak to her sister the rest of the way to the store. When they got there, Ryan went straight to work, which consisted of fiddling with a clothing display at the front of the store to take her mind off Justin.

When he called, it was all she could do to keep from doing one of those cheerleading jumps right there in the store. "Hey, Justin."

"Hey. Are you busy?"

Something's wrong. I can hear it in his voice. "We're about to close. What happened?"

"I just need to get away from here. Can we go for a drive?"

"Can I call you back?"

"Yeah."

She found her mom plinking on her computer in the back room. “Can I have the truck this evening?”

“Maybe. We can ride home with Dad. What for?”

Ryan bit her lip. *Please don’t read more into this than there is.* “Justin called. He wants to go for a drive.”

Her mom shook her head. “The whole thing is just so sad.” She leaned back in her chair. “You have to be pretty sick to put your kid through that. I heard that Justin found her.”

“He wrestled the gun from her.”

“Holy cow. Where was his dad?”

“Work? Can I have the truck?”

“Well, I don’t think he should drive upset. Where are you going?”

“I don’t know—probably just to Sonic.” *Just give me the keys already.*

Mom pulled her purse from beneath the kitchen cabinet and dug out a set of Ford keys and a twenty from her billfold. “Here. Be home by ten. It is a school night.”

“Thanks, Mom.” She turned to bolt from the room.

Her mom tapped her shoulder. “Wait.”

Great. Here comes the lecture about my behavior. She spun around. “What?”

“Justin’s dealing with some heavy stuff. I don’t know his situation with his dad, but if this is too much, bring him home. Dad and I can be great listeners.”

Totally didn’t expect that.

“Thanks, Mom.” She gave her mom a tight hug and reminded herself how lucky she was to have such awesome parents.

She tucked the twenty in her back pocket and called Justin. “I’m on my way. How do I get to your house?”

15

He lived less than five minutes from the feed store. He was waiting in the drive, and when she pulled in front of the house, he jogged toward the truck.

Her insides didn't know whether to be nervous or excited. When he opened the door, she smiled—and then her big, fat, lopsided lips did this crazy Elvis twitch.

Smooth, Ryan. Very smooth.

He smiled, but it was a sad smile. "Thanks for coming."

"No worries. Where do you want to go?"

"I need to walk. How about the park?"

The park was nestled in a grove of live oak trees. Spring Creek ran alongside the walking trail. She parked in the same spot Justin had taken her when he'd saved her from the fountain.

As they stepped onto the path, he took her hand and they walked in silence for what seemed like an eternity. It was sort of like that night at the gallery—except this time she wasn't all emotional. But the feel of his hand in hers was causing other sensations—like the desire to wrap her arms around him and press her lips against his. He gave her hand a squeeze and she thought her heart was going to burst.

They rounded a corner and there was a lookout over the muddy creek. Justin led her to the railing. “Thanks for coming.”

“Bad day?” She leaned on the rail and looked up at him. His eyes drooped at the corners and although he smiled down at her, his cheeks still sagged a little.

He placed his hands on her shoulders. “Better now.”

That was all she needed to hear. She wrapped her arms around his waist and he pulled her against him. He whispered into her hair. “Ryan, I need you. God, I don’t deserve you, but I need you.”

She looked into his face. “No. Believe me, I’m the one who doesn’t deserve you.”

He gave her a gentle kiss. “Does it hurt your mouth?”

“To kiss?” She gave him a slow smile. “No. Does it feel weird?”

“Let’s find out.” He lowered his mouth to hers. He kissed her deep and hard, and she couldn’t get enough. She pressed tight against him, welcoming his tongue. The kiss broke and he rested his forehead against hers. His breath was ragged. “It feels—awesome.”

She pulled back a little and placed her hands on his cheeks. “Good, because I want to take the sadness from your eyes.”

He squeezed them shut for half a second. “I’m sorry. I don’t want to infect you with my issues.”

She kissed the side of his mouth, his cheek, and the corner of his eye. “I’m here for you. I will always be here for you.” She caught his bottom lip between hers and then took his mouth with all the weeks of longing that had been building inside her. Desire flared—

The slut of Chicago was fighting for control.

She nestled against him. He ran his hands up her ribs and trailed his fingers over the sides of her breasts. Tingles spread through her and the Chicago side of her begged for more.

Justin pulled away from her mouth and trailed kisses down her neck. Somewhere in her mind, she pushed lust aside. "We can't."

"Okay." He stopped, wrapped his arms around her, and rested his chin on the top of her head. They held each other and swayed. He sighed deep and low and pulled from her completely. "Let's walk."

She nodded and they turned down the path again, only this time they didn't hold hands. But it was okay—they needed some distance between them.

"God, I feel like I haven't seen you in forever. How was school?"

"Good." She wanted to tell him about the doctor's appointment—that she had decided to have her lip fixed and that she was terrified something would go wrong. But this was his time. "How did it go with your mom?"

"It sucked." He ripped some leaves from a low-hanging branch. "The hospital is nice. It's just—I met the shrink today."

"Yeah?"

"Yeah. We barely got Mom settled when he wanted to jump right into therapy."

"Well, that's good. Right?"

He shook his head. "He talked to Mom first, then Dad, then me. I have no idea what they said, but by the time he got to me, I felt like he'd made some pretty big assumptions."

"Like what?"

"He said I needed to deal with Chelsea's death." He dropped the leaves he'd shredded. "I'm the only one who *has* dealt with it." His tone grew more animated. "I've cared for Mom while Dad has cared for the whole freaking county. I mean, he buries himself in work and *I'm* the one who isn't dealing?"

He wasn't yelling, but Ryan saw tension in his neck muscles. It was probably all he could do to stay in control. "What makes him say you aren't dealing?"

The trail continued alongside the cemetery, but Justin stopped and turned around. They walked in silence for a few hundred yards before he spoke again. "He asked how often I visited the cemetery." His voice was softer, but he didn't look any calmer.

"What difference does that make?"

"My mom goes every day—or did. On the days she could actually manage to get out of bed, she brought fresh flowers to Chelsea's grave. Every freaking day, rain or shine. That's out of control." He shook his head and spat on the side of the path. "Dad works all the time. He'll do like, six twelves in a row."

"But what does that have to do with you not dealing?"

"That's what I'm saying. Neither of my parents has dealt with Chelsea's death. I just want to go to school and play football. Who freaking cares if I go to the cemetery?"

"I take it the shrink cares. So when was the last time you went?"

His glance bounced off her and then away. "Never."

"Never? Like, ever? What about at the service?"

"I didn't need to see my sister's casket perched above some freaking hole in the ground. I didn't go to the graveside."

She reached for his hand, but he didn't take hers. She tried to dismiss the pang of disappointment. "You've never seen her grave?"

"It doesn't mean I haven't dealt with her death. I *deal* with it when I try to get Mom to eat. I *deal* with it every day that my parents don't." He shook his head. "Dr. O'Malley told me my homework was to visit her grave."

She stopped. "Go now. We're right here. I'll wait for you or go with you—whatever you want."

He kept walking and Ryan had to jog to catch up. "What's the point? It's not going to bring her back."

They passed the spot where they'd made out and Ryan wanted to pull him aside for a replay, but his long legs ate up the ground. Ryan couldn't keep up without half running. "Are you okay?" He slowed, but didn't say anything.

When they reached the truck, he leaned against the passenger door and ran his hands through his hair. "Look, I'm sorry. You don't need my shit."

She stood in front of him and ached for him to hold her again. But after the hand-holding rejection, she wasn't about to initiate anything. "I can handle it."

He pulled her close and wrapped his arms tight around her. She rested her head on his chest and felt his heart thudding in a steady rhythm. *God, this feels so good. No rumors. No past. Just here and now. This is exactly where I want to be.* His arms tightened around her and she pressed tighter against him. *Can we just stay like this forever?*

Her stomach growled. *Apparently not.*

He loosened his hold and smiled into her eyes. "Whoa, we need to feed that thing." He kissed her again and it was all she could do to keep from touching him in places that would get them both in trouble.

He dragged his lips from hers. "We'd better go."

"Yeah." She pulled away and walked to the driver's side. He waited until she was belted in and the engine running before he climbed in.

She looked at his flushed face and smiled. "Sonic?"

"Anywhere I can get a cold drink." He fastened his seatbelt and leaned back. "Talk to me about school? I need to hear about something normal."

She could have told him about her doctor's appointment. It was the perfect opportunity. But with everything he was dealing with, she wasn't going to burden him with her stupid fears. So instead, she told him about her Dating Respect idea.

"I'll help. It makes a lot of sense. Guys are stupid with girls." He leaned across the cab and planted a kiss on her cheek. "It's a great idea."

Her insides warmed.

She angled the truck into the drive-in and they placed their order. The Beatles played over the speakers. She looked at him and smiled, but if he remembered the last time they'd heard the Beatles, he didn't show it. In fact, he didn't show any emotion at all. He looked through the windshield completely blank-faced.

Shit. Shit. Crap. The last time we were here, his mom had just tried to shoot her brains out.

She reached across the truck and touched his arm. "Are you okay? Maybe we shouldn't have come here."

He snapped his gaze to her. "Why?"

His words didn't sound angry, but his eyes held a challenging look that made her stomach tighten. "I just thought it might remind you of the last time we were here."

"I don't work like that. If I avoided things because they were associated with a bad memory, I'd never go anywhere."

"Except the cemetery."

Why'd I say that? Too late. She couldn't pull the words out of thin air and stuff them back into her stupid mouth.

Justin's face flushed more brightly even than when she'd kissed him. "I'm not going to the cemetery."

Ryan put her hand on his. "Okay. I'm sorry. Let's drop it."

The carhop brought their order. Ryan pulled the money her mom had given her from her pocket and insisted she pay.

She nibbled on a few cheese fries while Justin wolfed down his dog. "Don't get mad... but there's something I don't understand."

He pressed his head into the headrest and sighed. "What?"

"Why do you hate Austin so much? You used to be friends. From what I see, he's a great guy." She was treading on dangerous ground, but if there was something about Austin that she needed to know, she wanted to hear it.

"You're new here, so you don't know the whole story."

"So what's the story?"

"You know Chelsea was answering his text when—" He shoved his half-eaten Coney into the paper sack. "—it happened."

Ryan had said too much already, but still her mouth kept spilling words. "Yeah. I feel bad for him, though. He couldn't have kno—"

"Really? You're going there." His voice trembled and she saw fury in his face.

Kelsey's warning surfaced. Did he have anger issues? She pressed on. "I'm sorry. I have to know something. Did you jump Austin in the coffee shop parking lot?"

Justin ran his hands through his hair. "It was stupid."

Ryan's stomach tightened. *Please have a good reason.* "What happened?"

He stared through the windshield and sighed. "Do you remember me telling you about the note my sister had written Eric?"

She nodded.

"I thought it was written to Austin. They'd spent a lot of time together. The thought of him doing that to my sister—I jumped to conclusions. Like I said, it was stupid."

Relief flowed through her.

"Why do you ask?"

"Kelsey brings it up a lot." She dropped the burger wrapper in the sack.

He pushed the leftover fries on top of the pile. "Not one of my finer moments."

She smiled at him. "We all have those." She set their trash and the window tray on the ledge by the menu. "Do you want to do something else?" *Please say yes.*

He looked at her and sighed long and loud. "I'm beat. I'm sorry."

"It's okay." She fake-smiled and hoped she hid the disappointment that filtered through her. She wasn't ready for the evening to end. She started the engine and pulled from the slot. Like everything else in town, it took about five minutes to get to his house. She parked and turned to him. "Are you okay? Really?"

"I am now." He leaned across the console and kissed her. She wanted to climb into his lap and spend the next hour making out. But he pulled away. "You wanna walk me to the door?"

"Sure." She got out of the truck and walked hand in hand with him up the walk. When they reached the door, she snaked her arms around his waist and looked into his eyes. She wanted him to ask about the appointment, and tried not to be disappointed that he hadn't. *Tell him.* But she couldn't.

He kissed her and her brain went straight into fireworks mode. When the kiss ended, he pulled her against his chest and whispered, "You saved me tonight."

Her heart felt so big and so loved. She squeezed him tight. This was the moment she'd heard about. The one when you knew you'd found *the one.* She felt his heart thump and wondered if hers was in sync with his. Then he ducked his head and kissed her neck. Her heart sped up.

She stood still and tried not to shiver as he trailed his kisses to her collarbone and back to her chin and then her lips. The kiss was slow, as though he was luxuriating in it. He pulled away and looked into her eyes. "You're the best thing that has ever happened to me."

"You saved *me*, remember."

He gave her a couple of quick pecks on the lips. "I need to go."

"Okay." But they both stood there staring at each other.

"I'll walk you to your truck."

She shook her head. "No, because then I'll want to walk you back to your door." She took a deep breath, pressed her lips against his one last time, and turned down the walk to her truck. But before she put it in gear, she took one last look at the house. He smiled and went inside.

*

It was only eight-thirty when she pulled up to their old farmhouse, where she parked next to Austin's truck. She hoped someday Justin would be welcome enough to hang out the way Austin was. He'd become a part of the family. Not that she minded. He was pretty cool and way better than Kelsey's old boyfriend. It was just that since Austin had made his way into the Quinn household, she wasn't sure Justin ever would.

She banged through the front door to the den. Austin and his best friend Travis sat on the sofa with Mackenzie and Kelsey playing a video game.

Kelsey spoke without looking up from the screen. "Where've you been?"

"Out. Where's Mom?"

Kenzie answered, "On the back porch with Dad."

Ryan dropped her purse on a table by the stairs and walked through the den to the kitchen and out the back door. Her parents sat at the patio table next to the pool sipping a glass of wine. "Mind if I join you?"

Her dad pulled out a chair. "Everything okay?"

She dropped into it. "Yeah. Justin needed to talk." She propped her feet on the chair next to her. "He's never been to his sister's grave."

Her mom shook her head. "Everybody deals differently."

"The shrink told him he hasn't dealt with it. But he's been so busy being angry and taking care of his mom that he thinks he has."

Her dad sipped from his glass. "Justin seems like a nice guy—just be careful. You don't need to take on his problems."

She tipped her head back and stared at the stars. "I'm not. I just want to be there for him. He doesn't have anybody else. I don't think he has any more friends than I do."

The screen door squeaked open and the gamers joined them on the patio. Travis and Kenzie sat next to each other a little to one side of the circle around the table. Kelsey and Austin sat next to Ryan, holding hands.

Ryan longed for Justin to be there too, holding her hand in front of everybody. She took a deep breath and turned to Austin. "I asked Justin about that night he jumped you."

Austin shifted uncomfortably in his chair. "Oh, yeah?"

She nodded. "He admitted that it was stupid."

Kelsey snorted. "Well, there's something."

Ryan snapped her gaze to her sister. "You don't know the whole story." She turned to Austin. "He'd found a letter his sister had written. He thought it was about you."

Austin nodded. "It was about Eric Perez."

Travis slammed his hands down on the armrests of his chair. "This is total crap." Everybody stared at him. "Justin goes through life being angry and blaming Austin and everybody makes excuses for him because his sister died. My sister died in that crash too. If you want to really look at it, I could be pissed at him because his sister was driving. I chose not to. All that anger doesn't do crap. It won't bring them back." He stood. "I'm sorry, Ryan. You're a cool chick, but don't let him pull you into his crap." He walked to the edge of the pool.

Silence filled the air.

Ryan's dad set his wine glass on the table. "He has a point."

Ryan didn't want to admit that Travis might be right. She wanted to think about how good it felt to be wrapped in Justin's arms. She wanted to dream about the day he could be a part of her family the way Austin was. She pushed out of her chair. She wanted to scream at Travis that he didn't understand.

But he did understand, better than any of the rest of them.

Instead, she yelled, "Maybe I *want* to be dragged into his crap." She stormed into the house and slammed the door.

By the time she reached her bedroom, tears were flowing down her cheeks. She didn't want Travis to be right. But the truth niggled inside her. She wasn't going to admit that out loud. Not to her family. Not to Austin. Not to Travis.

And sure as hell not to herself.

16

Justin dropped his keys on the counter. His dad was watching the news in the den. If he was lucky, he could head to his room without talking to him.

His dad stood and walked toward the kitchen.

Shit.

"There's some leftover Hamburger Helper on the stove."

"Thanks. I went to Sonic." Justin leaned against the counter. "Do you think this is going to work for Mom?"

His dad shrugged. "She's determined to work hard to get better."

"What does that mean—work hard? How do you work at not being depressed?" Justin grabbed a Gatorade from the fridge.

His dad folded his arms across his chest. "Well, she's taking her meds, attending group, engaging in activities. Stuff like that."

"And that's supposed to fix her."

His dad nodded, but his look held about as much hope as Justin felt. Zero.

Justin took a sip of his drink and hoped his dad would go back to the TV.

His dad rubbed the back of his neck. "Are you ready for the game Friday?"

"Yeah. It should be an easy win." *Not that you'd know.*

"I'm off Friday. I'll be at the game."

So you said. I'll alert the press. "It's a little late for you to act like you care, don't you think?" He grabbed the bottle of Gatorade and his backpack and headed to his room.

He pulled his calculus book from his backpack. He was half pissed and half relieved that his dad hadn't come after him. God, how many times had he said he'd be at a game and not shown up? The guy was full of such bullshit.

He opened his book and shifted his mind toward differential equations.

He'd managed to completely absorb himself in the problems when his dad knocked and came into the room. "It's late, I'm headed to bed. Don't forget, we have another family session tomorrow. And before you say anything, remember this is for Mom. Do you want me to pick you up from school?"

For Mom. He tapped the eraser end of his pencil on his notebook. He'd do it for her because he'd promised. "Just write me a note and I'll meet you there." He held out his spiral notebook and a pen.

His dad flipped to a blank page, scrawled a note, and handed it back. "The appointment is at ten. I put that you need to check out at nine-thirty. Okay?"

"I'll be there." He flipped back to his equations and turned away.

His dad left the room. Neither of them said good night.

*

Justin greeted his mom in the lobby at Garden Oaks. He hugged her and kissed her on the cheek. "You look good." And she did. She'd fixed her hair and makeup and the circles under her sagging eyes looked a little smaller.

"Thanks. Where's Dad?"

"We came separately. He should be here any second." He smiled at her, but the look in her eyes told him she didn't have any more confidence in his words than he did. His stomach churned and he prayed his dad wouldn't show up late. His mom deserved better.

She nodded and sat in one of the plastic chairs lining the wall of the lobby.

His dad rushed through the door of the lobby just as Justin and his mom were being ushered toward the therapy waiting area.

Typical.

Dr. O'Malley led Justin into the therapy room. An overstuffed leather sofa and love seat had been placed at right angles, with an end table nestled between them. Closing off the other side of the square were two high-backed velvet chairs. A coffee table separated the furniture.

"Have a seat, Justin. Your parents will join us in a few minutes."

Justin hesitated in front of the sofa Dr O'Malley indicated, and took a seat in the chair next to the doctor. If it bothered Dr. O, he didn't show it—not even a raised eyebrow.

Dr. O crossed his legs and balanced a pad on one knee. "Did you go to the cemetery?"

"No. I'm not going."

If he'd expected a lecture, he didn't get one. Dr. O only nodded. "Okay. What kind of grades do you make, Justin?"

"What?" That caught him off guard. They were supposed to talk about his mom and how to help her get her head together. "As, Bs, a couple of Cs. I have to keep my grades up to play football."

"Football is important to you?"

Was it? He hadn't really thought about it. It was something he did because he was good at it. Yeah, he enjoyed it, but was it important to him? "Yeah. Isn't it important to everybody?"

"Do you have a lot of friends at school?"

"Yes." Did he? Really? The only friend he cared about was Ryan.

"Enemies?"

"What kind of question is that?"

"Your dad tells me you've had some issues with a boy in your school. That you have had a couple of fights."

"How would he know?" Justin challenged.

"Is it true? Have you gotten into fights?"

"Maybe." *Shit. What kind of answer was that?* He looked at his hands. "Yes."

"Tell me about the fight."

"There is nothing to tell. There's this one guy. He killed my sister. He's responsible for my family being messed up. Sometimes when I see him…" He couldn't say *I want to kill him*. Then he'd be the one locked up in the nuthouse.

"What? What do you feel when you see him?"

"Anger. Loads of anger."

The doctor sat back. "Your sister pulled out in front of a cement truck. Why was it this boy's fault?"

“Because he was texting her. If he hadn’t been texting her, she wouldn’t have died.” The argument he’d clung to all these years seemed weak when he said it aloud. But it was how he felt.

“She didn’t have to answer.”

Dr. O’Malley had verbalized the argument Justin couldn’t dispute. It hung in the air in front of him, making him want to tear it apart. He couldn’t. He knew it was true. But if he accepted it, then who would he blame for the disintegration of his family? It sure as hell wasn’t his fault.

Time ticked by as seconds turned to minutes. Sweat formed on Justin’s palms and trickled down his neck. He closed his eyes and tried to swallow past the lump in his throat, past the air rushing out of his lungs in quick, shallow breaths. He opened his eyes and stared at the fibers of the tan carpet that stretched between him and Dr. O’Malley. Beginning with his gut, his muscles contracted, and he stood.

Dr. O watched him rise without moving his head. His eyes tracked him like those of a hunter tracking prey. Quietly he said, “How do you feel now, Justin?”

“Freaking angry.” Justin walked to the back of the room and stared out of the window. Some view. A parking lot and beyond that, a dried-up cornfield. The stalks were burned yellow by the Texas sun. He swallowed the anger that had surged and turned back toward the center of the room.

“Let’s back up a bit.” Dr. O spoke in an even tone that Justin figured must have been a technique to calm patients. He hadn’t flinched when Justin swore either. In fact, he hadn’t changed his position at all. He must have learned that in How to Deal with Crazies 101.

Justin walked back to the therapy area and flopped onto the leather sofa.

Dr. O'Malley looked at his notes. "Walk me through a typical day for you."

What kind of lame-ass question is that? "I get up. Go to school, football practice, come home. End of story."

"What happens when you get home? Is the TV on? Is it quiet? Where are your mom and dad?"

The lump in his throat grew. He leaned his head against the back of the sofa. "The house is usually quiet and dark. Mom…" His eyes stung and he squeezed them tight until the feeling eased. "Mom is in bed. Dad is at work."

"Who prepares the meals, does the shopping, and cleans the house?"

"Me." He barely squeaked the word. It was small, two letters, and yet it threatened to release a shitload of emotion. He toyed with the piping around the edges of the cushion.

"That's a lot of responsibility for a seventeen-year-old. How does that make you feel?"

Justin shrugged. "It has to be done."

"What about your dad?"

"He works. Like twenty-four seven. The sicker Mom got, the more he worked."

"Does he come to your games?"

"No. Never."

"And your mom?"

"She used to. It upsets her to see Austin."

"Austin?"

"The guy who texted my sister. She tried for a while. But it's hard to make it to a game when you can't even get out of bed to eat."

Dr. O'Malley uncrossed his legs and sat back. "You go to school and make pretty good grades. You're a starter on the varsity football team. But the other side of you manages the household. Do you pay the bills too?"

"No. Dad manages that." *Where the hell is he going with this shit?*

"What happened the night you found your mom with the gun?"

"I think you know." He wasn't going there. It was too fresh, too raw.

"I'd like to hear it from you."

"Why?"

"Were you frightened?"

"My mom had a fricking gun. How do you think I felt?" He was tired of this talking about your feelings shit. It was time to be done.

"Okay. Fair enough. I sense you have a lot of anger toward your dad."

Give the man a prize.

Dr. O set the notebook on the table. "It's okay, Justin. You've dealt with a lot. You've taken care of your mom, the house, the food preparation. When do you get to be a kid?"

That did it. When did he get to be a kid? Justin pressed into the back of the sofa and closed his eyes to fight the sting. "Never." He heard himself whisper. He hadn't meant to say it. He hadn't meant to let this doctor in on his secret. What kind of person resented—no, *hated*—taking care of his own mother? His cheeks were wet with tears and his nose filled with snot.

Justin pressed the heels of his hands into his eyes, but it didn't stop the flow of tears, didn't stop his torso from shaking as he bawled like a wuss. He looked up at Dr. O'Malley. "You son of a bitch."

Dr. O'Malley pushed a box of tissues across the table toward him. "I know."

Justin blew his nose, but it filled up again. "What kind of asshole hates taking care of his sick parent?" Dr. O didn't answer. "Just once, I want to come home to Mom cooking dinner, you know? Hell, I'd be happy if Mom were vegging out in front of the TV. But it's been the same damn thing every day. I come home and Mom is in bed. I beg her to eat, fix her dinner—which she barely touches—and then she goes back to bed. Jesus, she recounts the night of the accident over and over. And Dad." He stopped to blow his nose again. "And Dad is always at work. I mean, I know what he does is important. He saves frickin' lives, for Chrissakes. But he's forgotten us. Do you see? Do you see why I hate Austin McCoy? If my sister hadn't answered that freaking text, if she hadn't died, I wouldn't be in this shithole of a life."

"What about Chelsea? You're not angry with her for answering the text?"

Justin looked up at the doctor. "She's dead. What good would that do?"

"It's a normal part of grieving. Anger at the one who's gone is part of it."

"Nothing about my family's grieving is normal, Dr. O'Malley. That's why we're here." He thought he saw Dr. O's lip twitch toward a smile, but it didn't make it before it was replaced with the emotionless face.

Dr. O'Malley placed the palms of his hands on his knees and sat up straight. "Justin, I'm going to suggest something to you that you already know. What happened to your family is a sad and horrible thing. But you are not responsible for your parents' behavior and neither is Austin. There is a lot of strength in your story. You have taken care of yourself, your mom, and the adult chores. You probably saved your mom's life. From this point forward, I'd like you to work on being a kid. I am going to ask your parents to work on putting the family structure back in place."

It'd been so long since they'd been a real family that Justin couldn't imagine it. "What happens if Mom goes back to bed? What if it doesn't work?" Just asking the question made his heart beat a little faster. Could Dr. O help his family?

"I am going to give you all tools to keep it from happening again. Are you ready for me to bring your family in?"

"Yes."

Dr. O'Malley left the room. Justin blew his nose again and hoped his eyes weren't too swollen and red. He didn't want his parents to know he'd cried. Dr. O wanted him to work on being a kid. What did that even mean?

He knew one thing for sure. It was all well and good that Dr. O was going to give them *tools,* but his dad would always put the hospital before his family, and he doubted his mom was strong enough to pull herself out of the depths of depression for long. And as far as he could see, this was an exercise in frustration. There was no way they could be a family—that had died with Chelsea.

He just needed to hold his shit together until he graduated from high school—and hope to hell his mom could hold her shit together after he was gone.

*

Justin's heart raced as he slowed the truck. Sweat beaded his forehead and upper lip. According to the lady in the cemetery office, he should park next to the live oak tree with the wind chimes hanging from a branch and a bench beneath it. Chelsea's grave would be three rows from the street. He put the truck in Park and cut the engine.

He could do this. It was just a granite stone. It didn't matter that his sister's name was engraved on it, it didn't matter that she lay in a box beneath it.

He got out of the truck and tried to calm his pounding heart. He saw a pink granite headstone with a metal cross stuck in the ground next to it. A straw cowboy hat dangled from the cross, fastened to the metal with a zip tie. He read the name Lindsey Barnes and his throat felt tight. Travis's sister. She'd been in the front seat next to Chelsea.

He stepped carefully through the stone field until he found the third row from the road. Dried yellow roses slumped in the urn that was a part of the pink stone that bore his sister's name. He'd planned on looking and leaving. He just wanted to say he'd done it, to prove to Dr. O'Malley that he could.

When he saw her name, Chelsea Lynn Hayes, it was if he'd been sucker punched in the gut. He fell to his knees and all the air whooshed from his lungs. He gasped in a desperate attempt to drag oxygen into his body. His gaze was riveted to her name. "No. Oh, God. Chelsea, no." Tears flooded his eyes and streamed down his face. He dug his fist into the grass and sobs heaved from his chest. He imagined the white box beneath the earth and the girl asleep in that box. She was there, six feet and a lifetime away from him.

Pain filled every molecule in his body. She was gone. He would never tease her again—fight with her—see her. Why had she answered that freaking text? "Damn you, Chelsea! Damn you. You stupid girl. Don't you see? You ruined everything. Three people died because you couldn't put down your freaking phone. Mom is crazy out of her head. Dad is just gone. And I… I need you. Why? Why did this happen? Why did that truck have to be there? Why'd you leave us?"

He sat on the grass cross-legged, let his shoulders slump, and cried. Guilt for the things he'd said spread through him. He turned his face toward the sky. "And You, what the hell were You thinking? What did she ever do to You? You took her from us. She didn't deserve this. We didn't deserve this! We were a great family. We were happy. But You had to go and mess that up." He let tears fall freely until his eyes felt peppered with grains of sand.

He pulled his knees close to his torso, propped his left arm on his knee, and toyed with a blade of grass. *I didn't mean it. I'm sorry, Chelsea.* He bowed his head. *I'm sorry, God. Please don't take this out on my family. Make Mom better. Make us a family again.*

Tears dripped in an endless stream from his eyes. "I'm sorry I didn't come sooner. I miss you, sis."

He sniffed and stood. He took a deep breath and looked around at the stone field. Two graves from Chelsea's was the one marking the third girl's resting place. Abigail Yates. She'd been an only child. Her parents had moved to Dallas a few months after her death. He righted a brass cross that had toppled off the ledge of the headstone, turned, and walked to his truck.

Well he'd done it. He could tell the shrink he must be over Chelsea because he'd been to the cemetery. Sarcasm aside, he wasn't sorry he'd come. It was time.

He blew out a breath, started the engine, and headed back to school.

17

Ryan sat outside the counselor's office and willed Justin to text her. She had hoped to see him after lunch, but no such luck. She'd checked her phone between classes—no text. She was so consumed with looking for a message from him that she'd almost forgotten she'd been asked to meet with Mrs. Bettis after school.

She held her phone and stared at the screen, wanting so badly to text him and ask how the session had gone with his family. But how did one ask about a shrink appointment? Instead, she sent *Hi.*

Braden McGuire took the seat next to her. "Do you think they went for your idea?"

Ryan toyed with the rubber cover on her phone. "I don't know. Do you?"

He shrugged. "I guess we'll see."

Mrs. Bettis opened the door to her office. "Come in."

Ryan and Braden filed in and sat in the chairs in front of her desk. Pictures of twin girls hung on the wall behind her. They had the same auburn hair as Mrs. Bettis.

Mrs. Bettis folded her hands on top of her desk. "I talked to Mrs. Johnson about your idea, and we investigated the website." She stretched a little taller in her seat. "We like the idea of a replacement for the Purity Club. However, in light of—" She swept her hand in Ryan's direction. "—recent events, we feel we should broaden the group beyond dating violence."

Great. They're going to make me the anti-bullying poster girl.

Mrs. Bettis looked at Braden and back at Ryan. "There is a group called Teens Against Violence. It's very similar to Dating Respect but has a broader focus."

Ryan leaned forward. "So this is an anti-bullying group?"

Mrs. Bettis shook her head. "More than that. Abuse comes in all forms. Controlling behavior doesn't just occur between dating couples—friends can abuse each other as well."

She handed each of them a sheet of paper. Bold letters announced, *Red Flags to an Unhealthy Relationship.*

The first one on the list read *Does your friend/partner constantly put you down?*

Ryan looked up from the sheet. "I like it."

Braden read the paper and shook his head. "These things are pretty obvious. I mean..." He looked at the sheet. "*Does your friend/partner check your cell or email without permission?* Who doesn't know that's whacked?"

Mrs. Bettis said, "Unfortunately, a lot of people." Her forehead wrinkled and the corners of her mouth drooped a little. "It often happens slowly, insidiously. The abuser may start with a put-down and eventually break the person's confidence. They begin to control their victim's whereabouts, what they wear, who they can see. The victims often believe the abuser's controlling behavior is an act of love."

Braden shook his head. "That's crazy."

Ryan looked at him. "Which is why I want to do this. I mean, what if this is an education not only for the abused but the abuser? If they don't understand that what they're doing is wrong, we can teach them. Who knows—maybe I could save somebody from having to go through this." She drew an imaginary circle in the air in front of her face.

Braden looked at Ryan and back at Mrs. Bettis. "I'm in. What do we do?"

Mrs. Bettis pointed to the paper in his hand. "I want y'all to check out the website at the bottom of the page. Think of people you'd like to help you charter this club. I'd like to have a panel of eight—two from each class. I'd prefer a boy and a girl from each class. Let's meet back in a week. I'd like names of potential candidates."

Mrs. Bettis discussed the type of candidate she was looking for and Ryan and Braden were dismissed. Braden walked with her toward her locker. "Obviously I'm the sophomore male member and you're the junior girl. Do you think Mackenzie would be the freshman girl?"

Ryan tried to contain the smile that formed and it morphed into a smirk. "I guess you should go ask her." She pointed down the hall.

He visibly gulped. "Okay, then." He practically sprinted to where Mackenzie was talking to Travis.

Ryan pulled her phone from the back pocket of her jeans and looked for a message from Justin. Nada.

Her stomach tightened. The session must not have gone well. Should she call him? He probably wouldn't want to talk, but he probably needed to. Besides, she really wanted to ask him to be the senior representative. Was that cold? Here he was dealing with major stuff in his life and she was focused on asking him to be a leader in a club.

Texting was safer. He could ignore that.

Ryan: Hey there.

She didn't want to be too intrusive, just in case things were bad.

She stared at her phone as though she could make him answer. Nothing. Maybe he was with his parents and things were going great. Maybe not. She shook her head. She had never been the clingy type and she wasn't about to start now. She shoved the phone into her pocket and headed to her locker.

Someone, probably the janitor, had cleaned off the lipstick letters that had stained her locker. *That leaves a clean slate for whoever is doing it.* By tomorrow, another profanity would be scrawled across it. She got her books and slammed the metal door.

If they brought the Teens Against Violence club to school, would it stop? She doubted it.

Did she still want to be involved in Teens Against Violence? Absolutely.

*

Normally, if Justin missed school he had to miss practice too. Coach knew why he'd missed and probably figured how badly he needed to work out.

He'd answered Ryan's text with *Football practice.* He should've told her he'd call later. Part of him wanted to talk to her, tell her everything. The other side of him wasn't ready to share what had happened at the cemetery, but if he saw her, he'd find himself telling her. He wanted to hold on to it a little longer—to feel the pain and then release it. How sick was that?

He wasn't going to worry about that now. He had passes to catch. He and Austin might have been enemies, but they'd pretty much always been able to leave it off the field. Austin had an arm, and he had aim. All Justin had to do was be close to the spot he was supposed to be and Austin would get the ball to him.

Too bad Justin couldn't seem to hang on to a single pass. It was like the ball was greased or something. Every single pass slipped through his fingers. Coach blew the whistle and called him off the field.

"If you're going to play Friday, you'd better focus." He lowered his sunglasses. "Everything okay?"

"Yes sir." He rubbed his hands on his thighs. "I'm good."

Coach replaced his sunglasses and nodded. Justin ran back on the field. That's the way it was. Short and no extra bullshit words. The way it should be. They ran the drill again and focused on keeping the ball in his hands.

On the field it didn't matter that his family was effed up, or that Chelsea was gone. Here he could just be.

After they were dismissed, he took his time going to the field house. He had no reason to hurry home. If his dad was home, he'd have to talk to him and he wasn't ready. If he was at work, he'd have to face the echoes of the memory of the gun clattering to the floor. Either way, it sucked. Yep, that was his life.

Caleb James was at the door when he entered the field house. "Everything okay?"

"Yeah." Justin pushed past him.

Caleb followed. "Mickey and I are going to the Early Bird. Wanna go?"

Home with memories and Dad. Diner with guys from the team. "Sure. I got nothing better to do." *Why wasn't Ryan option number three?*

He wanted to see her. He wanted to wrap his arms around her and feel her against him. So what was his problem? She was the only good part of his life. She made him feel alive, happy.

But tonight he didn't want happy. Tonight he wanted to think about how much his life sucked. He wanted to wallow in it and let it suck him in.

*

As soon as they pushed open the screen door of the café, Justin regretted coming.

Ashley Boyd and Courtney Randall sat at a four-top in the middle of the restaurant. Ashley jumped up so fast when she saw them that she knocked her chair over. Couldn't they just ignore the girls and sit in the back corner?

Apparently not. Caleb was quick to help Ashley with her chair and then took a seat next to her. Justin sat next to Courtney, with Mickey Williams on her other side. It would've been great if at least the girls had been fixing to leave, but no-o-o. They hadn't ordered yet.

Great. Just effing great.

And as if the suck gods hadn't rained enough shit on him, Kelsey Quinn was the waitress *du jour*. She brought a tray of water to their table and passed around menus. "I'll be back in a sec to get your orders."

Justin jumped in before anybody else could order. "Can we have separate checks?" Not that he minded paying or everybody pitching in, but he wanted it to be clear that this was not a date—just in case Kelsey talked to her sister.

Courtney stuck one end of the straw in her mouth and blew the wrapper at Justin, hitting him on the cheek. Everyone laughed as though it was the funniest thing ever. All Justin could manage was a weak smile.

The girls droned on about something that had happened in the cafeteria. He laughed in the right places but his mind wasn't really into hearing about some poor kid spilling a tray full of food.

He sighed and leaned back in his chair. *Okay, really it isn't that bad. Better than sitting at home eating peanut butter sandwiches.*

That must have pissed off the suck gods, because before he could wipe the artificial smile off his face, he heard the screen door of the café squeak open. He turned toward the noise and a voice in his head screamed, *Nooooo!*

Yep. It was Ryan. In the few seconds of eye contact he saw—no, *felt* her emotions travel from shock to hurt in a nanosecond. One-two-boom. He wanted to explain himself, but she turned her back on him and walked straight to Kelsey, taking a seat at the counter.

He slumped back in his chair. "Crap."

Courtney fake-shivered. "Can you imagine having to go out in public with your face torn up like that? I'd just hide until it healed."

"Or at least cover it with some makeup," Ashley said. "They make stuff especially to cover scars."

"I'm done." Justin tossed his napkin on his plate and stood.

Courtney grabbed his hand. "Come on, don't leave."

He pulled his hand from hers and walked over to Ryan and Kelsey. “Hey.” His chest felt heavy. He should’ve texted her after practice. He should have been here with her.

She looked up at him. “How was practice?” The words came out flat.

“Okay. I’m sorry I didn’t text afterward.”

She shrugged. “It’s cool.” She turned back to her sister. He’d just been dismissed.

He leaned in so he could see her face. “Ryan, can we talk?”

“Not now. I’m busy.”

Kelsey didn’t say anything, but the look she gave him came through loud and clear: *Leave my sister alone.*

But he couldn’t. He’d screwed up and he had to fix this. “Can I call?”

Ryan didn’t look at him. “I can’t stop you.”

Shit. Shit. Shit. This was bad. “Please, don’t jump to conclusions. It wasn’t a date.”

She turned to face him full on. “I don’t own you.” Her words were clipped and angry. But the thing that tore at his heart was the hurt in her eyes. Not like there were tears—only pain.

Kelsey stepped closer to Ryan. “I think you need to leave.”

“Okay.” He stepped away. He’d effed up the best thing he’d ever had. And the suck gods rejoiced.

For now.

He walked to the cash register where the rest of his group waited to pay. Courtney slipped her arm around his waist and looked at him. “You okay?”

He backed away and put a hand up. “Not now.”

He tossed a ten on the counter with the check and walked out. His truck was parked almost front and center, facing the door to the diner. He climbed in and opened the windows, but he didn’t start the engine. He wasn't ready to leave. Not until he'd talked to Ryan.

So he'd just sit here until she came out.

18

The store closed at six and she could have ridden home with her parents, but the last thing she wanted was to sit at home staring at her phone. So, she'd asked them to drop her off at the Early Bird. She'd hang out there and ride home with Kelsey.

She was an idiot.

When she walked through the door and saw Justin with those girls, a piece of her died. She felt it. It shriveled up and died. She'd been crazy to think a guy like him could look past her face for long.

Sure, he felt bad. He'd been caught. But it didn't matter. She was done. Her heart couldn't take another battering. She was going to do what she should have done in the beginning, which was to focus on school, on getting the Teens Against Violence group together, and forgetting about Justin and his bag of shit. He obviously didn't need her to get through it. So fine, she could go on with her life without worrying about him.

After he left, Kelsey sat next to her on the swivel stool. "You're way better off without him."

"I don't want to talk about it." She toyed with a saltshaker. "How soon before you get off?"

"Twenty minutes." A group of middle-aged women entered the café and sat at a back table. Kelsey slid off the stool and pulled her order pad from her apron. "I need to get this order. Do you want a coke or something?"

"No. I just need some air. I'll be outside."

When she stepped out onto the sidewalk, the first thing she saw was a big black Ford F150. She didn't know whether to be happy or angry, so that meant both feelings churned in her. She had two options. She could sit on the bench outside the diner and wait for him to come to her, or she could go right up to his truck and talk to him. Either way, they were going to talk. He'd waited for her, so obviously it was going to happen.

She sat on the bench. She wasn't chasing anybody.

His door opened almost before her butt hit the weathered seat. She kept her eyes focused on the ground about ten feet in front of her.

He sat next to her. "I'm sorry. I didn't know Ashley and Courtney were going to be here."

"I'm not worried about those girls." It was true. It was obvious that Justin didn't want to be with either of them.

"You're not? Good." He studied his hands.

She could tell he was trying to sort everything out in his brain. She let the silence fill the tension between them.

He sat back and stretched his long legs in front of him. "I should've called."

She flopped against the back of the bench too. "Look Justin, you can hang out with whoever you want." She looked down. "It's just…"

"Just what? I want to hang out with you."

She tilted her head and shifted her gaze toward him. "I could tell."

"It's not like that. When we finished with practice, Caleb invited me to come here. I should've texted you. I just sort of—didn't."

Wow. That hurt. "You don't have to check in with me. I knew today was a big day for you. I just wanted to be there if you needed me. That's all." *And obviously you didn't.*

"But I do need you."

He sounded so fake it made her laugh. "Now you just sound like a player."

"I'm not. Not anymore." He raised his voice.

"Easy, boy. You don't want my sister running out here to rescue me."

He dragged his hands through his hair, leaving it all messy and sexy. "I don't want you to ever feel like you need to be rescued from me." He twisted to face her and stretched his arm along the back of the bench. "Today was big for me." He took a deep breath and let it out slowly. "I went to the cemetery."

"Wow. And?" *And then chose to share that earth-shattering experience with someone else.*

"It was—horrible—and good. Afterward I had practice. You're the only one I wanted to tell, but I—I just wasn't ready. When Caleb asked me to hang out—I don't know, it just seemed like a good way to not think about it."

Sucker punched. Right in the gut. "I'm glad you found someone to have fun with."

"That's not what I meant."

"The thing is, I don't want to be the girl you only talk to when you're down."

"But you're not. I want to be with you."

"I wish that were true. Think about it. You said yourself you weren't ready to talk about it. You went out with them to take your mind off it." He opened his mouth to argue, but she put a hand up. "Hear me out. Everything we've done together has been riddled with drama. We've never hung out just to have fun. That's not normal. No wonder you didn't text me. Being with me has always been heavy."

He didn't argue. She knew he wouldn't. But all the same, she wanted him to. As the seconds ticked between them, she willed him to deny what they both knew was true.

She picked at her thumbnail. "Maybe we should take some time to get our lives together."

"Why? Can't we just make it a point to do something crazy and fun? Come on, Ryan, let's just try."

"Right now, whatever we do will turn all serious and deep. We don't know how to have fun together. I need some time to get past what happened to me. You need to take time to heal with your family." She placed her hands on his cheeks. "Thank you for being my friend. Thank you for rescuing me. Let's not mistake this for love."

She dropped her hands and stood. He grabbed her hand and looked at her with pleading eyes. "Don't go."

Her heart pounded in her chest. Part of her wanted to sit back down and snuggle into his arms. It would be so easy to lose herself in him and pretend her life wasn't a hot mess. She bit her bottom lip. It was time to stand on her own two feet and face the people who called her *slut* and *whore*. "I can't—not now." She backed away and he let her hand slide from his fingers.

She turned and went back into the café, where Kelsey looked at her from the kitchen side of the counter. "You okay?"

Ryan flashed a smile that she hoped was more convincing than she felt. “No. But I will be.” Thankfully the place was almost empty and she was able to move close to the window. She watched Justin climb into his truck looking like he carried the world on his shoulders. It was good that she’d backed away from him. He didn’t need her drama.

She took a seat on the swivel stool across from her sister. “Can I have a DP?”

“Sure.”

As she waited, the reality of what had just happened squeezed her heart in her chest. She’d just let her only friend go. She’d just told the one person who had been there for her to give her space.

She took her phone out of her pocket and pulled up his name. She should tell him she’d been stupid and didn’t mean it.

Kelsey set the Dr. Pepper in front of her. “What happened out there?”

“I told him we needed space from each other.” She set the phone on the counter. “He’s dealing with so much, he doesn’t need my drama.”

“He is messed up. I’m glad you finally see that.” Kelsey snagged a sip of the DP.

“Hey. That’s mine.” She pulled the drink close. “He’s had a lot of stuff in his life. Who wouldn’t be a little crazy with all that crap?”

Kelsey put up her hands as though she were surrendering. “Sorry. It’s cool that you’re giving him space. It’s kind of the ultimate sacrifice. It’s really romantic—in a tragic sort of way.”

“Justin is not tragic.”

Kelsey grabbed a pitcher of tea and scooted from behind the counter. “Yeah, he is.” She walked to a table in the back of the room to fill glasses.

Ryan rested her elbows on the counter, cradled her head in her hands, and sipped her drink. He was tragic. He was a beautiful, sweet, sexy hot mess and she already missed him. She stared at his name on her phone. She hadn't intended to back off, but it was the right thing to do—for both of them.

She shoved the phone back in her pocket.

*

As she pulled away from him, dragging her fingers from his, a part of his soul went with her—torn from his chest and leaving ragged edges crying out to be whole again. *Let's not mistake this for love.* Those words made the first ragged cut severing the part of him that would be lost to her forever.

He wanted to tell himself that it was all Ashley and Courtney's fault, but he couldn't. The truth was that their relationship had been bundled with a whole lot of shit. It wasn't fair to ask her to deal with his crap while she was dealing with the assholes at school.

On the other hand, they could be stronger together. That was the thought he wanted to hang on to. Stronger together.

He could get up, walk back into the diner, and tell her so. And... she'd look at him like he was crazy. Nope. Theatrics was the last thing Ryan wanted. If he wanted to be with her, he'd have to win her. He needed to get his shit together and allow her to deal with what she needed to. He had to back away, just as she asked.

He trudged back to his truck. His body felt heavy, as though gravity were trying to suck him into the earth. Sadness had a way of doing that. He rolled his shoulders in a failed attempt to shed the feeling, pulled his body behind the wheel, and headed to the motherhouse of sadness.

The sky was pink when he parked in the drive next to his dad's car. The lights were off in the house—just like that night. He reached for the driver's door, but was seized by tightness in his chest as his heartbeat ramped up to thud against his chest wall. Sweat beaded across his face and panic rose in his throat like bile. His memory went to his mom sitting on the floor with the drawings in her lap and the gun in her hand.

He needed to get out of the truck, but he couldn't make his hand pull the door handle. He picked up his phone and found Ryan's number. His thumb hovered over her picture.

No. I can do this.

But he couldn't. What was freaking wrong with him? The image of his mom lifting that gun to her head flashed in his mind. He knew it wasn't real, but he couldn't stave off the panic that held him. He stared through the windshield, frozen behind the wheel.

A voice called through the fog in his brain. "Justin?"

He struggled to focus on the words that reached out to him like a lifeline to reality. But his memory went to his mom, unconscious, with a tube crammed down her throat.

The truck door swung open. "It's okay. I'm here. You're okay." His dad climbed into the cab, pulled him against his chest, and held him tight.

Justin's mind released him but not before making him blubber like a freaking baby. His whole body trembled with the effects of adrenaline coursing through it as he cried.

"It's okay. Let it go, it'll pass." His dad's voice was both calming and commanding.

When he could breathe again, Justin wrapped his hands around his dad's upper arms and held on, terrified he'd slide back into momentary hell. "Help." All he could manage was that single word.

His dad seemed to understand exactly what he meant. He kept his gaze focused on Justin and nodded. "Let's get you out of the truck. I'm with you."

Justin nodded.

Together they made it up the walk and into the house. His brain didn't kick back in completely until he heard his dad's sneakers squeak on the tile as he helped him onto the sofa.

"Let me get you some water." The sound of ice dropping into the glass brought reality one notch closer. His dad shoved the glass into his hand and sat on the coffee table across from him. "Drink."

The cold water felt good passing down his throat. He looked at his dad, who wore a sweat-soaked tee and jogging shorts. No wonder the house was dark. "What happened to me?"

"Post Traumatic Stress."

"I saw the lights off and I went back to that night. It was in my head. I knew it. But I couldn't stop the thoughts."

His dad nodded. "I was about a half a block away when I saw you freeze. Most of the time the feelings will fade. Still, I think you should mention it to Dr. O'Malley."

"Dad?" His heart thudded again. The question had to be asked—even if he wasn't sure he wanted to know the answer.

"Yeah."

"What if it doesn't fade? What if it happens again?"

"We'll deal with it. Dr. O'Malley will give you tools to help. That was a horrible night. No kid should have to go through what you did. Time is a wonderful healer. But we can't ignore it. You can't pretend you don't have those memories. You have to acknowledge and deal with them."

It made sense to Justin. Silently he prayed he wouldn't go back to that place. He wanted to talk to Ryan. To tell her what had happened. If anybody could understand, it would be her. Had she experienced PTS? Did seeing the fountain bring back that night of terror to her? God, he hoped not.

"You hungry?" His dad broke into his thoughts.

"No. I grabbed dinner at the Early Bird." He set his glass on the coffee table next to his dad and stood. "I'd better get my backpack out of my truck. I have Calculus homework." He stopped at the door and turned toward his dad. "Thanks for being there for me." Before his dad could answer, he pushed through the door and jogged to his truck.

Back in his room, he opened his book and stretched out in his desk chair. He tried to feel Ryan's hands on his cheeks.

Let's not mistake this for love.

No. Let's not. Because it's not a mistake. He clicked on Facebook and ran through status updates. Nothing new there. He clicked on Ryan's page. Absolutely nothing there either. He tried to focus on homework, but he kept going back to Ryan's words. He'd just about given up working on problem number five when his dad knocked and stuck his head in the room.

"Got a minute?"

"Sure."

His dad sat on the edge of the bed. "You doing better?"

"Yeah."

"Good." His dad nodded and looked around the room as though he were seeing it for the first time.

"Is there something else?" Justin's stomach clenched.

"I know I haven't made many games in the past couple of years."

"Any."

"What?"

Justin gazed at him. "You haven't made any games since I've been on varsity."

His dad looked at the floor. "Okay. I haven't made any games. I want to be there Friday."

"So you said." *At least twice. Who are you trying to convince? You won't come.*

"But..."

Ah, here it comes. The excuse.

"Dr. O'Malley wants to meet with me late in the afternoon. I'm not sure I'll be back in time for the first half."

The second half is more than you've seen before. "Okay. Is everything good with Mom?"

"I think so. He just wants to review her progress." He stretched. "So, how's school going?"

He shrugged. "Okay."

"What about Ryan? How's she healing?"

"Her face is still pretty messed up." He tipped his chair on two legs. "She blew me off tonight."

"What happened?"

"She said we have too much drama in our lives to be together. She wants space."

"How do you feel about that?"

"Sucks."

His dad leaned forward with his forearms on his knees. "One thing I've learned through all this mess is that if you stand back and hope things will get better, they won't. If you want her back, you can't hope it'll happen."

"But if I try to get her back, I might lose her too."

"But you might not—and at least you'll have tried." His dad stood and placed a hand on his shoulder. "Don't stay up too late."

"Hey, Dad?"

"Yeah." He stopped and turned toward Justin.

"Thanks for being there."

His dad nodded. "It's where I need to be."

Justin dropped the chair back on four legs when his dad left the room. His words mixed with Ryan's and swirled in his head.

Ryan was right. They'd met in the midst of drama and pretty much everything that had happened since had been riddled with it. His dad was right too. It was time to make a change. And he wasn't going to sit back and wait until his family got their shit together. God knew if or when that would happen. He wasn't going to wait until kids stopped writing crap on her locker—that had become routine.

Nope. He was going to prove to her they were more than two drama-ridden lost souls. He was going to show her that they could have fun, and at least for a while, forget the shit in their lives. And he was going to start tomorrow.

19

Ryan knew the moment she woke that the day was going to suck.

First, her face itched like crazy. It was all she could do to keep from clawing at her skin. She splashed water on it and leaned into the mirror. The swelling had disappeared, but she still looked like a freak. Swirls of tiny scabs covered her like a mask. She pressed her index finger into the lump that used to be the curve of her upper lip and tried to remember what she'd looked like before.

She raised the sleeves of her T-shirt and inspected her shoulders. She'd scratched the scabs from them days ago. Smooth tender skin remained—and so did a series of pink scars. She gripped the counter and tried to settle the anger that rose in her throat.

Why had it mattered so much to those girls that she'd had a past? Why had they taken their hatred to such an extreme?

"Hurry up, Ryan. I have to pee." Kelsey pounded on the door.

Ryan opened the door and brushed past her sister. "Gawd, I hate sharing a bathroom. I hate living in this house. I hate this town."

"Good morning to you too." Kelsey stared at her as though she were an alien creature—but in all fairness, she looked like one.

She trudged downstairs for a cup of coffee. Her parents sat at the kitchen table, each reading a section of the paper. Ryan grabbed a mug and dropped into the chair across from her mom. "I'm never going to have my face back, am I?"

Her mom lowered her paper. "Dr. Cooper seems to think you'll have very little scarring."

She slammed the mug on the table, spilling the contents over the edge. "I want to have my lip fixed."

"Of course. We've talked about the best time to have it done—"

"I don't want to wait. This whole thing was not my fault. They ripped my face up and they get—what—freaking alternate school?" Her control was slipping, and with it her ability to keep her voice at a normal level. "I will live with this for the rest of my life."

Her dad folded his section of the paper. "When is your next appointment with Dr. Cooper?"

Her mom answered, "Not for a couple of weeks."

Not good enough. "Can't you see if we can move it up?"

Her mom nodded. "I'll call this morning."

Moving the appointment up didn't do a thing to ease the anger inside her. She'd had enough of "dealing" with what had happened to her, with these people. "I hate this town. I don't want to go to school."

Her mom covered her hand with hers. "What's going on at school?"

Jeez, Mom, clueless much? "Oh, nothing. I just get looks from everybody who sees me. Stuff has been written on my locker so many times it has a permanent smell of cheap lipstick."

Her dad focused his attention on her. "What do you mean, written on your locker?"

"It's no big deal. I don't care. It's just annoying." She flicked her hand as if that would make it true. Day after day of seeing those words seeped into her bones. SLUT. WHORE. SCARFACE. MEATFACE. BITCH. Take your pick—they all hurt.

"We'll put a stop to it." Her dad stood with his hands on his hips. It was his *I'm in control* stance. "Does the principal know about this?"

"I shouldn't have said anything. Don't make a bigger deal out of it than it is. It's just kids being stupid."

Mackenzie bounced into the kitchen. "Who's being stupid?"

"Did you know Ryan's locker is being vandalized?"

Mackenzie's gaze went from her dad to Ryan, and Ryan felt the question in the look. She answered for her sister. "It's pretty hard not to notice. Pretty much everybody knows it. Look, if I do anything, they'll think they've gotten to me. I'm not giving them the satisfaction."

"I think we need to pay another visit to Mrs. Johnson. This needs to be stopped."

"Dad, let me deal with it. Please."

Her mom looked at her dad. "She's right, Tom. Let the kids handle this one." To Ryan she said, "The minute she needs us to step in, she knows we're here."

That was the problem with being a big talker—now she was stuck with acting brave. She didn't want to go to school, didn't want to face whatever was waiting for her at locker two-thirty-two. But she would because if she didn't, then they'd win. And no way was that gonna happen.

She pushed her chair away from the table. "I'd better get ready for school."

The rest of the morning wasn't any better. Her pixie haircut had grown to uneven lengths all over her head. She stood in the mirror for five minutes contemplating headband or no headband. On. Off. On. Off. When had she become so indecisive about clothes? That had always been Kelsey's thing. "Screw it." She settled the headband just above her bangs.

Kelsey scooted next to her at the sink. She loaded her toothbrush and looked at Ryan's reflection. "That's mine." She ran the brush under the water and began to brush her teeth.

"So? You're not wearing it."

"You didn't ask."

Ryan rolled her eyes at her sister. "Your Highness Kelsey. Can I wear your headband?"

"Okay. Next time ask first." White foam spilled down her chin and on to the counter.

"Gross." Ryan scooted from the bathroom and down the stairs, and tried to tell herself that she could turn her foul mood around. The truth was, she couldn't stomach one more day of plastering a stupid fake smile on her face and pretending everything was hunky-dory. Every day since Homecoming, she'd acted like she didn't care that her face had been shredded. She'd ignored the notes dropped on her desk or shoved in her locker. She'd laughed at the words written across her locker.

Today, she just couldn't get to that place.

She'd told Justin they had too much of their own baggage to handle each other's. And that pissed her off too. She still meant it. As much as she liked Justin, as much as his smile made her insides tingle, their whole relationship was based on drama. She was sick to death of drama. It wasn't fair. Neither of them had brought it upon themselves. They were simply victims of circumstance.

When Kelsey pulled into the parking lot, she saw Justin walking toward the building with his hands shoved in his letter jacket and his head down against the wind. A little place in her chest caught. He was alone. He needed friends. Friends who wouldn't drag their problems into his. Caleb and Mickey came up from behind and flanked him, and the catch in her chest eased. Of course he had friends.

He's lived here his whole life. He's a varsity football player.

The selfish part of her was a little sad that he hadn't fallen completely apart without her. What kind of person would wish that? Was she that kind of person? She wasn't sure how she felt. Lonely. Heartbroken. Angry at everybody. Confused.

As soon as Kelsey put the truck in Park, Ryan jumped from the cab and slammed the door. She hurried toward him, but not enough to catch up. She wanted to call after him. She wanted him to need her. She didn't want to need him. She couldn't. That was a dangerous place. She'd already opened her heart too much to him.

As if he sensed her behind him, he turned toward her and stopped.

Her feet froze to the blacktop. Her heart pounded in her chest. If he came after her, would she be able to keep her *we need space* rule?

He didn't smile. He didn't frown. He had no expression. Just those dark eyes peeking from beneath the bangs, staring into hers. He took three full steps back, turned, and rejoined his friends.

She wanted to cry. She'd done this. It all started because she was pissed when he didn't call, more pissed when he showed at the diner with other people. But it was true that the only thing they had in common was sorrow.

She was done with sorrow.

She took a deep breath and headed toward a door on the other end of the hall from the one Justin had entered.

She skipped her locker. It had remained word-free for two days, but for sure there would be something scrawled on it by this morning. *Slut, whore*, and *bitch* had been used. She wondered what they'd use next. She slumped into her desk.

A group of girls entered the room in one big clump. A couple of them were from the Purity Club. A note dropped on her desk. Half the time she didn't bother to open them. Today she chose to unfold the triangle football. She spread the paper and read three words: *God is watching.* She laughed out loud at the irony. Instead of wadding it up and tossing it in the trash, she took it to the PC girl's desk. She was blonde and wearing gold cross earrings—and she visibly recoiled as Ryan approached.

Ryan flattened the paper on the girl's desk and leaned in close. "Look at me. Look at my face." She grabbed the girl's hand and forced her index finger into the lump that had once been the arch of her lip. "Feel what they did."

The girl's eyes widened. "Leave me alone."

"What are you afraid of? What have I ever done to anybody?" She stood and looked around the room. Most of the class had entered and all eyes were on her. "I've never said a bad word about anybody. I've never touched a soul." She turned back to PC girl. "Can you say the same? You think because you wear a cross and are a member of the Purity Club that you're better than the rest of us? Read your own note." She turned and took a step back to her desk. She wasn't done. She faced the girl again. "And stop writing crap on my locker."

"It's not me," the girl squeaked.

"Then tell whoever it is to stop it. The cheap lipstick stinks." A couple of people laughed. The anger that boiled inside her eased. It felt good to stand up for herself. No, it felt better than good. It was freeing.

So this was the beginning of a new Ryan Quinn. This Ryan Quinn wasn't going to take it anymore. She would not shrink from the girl who always *accidentally* rammed a shoulder into her in the hall. She would gather the nasty notes shoved in her locker and dump them in the principal's lap. Besides, wasn't it her job now to make sure this kind of crap didn't continue?

When class ended she headed straight to her locker. Yep, this was a new day. A new her. When she got there, she saw a piece of red paper sticking out of the vent.

God, she was tired of this shit.

She dialed through the combination and pulled on the door. It was hung up and it took a second jerk to pop it open. When it did, paper cascaded onto the floor.

Not just paper. Red paper—cut in the shape of hearts. Big ones, little ones, and all sizes in between. A warm spot settled in the middle of her chest. Tears filled her eyes, but for once they were the good kind.

She dropped to her knees and gathered them up. They looked like something a first-grader would cut—all lopsided with ragged edges. She could see pencil marks where they had been cut outside the line. A visual of Justin cutting the hearts with a pair of safety scissors drifted through her mind. She stacked them as best as she could and shoved them into the front pocket of her backpack.

A heart larger than the others appeared in her field of vision. "You missed one."

She looked up and there he was. One look and her heart pounded in her chest. God, he was beautiful. His hair had just enough curl to be messy and just enough mess to make her want to run her hands through it. She loved the way it fell across his forehead, giving his eyes that smoldering, sexy look—until he smiled and exposed those boyish dimples. Those dimples were in full force as he waited for a response.

She dropped her gaze to the hand that held the paper heart. She wanted to take that hand. She wanted to crawl into the embrace it offered. But she wouldn't. She needed to stand on her own two feet. She took the heart and stood. "Thanks."

He flattened his back against the locker next to hers. "So?"

"So." They stared at each other and grinned. She could almost feel the air crackle between them. "You cut all those hearts."

"That I did."

"And stuffed them in my locker."

"One by one. I slipped them through the vents."

"That's a lot of work."

"I was hoping for a payoff."

"Oh? And that would be…?"

He dropped his gaze to the heart she held. "You haven't read it."

She turned the heart over and read the poem he'd written.

Roses are red.
Violets are blue.
My heart would flutter
If you let me bowl with you.
Tonight. 6:30?

"You want to go bowling?"

He pushed off the locker and moved closer to her. "Something fun. No drama."

"No drama? You've obviously never seen me bowl." She pulled the book she needed from her locker.

"Come on, Ryan. Let's have fun like normal people do."

Oh, how she wanted that. But the tiny mirror that hung on the inside of her locker showed her why it couldn't happen. For the most part, kids at school had gotten used to her face. But going to a crowded place like a bowling alley was a different story.

She closed her locker and leaned her forehead against the door. "I can't."

"Ryan, I'm really sorry about not calling you. It was stupid. Don't let it screw us up."

She felt his hands on her shoulders and blew out a deep breath. She turned and leaned her back flat against the locker. "It has nothing to do with you."

"Then what?" His voice had a desperate tone that made her feel stupid for what she was going to say, but it was the truth—no matter how shallow it sounded.

"You are so sweet to see past this." She pointed to her face. "I—I just can't. School is one thing, a crowded bowling alley..." She looked at her feet. "Sometimes it's all I can do to ignore the looks..."

The concern was replaced by a slow smile. "I don't care what we do. I just want to spend time with you. It doesn't matter if we bowl."

She nodded but couldn't quite make a smile form. She was ashamed that she wanted to hide away from everybody.

"What do you say? Can we do something tonight? Whatever you want."

She knew exactly what she wanted to do. "Would you want to come over and just hang out by the pool? I'll have to ask my parents, and the water is too cool to swim, but it's nice to hang out."

He nodded. "I'd like that."

She fired a text to her mom. "Okay, I'll let you know as soon as I hear back."

The five-minute bell sounded and she pushed away from the locker. "There will be plenty of drama if we're late for Shop. Come on."

They hurried down the hall to the breezeway leading to the shop. When they reached the classroom, Justin dropped his backpack on her table and headed to the project shelves. That simple act of moving from the table behind her to her table warmed her from toes to head.

So much for keeping her distance—she hadn't even made it twenty-four hours. But then, she never dreamt he'd stuff hearts in her locker either.

She retrieved her project and set it on the table next to him. "So how are things at home?"

"Ah-ah. No drama talk. But things are good. And you?"

She started to tell him she was going to have her lip fixed next week, but just thinking about it brought all of the anxieties associated with the surgery to the surface. She pushed the thought from her brain. "There is something I wanted to ask you."

"Yes, I'll be your boyfriend."

"Yeah, right." She knocked him with her shoulder. "Do you know Braden McGuire?"

"Don't tell me you want me to fix you up with him?"

"Yes. That's exactly what I want. No, silly. He was in the Purity Club."

"Five points against him."

"No. He's a good guy. He brought up some good points at the last meeting. The whole club shouldn't be punished because Macey went psycho."

"I don't know why not. Any other club would be disbanded if they did something less heinous than what those bitches did."

"Hear me out. We've talked to Mrs. Bettis and we want to start a new club called Teens Against Violence. The group talks to other schools about healthy relationships. Not just dating, but friendships too."

"That sounds cool. An anti-bullying group."

"Yeah, but more than that." She pulled a paper from her backpack. "Mrs. Bettis gave me some information." She handed it to Justin.

He looked it over. "This looks good. So what's your question?"

"Mrs. Bettis wants us to pick a representative boy and girl from each class. Would you be the senior rep?"

He rubbed the back of his neck. "I have a lot of stuff going on."

"Of course." *Duh. What were you thinking, Ryan?* "It was stupid of me to ask."

He leaned close to her. "I'm not sure if I can be a representative. But I will support the group. It's just…"

"I get it. And if all you can offer is moral support, that's good." She shoved the paper into her backpack. She didn't mean for the gesture to come off like she was mad, but from the way he winced, it did. "Seriously. I understand."

"Thanks. I will be a part of it, I promise."

"Okay." She smiled, but she couldn't help the disappointment that flowed through her. She pulled the wood she'd cut from her box.

It was different working alongside Justin. They worked on completely different projects. He was building a guitar—a far cry from the swirly end table she was putting together. She watched him run a bead of wood glue along one of the edges. "Do you play?"

He kept his focus on his work. "A little. I suck, but I keep trying."

"I'd like to hear you sometime."

"You say that now, but think really bad *Idol* audition."

"It can't be that bad." She snapped a wood clamp onto the two wedge pieces of walnut she'd just glued.

"Who knows, maybe this guitar will be magic and I'll actually learn to play the thing." He released a little chuckle and her heart warmed about a hundred degrees. This was the way it should have been from the beginning—flirting, smiling, and getting to know each other. Not rescuing her.

She worked on laminating pieces for her end table and he worked on his guitar for the rest of the class. They joked and talked some, but it was lighthearted and fun.

Her phone vibrated with a text, but she had to wait until the end of class to read it. She smiled up at Justin. "It's from Mom. She said you're welcome to come for dinner."

"Cool. Thanks."

Yeah, cool. Let's just hope it stays that way when Austin and Travis show up.

20

Practice was a bitch.

Coach was in a foul mood and took it out on the team—possibly because Austin couldn't hit the side of a barn. He overthrew, underthrew, threw too high, threw too low. It was a disaster. When Austin unraveled, so did the rest of the team. The few passes that reached Justin were dropped. And he wasn't the only offender. Austin's golden boy Travis Barnes dropped or missed every catchable pass. Tackles were missed, routes screwed up. They practiced like peewee players.

It was a welcome relief when Coach blew the whistle calling them to the sidelines. They spent the rest of the practice doing ball-busters. Justin just wanted to finish and get the hell out of there.

By the time they hit the showers, all he could think about was getting to Ryan. He breezed by his house and changed into shorts and flip-flops. When he called his dad to tell him he was going to Ryan's, he sounded relieved—probably because he was working late.

As much as he tried to hurry, it was after six before he turned down the gravel drive leading to the Quinn farmhouse. His heart fluttered in his chest when he saw the girl with the pixie hair waiting on the front porch.

When he parked, she walked to the top of the porch steps. She looked amazing in her khaki short shorts and green tank top. But that was nothing compared to the smile that lit up her face. And it was for him.

He stopped at the bottom of the steps. "Hey, you."

"Hey, yourself." She dropped down one step. Her eyes seemed to be three shades deeper than their normal blue and he couldn't take his gaze away from them.

He stepped up one step and stood eye level with her. "You look—beautiful."

"My face could use some help."

He cupped her cheek and stroked it with his thumb. He pressed his lips softly against her skin where his thumb had been. "It's perfect." He was about to drop his hand, pull her against him, and plant a solid kiss on her, when the screen door squeaked open. They both jumped back. Ryan would have fallen over the step if Justin hadn't grabbed her arm.

Mackenzie stepped out on the porch. "Mom said to tell you there are snacks on the back porch. Dinner is running late."

Ryan turned toward her sister. "Okay. We'll be right there."

Mackenzie shot a nervous look between Justin and Ryan and went into the house.

"Is she okay?"

Ryan shook her head. "She's been a little stressed lately." She grabbed his hand and led him up the steps and through the house to the back patio.

Justin had never seen the patio before. What a contrast to the rest of the house. The pool was pristine, with huge pots bursting with flowers situated around it. The patio furniture screamed *expensive* and his nerves amped up.

Mrs. Quinn poured lemonade from a pitcher with lemon slices floating in it. Fruit and crackers were displayed on a plate like something from a magazine. She flashed him a warm smile. “Hi, Justin. Make yourself at home. Would you like some lemonade?”

“Thank you, that would be nice.” He took a chair next to Ryan and hoped nobody would notice how awkward he felt.

Ryan pulled some grapes off the plate and munched them. “Help yourself.”

Mrs. Quinn said, “We’re pretty casual. Tom is going to grill salmon as soon as he gets home. Do you like salmon?”

“Sure.” He had no clue whether or not he liked salmon. But pretty much anything on a grill had to be good. He tried to relax. There was no reason to be uptight. Her family was all smiles and welcoming. Okay, her mom was. Mackenzie still looked a little freaked and Kelsey and her dad weren’t there. He blew out a deep breath and took a sip of his drink. “Beautiful place, Mrs. Quinn.”

“Thank you. It’s certainly different from Chicago.” An uncomfortable look crossed her face that made Justin wonder if this had been a good move for her.

Ryan put a hand on his forearm. “Want me to show you around?”

“Yes.” When he stood, he knocked into the table, jiggling everything. Thank God nothing spilled or worse, broke. *Jesus, Justin, relax.*

He followed Ryan off the patio and around the side of the house. They headed to the small red barn first. She opened the door to the tack room and he breathed in the smell of leather from the saddles stacked on racks that hung from the wall. "Do you ride?"

"No. Maybe one day. Kelsey is learning. Come on, I'll show you the horses." They passed through a door opposite the one they'd come in. There were four stalls, one in each corner.

"We only have two. They're my uncle's, but he doesn't ride much anymore. Austin rides them."

At the sound of Austin's name, his gut tightened. *Is there anything Wonder Boy can't do? Oh yeah, throw the freaking football.*

A chestnut with a blaze stuck its head over the door and Ryan scratched the side of his face. "This is Buster. The other guy is Harry. He's a paint." As if on cue, Harry hung his head out of the stall. "I have to say Harry is my favorite."

Justin rubbed the side of Harry's neck. "Nice." He watched her scratch the tip of Buster's nose. He wrinkled his upper lip, showing his teeth, and she giggled. It was the first time he'd seen her look so carefree and it took the breath completely from him. This was the way it should be. In that moment she wasn't thinking about the fountain or her face. She was taking in the simple pleasure of petting a horse. He wanted to give her a million more of those simple pleasures.

He moved from Harry's stall to stand behind her. He reached over her to pat Buster's forehead, but he couldn't keep his eyes off the length of her neck. He resisted the urge to place a kiss just below her ear and said, "It's good to hear you laugh."

She cupped the horse's face with her hands, but it pulled away and retreated to the water bucket hanging on the wall. "I like taking care of them. Someday I'll ride." She kept her back to him and watched the horse lap from the bucket. "Do you ride?"

"Not really. I've been on a horse a couple of times. But I don't really know what I'm doing."

She was so close, her shirt brushed his chest. They were having a normal, innocent conversation but the electricity between them could spark a fire and ignite the whole place. He placed a hand on her shoulder and refocused on her neck and how delicious it would be to trail kisses from her collarbone to her jaw.

He should resist. Take it slow. Let her make the first move.

Then she leaned against him.

He lowered his head to her neck and kissed her just below the ear. It tickled her and he heard the wonderful sound of her giggle. He wrapped his arms around her waist, pulled her more tightly against him, and kissed her neck again. That was all it took. She turned in his arms and wrapped hers around his neck. Her mouth found his. It was hot and wet and messy. It was perfect.

She pulled away, dropped her hands from his neck, and buried her head in his shoulder. "I can't stay away from you."

"I'm glad." He tightened his embrace. "Please, don't try." He rubbed his hands up and down her back, pressing her against him.

She lifted her head and kissed his chin. "We'd better get out of here before they miss us."

He relaxed his hold, but didn't release her. Instead, he looked into her eyes and smiled. "You are the best thing that has ever happened to me." He kissed her again, but this time it was sweet and gentle, like a first kiss.

When they pulled away, she grabbed his hand. "Come on. Let's meet the pig."

He let her lead him out of the barn, but all he wanted to do was yank her back and replay those kisses over and over. He wanted to hear her say how she felt, but he'd take what he could get. He could go a long way on smiles and a few stolen kisses.

They moved to a pen between the barn and the chicken coop. A big white pig snorted as they approached. "That's Winnie. I never thought I'd like pigs, but she's cool."

"Wow. Ryan Quinn has a pig." He squeezed her hand. "I bet that's different for the girl from Chicago."

"You have no idea. Come on. Chickens are next." She pulled on his hand and they went to the chicken coop. She squeezed through the gate to the chicken yard. They ran toward her and fluttered around her feet. "They think I'm going to feed them." She showed them her open hands and they actually looked disappointed, if that were possible. "I used to be terrified of them. Mackenzie still is. She won't even get close to the fence."

"What about Kelsey?"

"Kelsey is the true farm girl. She hated it when we first moved here. Oh my God, now she treats the chickens like they're her pets. She loves Winnie and the horses. I think she'd rather clean troughs and slop Winnie than just about anything."

"I would have never guessed."

"Neither would anybody else. I think about ninety percent of her love for the rural life is because of Austin."

There was that name again. He was beginning to understand why his mom freaked out every time she heard it. At least he didn't have to worry about his being competition for Ryan.

"Ry—an!" They turned toward the voice and saw Mackenzie standing about ten feet from the chicken fence. "Mom said dinner is about two minutes out."

"Okay." She grabbed his hand. "That concludes the tour of the Quinn farm. What do you think?"

He looked into her deep blue eyes and took a ragged breath. "I think it's awesome."

She squeezed his hand. "I think my guest is pretty awesome too." They walked to the back yard holding hands. It was a simple gesture, but he felt as though somehow their relationship had just taken on new meaning.

When they rounded the house, she dropped his hand. A twinge of disappointment filtered up his empty hand to his heart. But that was nothing compared to what he felt when he saw who sat on the patio. Austin and Travis. Austin joked with Mrs. Quinn and jealousy filled him. Would he ever feel that welcome here?

When they reached the table, he shook Travis's and Austin's hands. They were cordial, but the look Austin gave him said *this is my territory.* Whatever. He was here for Ryan.

Mr. Quinn left the grill he'd manned to join them at the table. He stuck his hand out to Justin. "It's good to see you again."

Justin shook his hand. "Thank you, sir."

To Mrs. Quinn he said, "I'm ready to pull the salmon if you want to get the rest of the stuff."

Mackenzie stood. "I've got it."

Travis stood too. "I'll help."

They went into the house together. Ryan and Kelsey looked at Austin for the answer to the obvious question. He shrugged. "I have no idea."

Ryan said, "They're both so shy, what would they talk about?"

"Maybe they don't." Kelsey winked and everyone around the table laughed.

Except Ryan. "Jeez, Kelsey."

Kelsey shook her head. "Lighten up."

Ryan ignored the comment, but Justin could tell she was annoyed.

Mackenzie carried a big bowl of tossed salad to the table, followed by Travis, who carried a platter stacked high with corn on the cob. Mr. Quinn served everybody a hunk of salmon and took a seat at the head of the glass topped table.

The Quinns and Austin crossed themselves and said a prayer he didn't know. What a concept—praying before a meal. His family used to hold hands and say a quick prayer, but only on Thanksgiving and Christmas—back when they were a family. He'd bet the Quinns were the every Sunday kind of church people too. He couldn't remember the last time he'd gone to church. Probably Chelsea's funeral.

Once again that longing for his family twisted in his gut. Austin seemed to have become firmly ensconced in this family. True, his dad was an abusive asshole, but it that didn't make Justin any less jealous.

It'd been so easy to hate the guy. He'd texted Chelsea. Chelsea died. Simple. He needed somebody to blame. But then Dr. O'Malley had taken it away from him. *She didn't have to answer the text.* Sadness rippled through him. *You didn't have to answer the text, Chel.*

Then it hit him. *She killed those girls.*

Cold dread spread down his spine and back up. He set his fork on his plate and looked at Travis, struggling to pull air into his lungs. *She killed Travis's sister.*

He picked up his glass, but his hand trembled. Ice cubes clinked and lemonade spilled over the edge of the glass.

Ryan looked at him. "Are you okay?"

Shit. The whole table was looking at him now. He went from cold to hot in a nanosecond. Sweat beaded his forehead. Ryan was so beautiful, even with the worried expression. He couldn't talk. Nothing worked. He was frozen, like that night in the truck, only this time it was worse.

He tried to turn his body back on. But his brain flashed from Chelsea's funeral to his mom on the floor with the gun. Chelsea had caused it all. Answering that text had forever altered three families. Had destroyed his mom. He didn't want to be angry with her. He loved her. Why did she have to pick up that damn phone?

He heard Ryan say, "Mom. Dad. Help."

He wanted to tell her he was okay. He couldn't. He was trapped. An arm circled him but it wasn't Ryan's—too motherly. He heard Mrs. Quinn telling him it was okay. God, how he wanted it to be okay.

Gradually, his breathing eased and he came back to himself. He focused on the seven faces staring at him in shock.

Mrs. Quinn quietly said, "Better?"

He nodded and she dropped her arm.

He wanted to escape the gazes and gaping mouths. He didn't belong here. This was a normal family with normal people who didn't have panic attacks. He stood. They didn't need his kind of crazy. "Excuse me. Thank you for dinner."

Ryan stood too. "Wait. You don't have to leave."

Beautiful Ryan. His heart loved her so much. "I'm sorry." It took every bit of control he had not to run around the side of the house to his truck. As it was, he walked as fast as he could without looking too stupid.

Ryan jogged to keep up. "Justin. Wait."

He didn't stop until he was safely in his truck. Safely away from grabbing her and hanging on for dear life. She deserved better.

She stood at the driver's door with tears in her eyes. "Justin!"

He couldn't leave her like this. He lowered the window. "I'm sorry, Ryan. You're right. I bring too much drama to your life."

"What happened back there? Was it Austin? We'll work it out." Her voice was desperate and tears fell down her cheeks.

He'd done this to her. What a shithead. "We shouldn't have to work it out. You deserve better than my kind of crazy. I love you and I won't put you through this." He slammed the truck into reverse and backed away.

He looked in the rearview as he turned the truck to head down the driveway. She stood in the same spot wiping her eyes.

Yeah, he was a shithead deluxe.

21

Ryan stared down the dirt drive long after he'd pulled onto the highway and sped away. What had happened? How could he say he loved her and then drive away? She eased herself onto the top step of the porch.

No doubt her family was already dissecting what'd happened. She couldn't blame them. One minute he was fine, the next he was frozen. Should he even be driving?

The screen door screeched open and her dad came through carrying a plate. "Mind if I sit?"

"No." She scooted over a few inches, although there was enough room.

He sat and held out the plate. "I thought you might want this."

"Thanks." She took it and forked up a bite of salmon.

"He seems like a good kid."

She nodded. "He is."

"Do you understand what happened back there?" He leaned back on his elbows.

"Not really—other than he kind of freaked out."

"Freaked out, anxiety attack, maybe more."

She looked at her dad. "Did I do something? Say something?"

He shook his head. "Probably not. He's been through some major stuff. There's no telling what caused his freakout." He made air quotes around *freakout.*

"What do I do? I feel so helpless."

"There's not a lot you *can* do. Listen when he needs you."

She set the plate on the step. "I don't think he wants to see me again."

Her dad sat up and put his arm around her, pulling her to his side. "What makes you say that?"

"He said I didn't need to be around his kind of crazy. I think he really hates himself."

"Do you think he'd hurt himself?"

She shook her head. "No. After what his mom did, I'm sure he wouldn't go there."

Her dad lowered his arm from her shoulder and sat forward with his elbows on his knees. "Ryan, you've been through hell the past couple of years. I'm really proud of how you've come through it."

"I haven't exactly come through it. I still have surgery on my lip and then there's what's left of my face."

He smiled. "That's cosmetic. It's the inside I'm talking about. You'll always be pretty on the outside."

"Thanks. Dad? Can I ask a personal question? I want an honest answer, not just one to make me feel better. I need to know."

"Okay, I'll do my best. Shoot."

"Did you lose your job because I got caught with Mr. Blankenship's son?"

He rubbed his hands across his face. "First, let's make something clear. I wasn't fired. I disagreed with the direction of the company and we came to a mutual agreement."

"You haven't answered my question."

He looked at her and she saw the pain in his eyes. Was he remembering that awful day when he'd walked in on them? She was so messed up she'd laughed when he opened the door.

"We'd been having disagreements. When—that happened, Blankenship blamed you. It was as if his son hadn't even been in the room. We had words." He shrugged. "It was just a matter of time before I was pushed out anyway."

"I don't understand how they could do that when you and Mr. Blankenship founded it together."

"He had more control. It's okay. It's the best thing that's ever happened to us. I'm happy to be back."

"Mom's not."

"What makes you say that?"

"I hear her crying at night."

He dropped his gaze to the ground. "It's been an adjustment, but we're okay."

She wrapped her hand around his bicep and leaned on his shoulder. "I wish I could have a do-over. Then none of this would ever have happened."

"We don't get many of those in life. The important thing is what we do with the lessons we've learned. You are the person you are because of your experiences. You're strong, smart, caring. I couldn't be prouder."

"Thanks," she whispered.

He stood and gave her a hand up. "Should we join the others?"

"I want some alone time." She turned toward the door just in time to see Mackenzie back away from the other side of the screen. *That's weird. Even for Kenzie.*

She grabbed her plate from the step and her dad held out his hand. "I'll take it."

"Thanks." They retreated to the house, but while her dad headed to the kitchen she went upstairs. She sat on her bed and grabbed her phone. *Should I text him? Should I give him some time? He says he loves me.* Her heart warmed and broke at the same time. *For some stupid reason he thinks he's protecting me by backing off.*

She set the phone down and hugged her pillow as a million other questions filtered through her thoughts. *Why was Mackenzie eavesdropping? We didn't say anything that she didn't already know. What did the others say after Justin left? What will I do now?*

What was the universe doing to her? It refused to let her be happy. She'd been accepted to the art-magnet school and—reset: date rape.

She'd changed, was ready to embrace a new life and—reset: attack by crazy girls.

She and Justin were happy for about a heartbeat and—reset: Justin runs.

She was tired of starting over. This was stupid. It was time to take control of the reset button for herself.

She jogged downstairs to the kitchen, where her mom was wiping down the counter. "Can I run to town?"

"It's getting late."

"I know. I'll be back by ten."

Her mom hesitated before nodding. "Okay."

"Thanks, Mom."

She'd made it almost out of the kitchen before her mom stopped her. "Ryan."

"Yeah?"

"Tell him he's welcome here anytime."

"I will."

"Call if you're going to be late."

She was determined to convince him that she could handle whatever was going on with him. Her plan was to march up to his door and pound on it until he answered. But by the time she parked behind his truck, her bravado had begun to waver. She texted instead.

Ryan: You okay?

Justin: I'm sorry.

Ryan: Don't be. Don't run from us.

She stared at the screen. Nothing. *Okay, maybe I shouldn't have gone there. So now what? Do I pound on the door or drive off?*

Ryan: ???

Seconds ticked by and with every one, her heart seemed to beat a little faster. *Screw it. I didn't come all this way for nothing.* She opened the door of the old blue truck and took a deep breath before getting out. *Here goes nothing.*

She walked up the driveway to his door. With each step, her feet seemed to want to turn the other way and retreat to the truck. When she made it to the front door, she hesitated before raising her hand to the doorbell. What if he didn't answer? What if his dad answered? Her hand shook as she pushed the little white button.

It seemed like an eternity before the door opened. *Shit.*

Mr. Hayes stood on the other side of the door. At least he smiled when he saw her.

"Hi Ryan. Come in. I'll get Justin." He stepped back and she stepped into the entry.

Mr. Hayes walked down a short hall and knocked on a door before opening it. She couldn't hear what he said, but he closed the door and returned to her. He had a fake smile on his face and she was sure he was going to tell her that Justin didn't want to see her. She held her breath and waited for him to speak.

"He'll be out in a minute. Come in and have a seat."

"Thanks." She followed him to the den and sat on the leather couch he indicated.

"Can I get you a coke or water or something?"

"No, thanks." This was crazy awkward. Why hadn't her plan included running interference with Mr. Hayes?

He sat in a chair across from her and muted the TV. "Your face looks good."

"Thanks." She almost giggled. Out of context, that statement would have been hilarious. "I'm having my lip fixed on Tuesday." Wow, she hadn't expected to tell him that. She hadn't even told Justin.

"Here?"

She nodded. "Dr. Cooper said he could do it here or in Dallas. It didn't make sense to drive all the way to Dallas."

"He's a good surgeon. You're in good hands."

"Good to know."

And then the uncomfortable silence settled in. They smiled at each other and waited. Mr. Hayes stood and walked back into the kitchen. "He should be right out."

"Yeah." She gave a jerky nod. *That didn't look weird.* She was about to ask for a glass of water just for something to do when Justin entered the room.

"Hi." He looked at her beneath the bangs that almost covered his eyes and her breath caught.

She stood. "Hi."

"Do you want something to drink?"

"No. I'm good."

He took a step back. "Let's go to my room." He reached for her hand and led her down the hall. She loved the strength and warmth of his skin next to hers. He pulled her into his room and closed the door most of the way. "Open door rule."

"We have the same one."

He dropped her hand and for a few seconds they stood a foot apart and stared at each other. When she looked into his eyes, it was as though she could see a war going on in there.

He opened his arms and she stepped into them, wrapping her arms around him. He let out a sigh and pulled her against him. He kissed her head and tightened his embrace. Neither spoke, they just held on.

When he released her, he pulled her over to sit on the bed. "I'm sorry I left like I did. I just had to get out of there."

"What happened?"

"One thing triggered a memory and the next thing I knew my mind was out of control." His voice sounded strained. He lifted his gaze to hers and she saw fear in his eyes. "I don't know how to stop it."

Crap. This was way bigger than she imagined, and she had no clue how to make him feel better. "What does your dad say?" *Really, Ryan? That's the best you can do?*

"I'm going to meet with Dr. O'Malley." He focused on his hands. "The thing is, until I can get this thing under control, there will always be drama." He looked at her again. "I'm scared." His voice was so hoarse she barely made out the last words.

She looked at his beautiful sad eyes and her heart pounded in her chest. She had to show him that he didn't have to do this alone. She cupped his cheek and guided his lips to hers. He opened his mouth under hers, allowing her deepen the kiss. It was awkward sitting beside him, especially when what she really wanted to do was crawl into his lap.

He broke the kiss and slid up the bed to lean against the headboard. "Come here."

She snuggled into his arms. He trailed the back of his hand down her arm, leaving chills in its wake. He pressed a kiss against her forehead and trailed his fingers back up her arm. Her heart pounded heat through her.

Silence stretched between them. She'd come here to talk, but now all she wanted to do was feel his mouth on hers.

He wrapped his arms tight around her. "I want to be with you more than anything. But I have to get my shit together first."

"No. You don't." She pushed away from his chest and faced him. "Look, I know I said that I was tired of the drama. Drama brought us together and maybe that's part of what *us* will always be about. We're both a little screwed up." She hovered over him and waited for him to say something. He brushed his fingers across her cheek. She was a heartbeat from pressing her mouth to his when he let his arm fall to his side.

"What if I'm crazy?"

She scooted higher and rested her back on the headboard next to him.

A tear slipped down his cheek. "What if it happens at school? What if it gets worse?"

She wrapped her arms around him and pulled him against her. He rested his head on her chest, curled his body next to her. She brushed his hair away from his face and the tears from his cheeks. She wanted to tell him it was going to be okay. But she couldn't, because she wasn't sure it was. What if he was crazy? Could she handle it?

He rolled onto his back and pressed his fingertips against his eyelids. "I'm sorry." He gave her a sideways look and smiled. "I finally get to feel your boob and I cried all over it."

She threw a pillow at him. "Ah, so that was the plan all along."

He caught it and tossed it back. "No, this is my plan." He crawled to her and tickled her.

She laughed and grabbed his hands. She used them for leverage and pushed up to her knees. They both knelt facing each other. She let go of his hands and launched a counter attack, managing to get a few tickles in before he grabbed her wrists and held them together. She tried to wriggle free, but he was too strong. "What now, big guy?"

He kept hold of her hands and closed the gap between them. "This." He pressed his mouth to hers. He pulled her arms down, causing her to fall forward against him. They both laughed, but never broke the kiss. He let go of her wrists and wrapped his arms around her, rubbing his hands up and down her back and stopping every few inches to squeeze. And with each squeeze, she wanted to press her body harder against him.

A knock sounded on his door. "Justin?"

They jumped apart like they'd been shocked.

*

"Yeah, Dad?" He moved to the edge of the bed as he answered. Ryan just sat cross-legged in the middle of the mattress.

His dad pushed the door open and half-stepped in. He looked at Justin with slightly raised brows—a look that said he knew what they were up to. "I have to run in to the hospital. I'm sorry. I know I promised…"

"It's okay, Dad." *Just leave already.*

"I shouldn't be long—maybe a couple of hours—just long enough to transfer a patient."

Justin nodded. "It's cool. Really."

He nodded. "Ryan, it's good to see you again."

"Thanks."

He looked at Justin. "I'm leaving as soon as I change. Don't forget it's a school night."

Ryan looked at her watch. "I have to leave in a few minutes anyway."

He nodded and stepped from the room… leaving the door open a little wider as he left.

Ryan sat on the edge of the bed next to Justin. "Are we good?"

Justin grabbed her hand. "*We're* great." He stood, pulling her up with him. "The question is, do you really want to ride this crazy train? Ryan, I'm serious. It could happen again."

"I know. If it does, I want to be there. Teach me what to do. How do I help you?"

"I don't know if you can. See crazy."

She shook her head and pressed her palms against his cheeks. "No. I see amazing."

"You need glasses." He barely got the last word out before she gave him a quick kiss.

She moved her hands to his waist, while he rested his just above her hips. "You amaze me, Ryan Quinn. You and your super sexy short hair, and your perfectly beautiful face, and your freaking amazing body."

She laughed. "My hair is short because I'm too lazy to mess with long hair and my face is a mess. And well, I think you're too blinded by one and two to see the flaws in three."

"No. You're not only beautiful, you are also the strongest person I know." He stared into her eyes. How could he make her understand that he meant every word? She was amazing. She was incredible.

"We're strong together."

Her gaze was locked with his and he felt energy build in the space between them. He bent his head to give her a kiss, when his dad appeared in the doorway wearing navy-blue scrubs. "Justin, can I have a quick word?"

"Yeah." He looked at Ryan. "I'll be right back." He followed his dad to the den. "What's up?"

"This is the first night I've had to leave you alone in the house since you found your mom. I want to make sure you're okay."

"I'm good."

His dad nodded, but Justin could tell there was something else he wanted to say. He rubbed the back of his neck and said, "Ryan seems like a special girl."

Jesus, not another keep-it-covered talk. "She is special. Just so you know, I don't want to blow what we have by having sex. We're not ready. When we are, I won't be stupid." *Wow, I sounded freaking mature.*

His dad smiled. "Good kid. Okay, I'd better get moving." But he stood where he was.

"I'm okay, Dad."

Then his dad did something that totally shocked him. He grabbed him and hugged him. “I’m really proud of you.” As soon as the words were out, he let go and stepped back. “I’ll have my cell if you need me.”

“Okay. Go.” He watched him grab his keys and exit through the front door before turning back toward his bedroom. Wow, they were in the house alone. No interruptions. Anything could happen.

But he’d been honest with his dad. Ryan was too special to him to rush into sex before they were both ready.

“Ryan?” he called as he neared the door.

She peeked around the door frame. “Everything okay?”

“Yeah. How much longer before you have to leave?”

She stepped into the hall. “I texted and asked for an extension. I have an hour. Is that okay?”

He couldn’t help the grin that he flashed her. “Yeah. I think I can handle more time with you.”

A slow smile formed on her face. “Are we alone?”

He nodded.

She sprinted the few feet down the hall and practically jumped into his arms. He lifted her and she wrapped her legs around his waist as they kissed. He carried her to the den—it was safer. He sat on the leather sofa with her straddling him and deepened the kiss. He wanted to pull her shirt over her head and to slide her shorts from her perfect butt. It was all he could do to keep his hands from exploring her body. God help him. How was he going to keep his word to his dad?

He pulled from the kiss. They stared at each other, both breathing hard. He smoothed his hands down her ribs, brushing his thumbs over her breasts. “God, Ryan, I’ve never wanted anything so much as I want you right now.”

She closed her eyes and he saw a flash of pain cross her face. She whispered, "Me too. But I can't." She slid off his lap and stood. "I'm sorry."

He stood too. "Don't be. When it's right, we'll know. I'll wait as long as you want."

"Thank you."

"I love you, Ryan Quinn."

"I love you too, Justin Hayes." She stepped closer for another kiss.

He cradled her face between his palms. Her hands clung to his triceps. He pulled from her lips and pressed his own down her neck to the notch in her collar. Was this too much? He squeezed her shoulders and looked into her face for the answer.

Fire burned in her eyes and she ran her hands up his chest. "If we don't stop now, we won't."

"Okay." He breathed the word. It was the right thing to do, but damn, he wanted it to go the other way. "We need to do something that doesn't involve kissing." He slid his fingers into the belt loops of her shorts and took a step back. "Do you want a snack?"

She shook her head. "No."

"How about some Xbox?"

"Sure."

She set the timer on her phone and they killed zombies for the next forty-five minutes. She was horrible at it, but he wasn't much better. He was too distracted watching the way she contorted her mouth to try to make the shots. Time went too quickly before the alarm sounded.

He ended the game and they set their controllers on the coffee table. She stood. "I'd better go."

"Yeah. I'll walk you to your truck."

He pulled on flip-flops and held her hand as they walked to her truck. Before she opened the cab door, he kissed her again. "Thanks for coming. I feel like a real jerk for leaving your parents that way. They must think I'm a real tool."

"Nobody thinks that. We were just all so worried. You'd be surprised how much people care if you let them."

Could eyes actually smile at a person? Because that's what her gaze felt like. Just being with her gave him a sense that everything was going to be okay.

She leaned back against the truck door. He placed a hand on either side of her and dropped his mouth to hers. His hands remained on the truck, never touching her. She wasn't touching him either. It was just the kiss they shared. And what a kiss it was. Heat built between them and with every flick of her tongue, tingles shot through him.

He pulled away. "I don't want you to leave."

"I don't want to leave." She wrapped her arms around him and snuggled her body against his. "I'm so glad you pulled me from the fountain."

"Me too." He dropped a kiss on her bottom lip. "You'd better go before you get into trouble." He stepped back and she opened the door. He kissed her again before she climbed in the cab and again before she closed the door. She rolled the window down and they kissed again.

He didn't step away from the truck until she started the engine. "Call me as soon as you get home."

"Okay." She stuck her head out of the window and smiled. "One more for the road."

He pressed his lips hard against hers, then took three steps back. "Go before I drag you from the cab."

"Promises, promises." She blew him a kiss and pulled away from the curb.

22

He stood in the street and stared after her until the taillights disappeared. He was still smiling when he turned and faced the house. The lights were on. The only barrier to the inside was the screen door. His chest squeezed. *Not tonight.* He took a deep breath and reminded himself that this was not the sad house where he'd found his mom. Tonight it had been a place of joy and love. He walked up the lawn to the door and walked in without hesitating.

He scrounged chips and salsa and plopped in front of the TV. He'd barely settled into ESPN when he got a text from his dad.

Dad: About to leave ED.
Justin: Okay.
Dad: Everything okay?
Justin: Yeah. Ryan just left.

His dad responded with a thumbs-up. Wow, it could have been different. What if they had decided to take things to the next level tonight? His dad could have walked right in on them. As much as he wanted to make love to Ryan, he didn't want it to be something hurried—something they did as soon as their parents turned their backs.

His mind drifted back to dinner at her house. He had been a jerk to run away. He had to apologize. He had other fences to mend too.

Two years of hating Austin McCoy was going to be a hard thing to ask forgiveness for, but he was going to do it. The easy thing would be to pretend none of it had happened. It'd be great if he could just show up at school tomorrow and not hate Austin. But it wouldn't make him a better man. He wanted to be better—no, he *needed* to be better. He couldn't love Ryan the way she deserved with hate crowding his heart.

He'd finished the last bite of salsa when his phone rang.

"I'm home." Her voice was like a ray of sunshine in his crazy life.

"Good. I had fun tonight."

"Me too. Are you playing tomorrow?"

"I plan to. Are you coming to the game?"

"Yeah. Is that okay?"

"I've always wanted my girlfriend cheering me on."

"Is *that* what I am?"

"I hope so."

"Hmm. Let me think. What do I want in a boyfriend? He has to be the sweetest, kindest person on earth. Check. He has to be an unbelievable kisser. Check. And, I have to love him more than anything. Check. Sounds like you're officially my boyfriend."

"Yeah. I win. Hey, what are you doing Saturday?"

"Working."

"Can we hang out Sunday?"

"Yeah. The store is closed on Sunday."

As they hung up, his dad came in. “Still up?”

“Yeah. I was talking to Ryan.”

His dad sat in the chair to the right of the sofa. “I like her.”

“Me too.” He looked at his dad. “I’m ready to talk about what happened at Ryan’s house.”

“I’m all ears.” His dad leaned forward and focused on Justin.

“So, Austin and Travis were there. It was awkward but I was dealing, you know? Then out of the blue I realized that Austin was as much of a victim as the rest of us—if not more. Dad, for two years Mom has blamed Austin and I’ve bought into it.” He waited for a reaction.

His dad sat back in the recliner and nodded. “I think it’s part of why she can’t move past the accident.” He let out a sigh like he’d been holding it in for the past two years.

Justin leaned forward with his forearms on his knees. “Dad, Chelsea killed those girls.”

His dad closed his eyes tight and nodded his head. “Yes. She did.” When he opened them again, Justin was a little surprised that they were dry. No tears—just a look of relief. “To be honest, I’m not sure your mom will ever see it.”

“She has to. Have you said anything?”

“In the beginning, it was a daily thing, if not more often. After a while, I gave up.”

“I need to apologize to Austin and Travis. I’ve hated them.”

“Do you want me there?”

He shook his head. “I’m good. This is something I need to do. How could I have been so sucked into Mom’s delusions?”

“When someone dies, especially someone so young, that you love so much, it’s hard to place blame on them.”

“Mom has to see. It’s not right for her to hate him.”

"I know." His dad rubbed his hands over his face. "I hope Dr. O'Malley can get her there."

"We have to." Justin stood. "Do you think I could see him tomorrow?"

"You have an appointment for Monday."

Justin carried the empty salsa bowl and the half-eaten bag of chips to the kitchen. His dad followed him and pulled a beer from the fridge. He popped the top and took a sip.

Justin leaned against the counter. "You said Dr. O'Malley would give me tools to stop the anxiety attacks. I don't want to wait until Monday. What if I have one in the middle of the game?"

His dad nodded. "I'll see if I can get you in tomorrow."

Justin let out a sigh. "Thanks. I'm heading to bed." *And figure out what the hell I'm going to say to Austin and Travis tomorrow.*

*

About two seconds after Ryan clicked off with Justin, her mom appeared in her bedroom doorway. "I take it things went well."

"Yeah." She shook her head. "He's been having anxiety attacks since his mom—you know." *Great, I've just given Mom a reason not to want me to see him.* "He's seeing a shrink, though." *That probably didn't help.*

Her mom sat next to her on the bed and wrapped her arm around her shoulders. "Just be careful. We're here if you need to talk about it."

She gave her mom a sideways look. "You're *not* going to tell me not to see him?"

"Do you want us to?"

"God, no."

Her mom smiled. "We all have—stuff—in our lives. He's a nice kid. As long as he treats you well, we're okay with it."

Ryan hugged her. "I'm the luckiest kid on the planet to have you guys as parents."

Her mom laughed. "Remember that the next time you have to help with the barn chores." She stood and said, "I'm headed to bed and you should too."

Her mom had barely left her room before Kelsey and Mackenzie came in. Mackenzie twisted her hands. "Is he okay?"

"Yeah."

Mackenzie had a freaked-out look in her eyes. "I've never seen anything like that."

"It was an anxiety attack. Are *you* okay?"

She nodded. "It's just all the stuff that's happened. First you get attacked at the fountain, then Justin's mom..."

"But none of those things have anything to do with you. It's just life."

"Yeah, well, I'm glad he's okay." She scooted from the room like a scared rabbit.

Ryan looked at Kelsey. "What's up with her?"

"I don't know. She's been on edge a lot lately. Do you think there's something going on that she's not telling us?"

"Who knows?" Ryan pulled a throw pillow into her lap. "Did Austin or Travis say anything after we left?"

Kelsey sat on her desk chair and propped her feet on the end of the bed. "No. We just all stared at each other for a few minutes. Does it happen a lot?"

Ryan shrugged. "I don't know. It's the first time I've seen it. It's got him freaked out. He's afraid he's losing it."

"I think he kinda did."

"Yeah." Seconds ticked between them. What else could she say? Kelsey was right. He had freaked out. Would it always be this way? They hadn't had one night together without some sort of craziness.

Kelsey broke into her thoughts. "Hey, are you okay?"

"Yeah. Just thinking."

"Well, I came in here to ask a question."

"Okay?"

"Do you want to hang out with us at the game tomorrow?"

Us being Shelby Cox and Hannah Ellis, Kelsey's two best friends. "Yeah. Shelby and Hannah won't mind?"

"Are you kidding? Of course not. They love you. After the game we'll go to Pepperonis."

That made Ryan smile. She hadn't had a friend since—well, she couldn't remember the last time she had a real friend. In Chicago she hung out with a group from The Fine Arts Academy. But she wouldn't really call them friends. There was always an underlying competition with their work. She thought she'd found friends with the Purity Club. Ha! "Thanks for asking me."

Kelsey tipped her chair on its back legs. "Do you love him?"

Ryan nodded. "I do. With all the shit that's happened, I think I love him even more. What about you? Do you love Austin?"

Kelsey dropped the chair on all fours. "You know I do. I hate it when we're not together."

Ryan took a deep breath. "Have you done it?"

"No. We've come close. I'm terrified."

"Just don't rush in. Make sure it's what you want—not just in the moment."

"Do you think you will with Justin?"

Ryan nodded. "I'd be lying if I said no. Once you've gone there, it's really hard not to. But in a way, I'm terrified too. I don't want to rush it. When we do it, I want it to be magic. I want everything to be perfect."

"Wow, it's weird, huh? The two of us talking about sex."

Ryan smiled. "Does that mean we're growing up?"

Kelsey nodded. "So on another topic, are you ready for the Teens Against Violence meeting Monday?"

"Don't remind me. When she asked me to talk, I thought it would be a regular meeting. Now she's made it a freaking assembly."

"You'll do great. Everybody has their version of what happened at the fountain. It's your chance to tell what really happened."

Ryan nodded. "Yeah. Hopefully, whoever has been writing crap on my locker won't be there."

"You know that's probably one or two people. The rest of the school feels like those bitches got what they deserved."

"One or two who've been heard above the majority."

"I think this club will change that. Who knows, maybe the jerk who's doing it will learn something." Kelsey yawned big and loud. "I'm going to bed. Chickens to feed in the morning."

Ryan said good night to her sister and sank onto her bed. *Wow. Kelsey's thinking of having sex with Austin.* A few months ago she'd never have imagined her sister thinking about having sex with anybody, much less talking about it.

Her phone signaled a text.

Justin: Can't stop thinking about you.

Ryan: Me either.

Justin: Sweet dreams.

Ryan: You too.

Justin: Love you.

Ryan: Love you too.

She set her phone on her bedside table and thought of the kisses they'd shared just an hour ago. What would *it* be like with him? The times before, it had been all about the physical feeling. And afterward, she'd felt ashamed and empty. What if that was just the way it was? Pleasure in the moment, hollowness afterward?

Surely not with Justin. She loved him. Kelsey had said she was terrified. Ryan was terrified too, but for a completely different reason.

23

Justin arrived at the field house early. Austin was almost always the first one there on game nights and Justin hoped to talk to him without a bunch of people around. He'd tried to corner him all day, but the timing never seemed right. But he was going to do it before the game come hell or high water.

He sat on the bench across from his locker and fished his phone out of his pocket to check out his Facebook page while he waited. He'd tried to plan what he was going to say. Too bad his dad couldn't get him in to see Dr. O'Malley until Monday. Surely Dr. O would have been able to help him explain away two years of hate? *I'm sorry* just wasn't enough. He sure as hell hoped he'd come up with something when he opened his mouth.

He'd clicked off the app on his phone when he heard the door to the field house swing open. Austin walked in, followed by Travis. Justin stood and walked toward them.

Austin dropped his backpack and immediately took a defensive stance—feet wide apart, elbows slightly bent, hands fisted. "You're here early, Hayes."

Justin took a step back and ran a hand through his hair. "Yeah, I wanted to talk to you." He looked at Travis. "And really, what I have to say goes for you too."

Austin picked up his pack but didn't take his eyes off Justin. "Okay. Talk."

"Shit. I don't know where to start."

Travis stepped toward him. "Is this about your little freakout?"

Justin hated the sarcasm in Travis's voice, but he guessed he deserved it. "Yeah. Kind of." He sat on a bench. "Look. I—ah—have come to realize a few things—many things, actually. One of those is that I've been wrong."

Travis shook his head. "About frickin' time."

Austin nodded. "You've been wrong about a lot of shit. So just what shit are you talking about?"

"Austin, I hung on to blaming you for the accident, for my messed-up family, for everything… because if I didn't, then I'd have admit that Chelsea caused the accident and that didn't seem right. But she did. You were innocent and I made you a victim too. I'm sorry."

Austin sat across from him. "It sucks. Your sister was my friend and I texted her. Nobody even talked about the dangers of texting back then. We all did it. Dude, wrong place, wrong time."

He didn't expect the tears that showed up in his eyes. Damn it. He would not cry. He forced them back and looked at Travis. "My sister killed your sister. I wish I could change that."

"It happened. We learn to live with it and get on."

Justin nodded. "I guess my family is a little late with all that. So—I wanted to say I'm sorry."

Austin stuck his hand out. "Thanks, man."

Travis shook his hand too. "Let's just kick ass on the field, huh?'

Relief flooded Justin. "Yeah."

They changed and stretched for the game. It was going to be a great night. Justin was totally pumped.

It only got better when they stepped onto the field. He looked at the student stands on the home side and there she was. His awesome girlfriend was yelling her head off as the players raced down the field. It didn't matter if his dad blew off the game tonight, because she was there for him.

As the team walked to the benches on the sideline, he heard his name called. Ryan hung on the fence that divided the players from the fans. "Justin! Look!"

His gaze followed the direction of her pointing finger. Holy shit. His dad was making his way down the stands toward Ryan… and holding his hand was *his mom.*

Justin reached the fence about the same time as his parents. He climbed up the chain links and hugged them over the top. "You're here. How?"

His mom brushed his hair from his face. "I wanted to tell you, but dad insisted on it being a surprise. I hope you don't mind."

"No! Are you home for good?"

His mom flashed a nervous glance toward his dad. "Alan?"

His dad nodded. "If this weekend goes well, yes. And I can't see why it wouldn't."

Justin hugged his parents again and then gave Ryan a quick kiss.

"Hayes! You gonna play?" Coach Peterson tipped up the brim of his ball cap. "Pleased to see you, Mrs. Hayes. Mr. Hayes."

Justin ran toward the bench feeling totally and completely invincible.

The game was slated to be the battle of the season. The Panthers were undefeated and had trounced the Hillsdale Hornets last year. The Hornets were playing like pros. McCoy to Barnes—touchdown. McCoy to Hayes—touchdown. McCoy scrambled and ran it in—touchdown. By halftime they were ahead twenty-one to zero.

The energy in the locker room buzzed. They could hardly contain themselves while Coach gave his *here's what to expect in the second half* speech. This was what it was all about. They were a machine and they played like they could read each other's thoughts.

The first play of the second half, the Panthers ran it in and nailed the field goal. It was cool, they could handle it. Justin wasn't worried as they huddled up—they were on fire.

And then it happened.

He could see the scoreboard behind the guys in the huddle and his mind flashed to Chelsea's painting—the one in the gallery. He felt his heart speed up along with his breathing. The freeze was coming. His brain shifted to the drawings in his mom's lap. *No. Not now. Not tonight.* He tried to refocus. Austin called a play, but all he could hear was his pulse drumming in his head. He focused on Austin but couldn't get his brain to engage. It was like the sound had been turned off.

The whistle blew and the sound of the crowd filled his ears. The ref announced a delay of game. Austin shook him. "Dude, what happened?"

"I'm good now." What else was he going to say? *I flipped out?*

They called a time-out and ran to the sideline. Coach yelled at the group. "Delay of game? What the hell happened?"

"Hayes freaked," one of the guys offered.

Coach looked at him. "That right?"

Austin stepped in. "He's cool. Let's just finish this thing."

Coach gave the go-ahead and they ran back to the field.

The team lost momentum in the third quarter, but by the fourth they were back on their feet. They beat the Panthers twenty-eight to ten. It was the best game Justin had played—and the worst.

He'd frickin' frozen out there.

The guys celebrated in the locker room, but the energy had been zapped from him. He stood in front of his locker and stripped off his jersey.

Coach appeared at the end of the row of lockers. "Hayes. Before you leave, in my office."

"Yes, sir." After he showered and dressed, he made his way to Coach's office. He passed Austin leaving. "Hey man, thanks for taking up for me."

Austin nodded and fist bumped him.

Justin stepped into Coach's office. "Sir?"

"McCoy said you froze. Is that right?" Coach stood with his arms crossed and his jaw clenched. When he spoke, he looked like he had to force the words from his mouth.

"Yes, sir."

"Is it going to happen again?"

"I don't know, sir." Shit. He had to tell him. "My dad says it's sort of a PTSD thing. I'm working on it."

"Anything I can do?" Coach's arms remained crossed, but he no longer looked like he was spitting words out of his mouth.

"No, sir. I just want to play ball."

Coach nodded. "I got no reason not to let you. I'll see you Monday."

Justin couldn't wait to get out of the locker room. The girlfriends tended to wait outside the field house door. There was something about having a girl waiting that made you feel like a star.

Tonight it was his turn. He stepped from the field house with a grin on his face.

*

Ryan stood with Kelsey, Mackenzie, Austin, and Travis. “Great game!”

Travis nodded. “Yeah, it was. Let’s head to Pepperonis.”

Ryan looked across to the field house where Justin’s parents stood. She’d planned to go with Justin, but now she wasn’t sure. He probably wanted to spend the evening with his parents. She checked her phone again. “I’m not sure what I’m doing.”

Kelsey sighed. “Well, we can’t wait all night. Text him.”

Ryan looked at her phone. What should she say? *Are you taking me to Pepperonis? Do we have a date?* She didn’t want to pressure him. It was right for him to be with his parents. She settled for *Hey there!*

She’d barely fired off the text when he exited the field house. He had to have been the last one to leave. He looked around, but he didn’t see her. She started toward him, but his parents beat her to him so she hung back and let them have their time. He had a boyish grin on his face, like he’d just received the best Christmas gift ever. He hugged his mom and kept his arm around her as though he was afraid to let go.

Then he saw her. “Ryan!” She walked to them. “Mom, have you met my girlfriend?”

His mom nodded. “We met before the game.”

Ryan wanted to ask what the plans were, but the timing was all wrong. On the other hand, her sisters were waiting.

Kelsey called, "Ryan! What's the deal? Are you coming with us or not?"

She cringed. "Sorry." She really didn't need her sister pressuring her right now.

Justin released his mom and took Ryan's hand, saying to his parents, "We were going to Pepperonis. Do you want to come?"

His mom shook her head. "No. Go have fun. You earned it."

"But it's your first night home."

His dad wrapped his arms around his mom's waist. "Yes, it is. So go. Have fun. Don't stay out all night."

"Jesus, Dad." He shook his head and gave his mom a peck on the cheek. "Later."

Ryan smiled at his parents and pretended she hadn't caught his dad's meaning. "It was nice to see you again."

"Likewise." Mrs. Quinn leaned against her husband's chest and waggled her fingers.

Justin pulled her away from his parents and toward the group waiting. "Awkward."

"I think it's cute."

"Yeah, how often do you want to think about your parents bumping pubes?"

She smacked his arm. "Yuck. Not a visual I want."

"Exactly." He tugged her closer and planted a kiss on her in mid-step.

Kelsey took charge when they joined the others. "We're going to be the last ones there. Who's riding with us?"

Ryan looked at Justin. "Not us."

Mackenzie looked around as though she were looking for somebody. Travis kept his eyes focused on Mackenzie and spoke up. "Come on, Short Stuff, you can ride with me."

Well, isn't that interesting?

Mackenzie glanced up at him and gave a shrug. "Okay."

Looks like a one-sided attraction.

Kelsey grabbed Austin's hand. "Let's *go* already."

Justin pulled Ryan in the opposite direction. "We're parked this way." By the time they reached the parking lot, it was almost empty.

A cool breeze kicked up and made Ryan shiver. "Brr. Cold front's here."

"I thought you northern girls were immune."

"Not this one." She hugged herself, trying to ward off the chill.

Justin shrugged out of his jacket and wrapped it around her shoulders. "Better?"

"Much." When they reached his truck she slid her arms around his waist and he hugged her to his chest. "This is even better." She went up on her toes and kissed him.

It was slow, but the heat that accompanied it was instant. She pressed her breasts to his chest and he cupped her rear, pulling her tight against him. They were alone. They could climb into his truck. This could be the moment. She wanted it to be the moment. Or did she?

No. Not in the back of a truck. It had to be perfect.

She pulled from the kiss. "Pizza?"

He smiled, but she could see the same longing in his eyes that she felt in her soul. "Yeah. Pizza."

When they climbed in the truck, she reached across the console for his hand, but he pulled it away like she'd burned him.

He gave her a sideways grin. "Give me a minute."

She faced her window and stared at the empty parking lot. Awkwardness aside, it was pretty cool that she turned him on so much he couldn't touch her.

He sighed and started the engine. "Okay, we need to talk about really stupid stuff."

"Like what?"

"Anything to take my mind off kissing you… and things."

"Okay, well, my favorite Popsicle flavor is grape."

"Not helping."

"Hmm. I like to blow bubbles with my gum."

"Still not helping. You're killing me here."

"You come up with something."

"I want to, but all I can think about is the color of your panties or whether you have a front clasp or back."

"Pink and a pink front clasp."

"Really. You had to go there. I want to crawl across this console and see for myself."

She grabbed his hand. "Justin, I don't want to wait. But I don't want our first time to be in the backseat."

He squeezed her hand. "Me either."

She stretched across the console and kissed him, hard. He pulled away. "Pizza."

Ryan fell back into her seat and did up her seatbelt to keep herself there. "We'd better go. Now."

They drove to Pepperonis in silence, but Ryan was okay with it. They both needed time to check their emotions. She'd never felt anything close to what she felt with Justin. She was in love—the real thing. It wasn't supposed to happen to a seventeen-year-old. She hadn't planned on loving anybody until she was in college, and here she was a junior in high school and she was madly, truly, out of her mind in love with Justin Hayes.

And that scared the ever-living snot out of her.

At the restaurant they made their way to the back room that was reserved for the students. They met Kelsey coming back from the buffet. "About time. What took you so long?"

Ryan just looked at her and blushed.

"Whatever. We saved you a seat." She led her toward the table in the back of the room. Hannah and Shelby waved from the end of a long row of tables. Shelby shouted over the cacophony of chatter, "It's about time y'all showed up."

Ryan's insides warmed. *Normal people, normal friends.* She set her purse down at the place Kelsey had saved and followed Justin to the buffet. This was the way it was supposed to be.

What a contrast to the first time they'd had pizza together at a school function—on the first day of school at the Meet and Eat lunch sponsored by the Purity Club. Kelsey was angry they'd moved to Texas and blamed it all on Ryan. She'd threatened to divulge Ryan's disqualification for the PC. Now, Kelsey was Ryan's biggest protector.

Justin squeezed her hand. "You okay?"

"Yeah. I was just thinking about the PC. The first time I had pizza in Texas was at a PC meeting. It was disgusting."

"The meeting or the pizza?"

Ryan laughed. "Looking back, I'd say both." She turned more serious. "It's weird how seeing Kelsey with that slice on her plate made me think about that meeting. Is that the way it happens to you?"

"Yes. Only my mind takes me all the way to that bad place and freezes. It's like I relive that night every time. I know it's not really happening, but I have the same emotions. Crazy, huh?"

"No. Not crazy. Maybe your mind is just trying to make sense of it all."

He shrugged, "I guess. Come on, let's sit."

This was the first time Ryan had come to a postgame celebration. Before, she'd gone to slumber parties at Macey Brown's with the PC girls. This was way more fun.

As quarterback, Austin stood on the bench at their table and gave a postgame speech about how awesomely everybody had played. The crowed cheered like mad. It was a perfect postgame night.

Afterward, they decided to move to the little coffee shop across from the courthouse, so Ryan and Justin left first to save the seats. This time they didn't spend time making out. Little kisses were enough. Make-out time would happen later.

The Grind was packed. Several groups of people sat on the wall that surrounded the courthouse across the street. She pulled Justin's jacket closer around her and hoped they'd find a place to sit inside. But when they reached the coffee shop, a figure stepped from the shadows like a scene from a scary movie.

Macey Brown stood between them and the door.

Macey's eyes held that same crazy look as they had the night at the fountain. "Well, if it isn't the slut of Hillside."

"Move, Macey." Ryan took a step toward her, but she held her ground.

"This isn't over. They may be able to keep *me* from school, but there are people who know what you are."

Justin put his arm around Ryan. "Come on, let's find seats."

Ryan didn't move. Here was her chance. "What difference does any of this make to you? What did I ever do to make you hate me so much?"

"You tainted the club. You lied."

Ryan shook her head. "Why not just kick me out?"

Justin shook his head. "You can't argue with crazy. Come on."

"Hang on." To Macey she said, "Tell the truth. Why pick on me?"

Hatred flashed in the other girl's eyes. "You want to know why? Because you ruined everything. You came along and all anybody could talk about was the Quinn sisters. All Eric could talk about was you. He liked me until you came. He knew you weren't a virgin the minute he saw you. Guys can tell by the way you walk."

"That's a load of bullshit," Justin snapped.

Macey narrowed her gaze at Ryan. "Eric could tell and he wanted you. He said you had the face of a goddess." She raised a brow. "Not anymore."

Ryan slapped Macey across the face with all the pent-up anger she'd felt over the past few weeks. "Come on, Justin."

Macey put a hand to her cheek and glared at them as they passed her. "This isn't over."

Ryan stopped and turned toward her. "Yeah, it is."

She let Justin lead her to a just-vacated sofa in the back of the shop, where she sat with a plop. "She is twisted. Eric hardly talked to me."

Justin sat next to her. "I knew he had a thing for you and I don't doubt he said those things to her. He's a jerk." He shook his head. "I didn't know he'd talked to Macey, but if he saw her as somebody he could screw, he would."

"Jeez, and you were friends with him?"

"Key word—*was*."

Kelsey and Austin walked up, followed by Mackenzie and Travis. Kelsey wrinkled her brow. "Everything okay?"

Ryan nodded. "Macey stopped me on the way in."

"You're kidding." Kelsey and Austin sat on the loveseat opposite them. Mackenzie sat on the sofa next to Ryan and Travis took a chair.

Ryan said, "I wish. That bitch is crazy. I slapped her."

"She deserves more than that." Kelsey leaned against Austin's shoulder.

Ryan rubbed the scars on her cheeks. "She's glad she scarred my face. She did it because Eric Perez said I was pretty."

"You're kidding." Austin put his arm around Kelsey and pulled her closer.

Mackenzie stood. "I'll be right back." She headed toward the bathroom, but not before Ryan saw the tears that welled in her eyes.

"She okay?" Ryan asked the group.

Kelsey looked at Travis. "Anything happen on the way here?"

"No. She has taken this whole thing pretty hard, though."

Ryan sighed. "I don't want to think about it anymore. Let's get some coffee and hit the reset button to the fun we were having at Pepperonis."

"Agreed," said Kelsey.

Justin stood. "Tonight is my treat." Mackenzie returned just as he was getting everybody's order. "What do you want, Kenzie? I'm paying."

She smiled—almost back to her normal self. "Nonfat, two raw sugars, latte with whip."

Justin shook his head and repeated the litany of complicated orders.

Travis stood. "Come on, I'll help you carry."

Kelsey shot Austin a look and he stood too. "Hang on."

As soon the guys left, Ryan turned to Mackenzie. "Hey there, what's going on?"

Mackenzie gave a subtle shake of her head. "Nothing."

Kelsey leaned forward. "You and Travis?"

Mackenzie rolled her eyes. "We're friends."

Ryan said, "I don't know about that. He seems to stare at you—a lot."

"He's like a brother to me."

Kelsey shrugged. "Shame. He's one of the good ones."

"I know—which is why I don't want to screw things up by being more than friends." Mackenzie smiled, but Ryan saw sadness in her face.

Something was up with her little sister and she needed to find out what.

24

Friday had been perfect. Justin's parents had come to the game. His mom was home. He'd made amends with Austin. Best of all, he'd spent the evening with Ryan Quinn.

Saturday she had to work and it was all Justin could do to keep from hanging out at the feed store. Instead, he'd hung out with his parents. He'd tried to teach his mom to shoot zombies, but she was worse than Ryan. It didn't matter, though—because she was laughing. When the Aggies played, they gathered around the TV with a bowl of popcorn and yelled them to a victory. After the game, he cleaned up and let his parents relax on the sofa. His dad's feet were stretched onto the ottoman while his mom was laid out on the couch with her head in his dad's lap.

They weren't the same family as they'd been two years ago. This was the beginning of a new family—a family of three. It would never be the same and he would always long for the one he'd lost. But this was the beginning of something new and good.

By the time Sunday rolled around, he couldn't wait to see Ryan. When she texted that she was home from church, he bolted from the house, but not before noticing his parents snuggled on the sofa in the den. Life was good.

The wind had dropped the temperature to the freeze-your-ass-off degrees. He grabbed a jean jacket because she still had his letter jacket. The thought of his jacket hanging below her butt and long on her arms made him smile.

The gate to the Quinn property had been left open. His gut clenched when he saw Austin's truck parked in front, but he reminded himself that the guy was okay. He parked and jogged up the steps. The front door swung open before he had a chance to knock.

Ryan stood on the other side of the screen wearing a green sweater, super tight jeans, and a huge grin. "Hey there. Come in."

"Hi." He dropped a kiss on her lips. He was met by the smell of roast cooking and the sounds of a family enjoying a Sunday together. A fire crackled in the fireplace and a football game was on. Austin sat next to Mr. Quinn watching the game. Kelsey walked into the den carrying a bowl of chips and another of salsa. "Hi, Justin."

Austin didn't move but held his hand out for Justin to shake. "Dude."

Mr. Quinn shook his hand and said, "Have a seat."

He looked at Ryan. Not that he didn't want to watch the game, but he'd waited all weekend to see her.

"Do you want a soda?"

"Sure, I'll come with you." He followed her into the kitchen, hoping to wrap her in his arms and lay one on her. No such luck. Her mom sat at the table snapping green beans.

"Hi, Justin. I hope you like roast."

"Yes, ma'am." Was she kidding? The smell wafting through the house made his mouth water.

Ryan opened the refrigerator. "Dr. Pepper?"

"Sure." He wanted to ask her if they could hang out without the rest of the family around, but that wasn't going to happen.

She handed him a can and grabbed one for herself. "Come on. I want to show you something."

He followed her up the stairs to her room. She didn't close the door, but when they crossed the threshold she took his can and set both hers and his on the dresser. She smiled up at him and he felt his gut clench again, but for a different reason. She snaked her arms up his chest and around his neck.

He pulled her close and lowered his mouth to hers. She opened to him, her tongue warm as it slid over his. She pressed her breasts tight against his chest and as much as he told himself he would resist, he ran his hands up her ribs to the sides of them. When the kiss broke, he nestled her hips against his and lost himself in her gaze. "I've missed you."

"I've missed you too. We can't be up here long. I'm sure one of my parents will find a reason to check on us. But I thought I was going to die if I didn't get to kiss you."

He liked that she wanted him as much he wanted her. He hugged her and whispered in her ear, "I can't imagine my life without you." He pressed his lips just below her earlobe and felt her shiver against him. He ran his hands beneath her sweater and up her back, where her bare skin was soft and warm.

"Ryan." Her mom sounded from somewhere around the stairs. "Could you come here, please?"

She pulled away from him and rolled her eyes. "See?"

Justin leaned against the wall and watched her pad to the top of the stairs.

"What's up?"

"Would you please gather some eggs? I need them for dessert."

"Be right down." She turned to Justin. "Have you ever gathered eggs?"

He shook his head.

"Come on—it's kind of fun." They jogged downstairs and she grabbed his letter jacket off the coat tree by the front door.

He followed her outside, but they both stopped abruptly as soon as the door closed behind them. Travis's truck was parked across from the house close to the chicken coop. He could only see their backs, but judging by the way her shoulders shook, Mackenzie was crying. Travis was angled in his seat with his arm stretched across the back. He rubbed the back of her neck, but she pulled away. Travis shook his head and turned sideways in his seat.

Ryan dropped Justin's hand. "Wait here." She ran down the steps to the truck.

Travis looked through the back window, spotted them, and said something to Mackenzie. She jumped out and ran toward the barn.

"Kenzie!" Ryan went after her.

When Kenzie reached the barn door, she turned toward her. "Leave me alone."

Justin walked to Travis's truck. He had no idea what was going on, but he couldn't deny the pain in the guy's face. Travis lowered the window. "Before you say anything, this is not about me. Ryan needs to talk to her."

"About what?"

"I can't tell you. I promised. But Ryan needs to make her talk."

Justin shook his head. "You're going to have to give me more than that."

"All I can say is that she needs Ryan right now." He started the engine.

It was none of Justin's business, but this didn't seem right. "You made her cry and now you're leaving? That ain't right."

"*I* didn't make her cry. I'm just trying to pick up the pieces."

"Who the hell did?" Justin's mind began to search through the jerks at school.

"Ask her." Travis shifted into reverse and backed away from them.

*

Ryan found Mackenzie sitting on a trunk in the tiny tack room just outside the stalls. When she walked in, Kenzie held up her hand. "I need to be alone."

Ryan sat next to her sister. "Kenzie, what's going on? This isn't like you."

She shook her head and hicupped. "I can't," she whispered.

"Did Travis do something?"

"No. Look, I can't talk about it."

Ryan put her arm across Kenzie's shoulder, but her sister recoiled. Ryan let her arm fall away. "Whatever it is, you can tell me. Maybe I can help."

She studied her hands and shook her head. "It's just—school stuff." She sniffed and placed a fake smile on her face. "It's stupid. Hormones. I'm good."

"You're not good."

Kenzie took a deep, ragged breath. "I am. Promise you won't say anything to anybody. I'll be up in a few."

Ryan wanted to stay and make her talk, but she knew her little sister. Once she set her mind to something, nothing was going to change it, and right now her mind was set on not talking. She stood. “Okay. But Mackenzie, remember, you can trust me. When you’re ready, I’ll be here for you.”

Mackenzie nodded and Ryan left the barn.

Justin was waiting just outside the door. “Everything okay?”

“Not really.” She walked toward the coop. Justin matched her stride. “Where’s Travis?”

“He left. He told me to tell you to make her talk.”

She shook her head. “He obviously does not know my sister. She won’t talk until she’s good and ready.” She grabbed a galvanized bucket from a nail on the outside of the coop and proceeded to look for eggs beneath the chickens in the nesting boxes. She collected four bluish-green eggs.

Justin held his hand out. “Here. I’ll take that.”

She handed him the bucket with the eggs in it, although she wasn’t sure why. It wasn’t like she’d never carried them to the house before. “She said it was school stuff. Do you think she’s being bullied?”

“Maybe. But why wouldn’t Travis just say so?”

“She could’ve made him promise not to tell.”

He shook his head. “He said he’d promised her he wouldn’t say anything. It doesn’t make sense for him to keep a secret like that.”

He was right. There was something else going on with Mackenzie.

She heard gravel crunching beneath tires and headed out of the coop, bucket in hand. When she saw who it was, an instant grin formed on her face. “Have you met my Uncle Jack and Aunt Susan?”

“Sort of. I mean, everybody knows pretty much everybody in this town. They used to own the feed store, right?”

"Yeah, and this house too. Come on, you'll love them." She practically ran to Uncle Jack's Suburban. When they got out of the truck, she gave them both a huge hug. "This is my boyfriend, Justin Hayes."

Aunt Susan raised her brows at Ryan. "Boyfriend? Well, well, somebody has been busy." She shook Justin's hand. "You're Alan's boy."

"Yes, ma'am."

"Pleased to meet you."

Her uncle shook his hand too. When he released it he said, "Well, if you're Ryan's boyfriend you might as well make yourself useful and unload that cooler from the back."

Justin handed the bucket to Ryan and retrieved a Yeti from the back. Ryan liked the way his biceps bulged as he carried it up the steps.

Aunt Susan ran up the steps and held the door. Ryan led Justin to the kitchen, where she handed her mom the eggs and pulled homemade ice cream from the cooler. The rest of the family joined them in the kitchen. She loved days like this—everybody talking at once. Her dad and Uncle Jack talked football with Austin. Her sister, mom, and aunt were discussing the latest celebrity scandal. Justin stood a little back from the men looking slightly awkward. She was about to rescue him when Austin turned toward him and asked him some football question. He stepped into the circle and joined the conversation. She sighed. Everything was perfect.

Almost. Mackenzie still hadn't made an appearance.

As if her aunt could read her thoughts, she looked around the kitchen and said, "Where's Kenzie?"

Her mom answered, "She rode home from church with Travis. They should be here by now."

Ryan wasn't sure if she should say something or not. Travis had been invited to Sunday dinner, but that clearly wasn't going to happen. She was about to tell her mom that Kenzie was home when she walked into the kitchen.

She had manufactured a smile and hugged her aunt and uncle, but Ryan still saw the pain in her eyes. Travis was right—she had to make her talk.

Her aunt gave her a squeeze. "Did you and your friend find everything you needed?"

Kenzie blushed. "Yes. Thanks."

Ryan's wasn't the only stunned expression that flashed at Kenzie. Her mom looked from her to her sister-in-law. "What's this?"

Aunt Susan swiped her hand through the air, dismissing her statement. "Kenzie and her friend came by to look through our old yearbook stuff." She turned to Kenzie. "Did you get enough for your story?"

Kenzie pulled away from her aunt. "Yes. Thanks." She looked at her mom. "I need to work on some homework." She practically bolted from the kitchen.

Aunt Susan looked at the Quinn women. "Did I say something I shouldn't have?"

"No." Ryan's mom asked the question that was burning in Ryan's mind. "What story?"

Aunt Susan said, "Kenzie and…" She turned to Uncle Jack. "What's the name of that curly-headed kid Mackenzie brought around?"

"Braden. He's John McGuire's grandson."

"That's right. Braden. Cute kid."

Their mom's gaze volleyed between her and Kelsey. "Do you girls know this Braden McGuire?"

Ryan shrugged. "Sort of. He's the guy I'm working with on the Teens Against Violence stuff. I didn't know Mackenzie really knew him." She tried to look completely nonchalant about it. On the inside her brain was reeling. This had to be connected somehow with the tears in the truck.

Aunt Susan smiled. "He's a good kid. They're working on some story about the history of Hillside High." She turned to Ryan's dad. "Tom, we found the award you got for MVP your freshman year. I should have thought to bring it over."

"What would I do with a relic like that besides toss it?"

"No." Kelsey almost shouted. "Dad, if you don't want it, let one of us have it. You may not embrace your high school football career, but we do."

He shrugged and grabbed a beer from the fridge. "The second half is about to start. Who's watching football with me?"

Austin and Uncle Jack followed him into the den. Justin looked at Ryan and back at the door through which the other men had gone, and Ryan almost laughed. It was obvious he was dying to watch the game. "Go. I'm going to help Mom anyway." He grinned and joined the others.

Aunt Susan cocked a brow at her. "So—boyfriend?"

"Yeah. I couldn't not fall for him. He saved me from the fountain, after all."

Aunt Susan shook her head. "He's had a tough couple of years. I'm glad to see something good happen to him, like you."

"Thanks." She turned to her mom. "Do you need help with the pie?"

"Not yet. Is something going on with Mackenzie? She doesn't seem herself."

"I dunno. I'll go check on her." Ryan jogged upstairs to Kenzie's room. The door was closed. She knocked and pushed it open—no sense in giving her a chance to tell her to go away.

Mackenzie was curled up in the corner of her room with a pillow in her lap. Her eyes were wide, her stare distant.

"Kenzie?"

She didn't answer. She didn't even acknowledge that Ryan had entered the room. No movement at all.

Ryan sat next to her sister, put her arm around her, and pulled her head to her shoulder. "I don't know what's going on, and you don't have to tell me. But know that I'm here for you. I always will be."

Kenzie nodded but kept silent. They sat like that until Ryan's arm was full of pins and needles. "Kenzie, we need to go downstairs."

Her sister sat up. "Yeah." She stood and walked to the door, then turned to Ryan. "You shouldn't be nice to me. I don't deserve it." She left the room, closing the door behind her.

"What? Kenzie, wait. You can't say something like that and leave." Too late—she'd already fled down the stairs.

On the way to the kitchen, Ryan traipsed through the den. She wanted to tell Justin what had happened with Kenzie, but he was in total guy football mode. It was cool to see him sitting with Austin, her dad, and her uncle. They groaned in unison when a pass was fumbled. She smiled to herself. Guys bonded over football the way girls bonded over shopping.

Wow, how stereotypical is that?

She was still smiling when she entered the kitchen. Mackenzie sat at the kitchen table with Aunt Susan. She had erased the troubled expression that Ryan had seen and was listening to Aunt Susan talking about their latest trip in the motor home.

Kelsey stood at the counter slicing apples. She turned to Ryan. "Want to help with these? The sooner we finish, the sooner we can watch the game."

Aunt Susan said, "I'll cut those apples. My goodness, I didn't know you were such a fan." She said it with a smirk on her face.

"Well, I've learned a lot about it since Austin has been hanging around. It's fun." She handed Ryan a knife.

Aunt Susan looked at Ryan. "Are you into football too?"

"It's cool."

"And you?" Aunt Susan said to Mackenzie.

"Not so much. But it's hard to avoid in Texas."

"Hand me that." Aunt Susan indicated the knife Ryan held. "My, my, how the Quinn girls have changed. The day you three drove up to this house and met us on the porch just about ripped my heart out. Kelsey was convinced her life had been ruined. Ryan was full of spit and vinegar and looking like she was ready to tear the world a new one. And Mackenzie, bless your heart, I've never seen such a sad person in all my life." She shook her head. "Look at you now. Kelsey has embraced the farm. Ryan, you've handled what happened to you with enough courage to be a lesson to the rest of us." She turned to Mackenzie and winked. "I can't wait to read the story you and that McGuire boy ferreted out."

"I'm proud of the way the girls have adjusted." Ryan's mom smiled at Aunt Susan, but the corners of her eyes sagged a bit and Ryan wondered how well her mom had adjusted to the move.

Aunt Susan peeled and chopped the apples twice as fast as Kelsey and Ryan. "All right, girls, I'll take over. I don't give two figs for football. Go watch the game."

Ryan looked at her mom.

"Go on."

They didn't have to be asked twice. Kenzie practically sprinted from the room. Kelsey grabbed a soda and joined the guys in the den.

Ryan went upstairs after Kenzie. She found her little sister changing into running clothes. "You're going for another run? You ran this morning."

"I need to clear my head."

Ryan stood in the doorway. "What's going on?"

Kenzie shook her head. "I can't talk about it. Not yet. I will, just not yet. I have to figure things out first."

"Are you and Travis okay?"

"I hope so." She pulled her running shoes on. "Look, Ryan, I know this doesn't make sense and I don't mean to be so dramatic. I'll tell you everything. I just have to figure a few things out first. Don't push me."

"Okay." She stepped away from the door. What else could she do?

Mackenzie pushed past her, down the stairs, and out the door.

Ryan jogged more slowly down the stairs. She shot Justin a look that said *I need to talk* and went onto the porch. The wind had died, but it was still cold—too cold to be outside without a jacket.

She had turned to retreat to the house when Justin came through the door holding his letter jacket. "Here. I thought you might need this."

She shrugged into the jacket. "Thanks."

"What's going on?"

"Something's up with Mackenzie. I'm worried about her."

Kelsey came through the door with Austin on her heels. "Did Mackenzie just go on another run?" The group moved to the wicker furniture nestled in the corner of the porch. Ryan and Justin sat on the glider and Austin and Kelsey snuggled on the loveseat across from it.

Ryan nodded. "Yep. She said she had to clear her head."

Kelsey shook her head. "She ran three times yesterday."

"Wow. There's more." Ryan explained what had happened earlier.

Austin nodded. "I wondered what'd happened to Travis. When I texted him, he just said he needed to be home."

Ryan said, "I guess there's nothing we can do until she decides to talk."

"I think Mom should know that she's running like two to three times a day. That can't be good."

Ryan shrugged. "I don't know—I mean, she used to work out six hours a day when she was in gymnastics."

Kelsey shook her head. "That's different. I get the feeling this all has something to do with Braden McGuire."

"Aunt Susan mentioned a couple of times the story they're working on. What's up with that? Did you know she was doing this?"

Kelsey said, "No. I know Braden has the hots for her, but I didn't think she was even talking to him."

Austin nodded. "She and Travis are always hanging out, but he says they're just friends."

Ryan pulled the jacket more tightly around herself. "Well, we're not going to solve this today and I'm freezing."

They stood and filed back into the house. Ryan and Justin took a seat on the hearth in front of the fire. *Thank God for gas fireplaces.*

When Kenzie returned from her run, Ryan resisted the urge to follow her upstairs and quiz her. Instead, she focused on enjoying the day. Justin seemed to feel more comfortable with her family. He even joked a little with her dad during dinner.

It was the perfect Sunday. Football, family, and a feast. Her mom had outdone herself. Aunt Susan had brought homemade vanilla ice cream laced with Baileys Irish Cream. The day seemed to fly by and in a blink of an eye, she was standing next to Justin's truck saying good-bye.

"I had a great time." He wrapped his arms around her.

She nestled against his chest. "I wish you didn't have to go."

"Me too. But I need to spend some time with my mom."

She pulled away enough to look in his eyes. "I didn't even think about this being your mom's first Sunday home."

"It's okay. We spent all day yesterday together." He kissed her softly. "There's nowhere I'd rather be than right here." He lowered his mouth to hers again.

This time it wasn't a sweet kiss. It was full of heat. He leaned against the side of his truck and she leaned against him. The more the kiss deepened, the more tightly he held her. When the kiss broke, they were both breathless.

"I'd better go."

She pulled away. "Okay. I'll see you tomorrow."

"I have a shrink appointment in the afternoon. I'm going to miss your meeting."

"Let me know how it goes." This would be the perfect time to tell him she was having surgery on Tuesday, but she couldn't make herself say the words. She'd told his dad without a second thought, but Justin was struggling with his own stuff. It didn't seem fair to give him her stuff too.

She'd tell him tomorrow—after his appointment.

25

Justin waited outside Dr. O'Malley's office with his parents on either side of him. Was it weird for his mom to be there without being an in-patient? The white-knuckled grip she had on the armrests of her chair told him it was.

He rubbed her back. "Hey, are you okay?"

She shot him an anxious glance. "I'm sorry that my illness has affected you so much."

He shook his head. "Don't do that to yourself. We're all going to be okay."

She let go of the armrest and twisted her hands in her lap. "I want to be. Letting go is—difficult."

"I don't see moving on with our lives as letting go. We will always remember and love her."

His mom nodded. "In my mind I know that. I know she'll never be back. But I miss her with every beat of my heart."

His dad stood and moved over to sit next to his mom. "Sandy, we all miss her with every beat of our hearts."

She gave his dad a weak smile. "I know. I know I have to get on with my life. I have to let y'all live yours." She grabbed each of their hands. "This is our family now. A family of three."

Justin's dad covered her hand with both of his. "Yes. But she's always with us, in our hearts, in our memories."

Dr. O'Malley walked through his office door and smiled at the scene before him.

He must think we're the freaking Brady Bunch.

"Justin, are you ready?"

He stood. "Yes, sir." Justin followed him into his office and sat on the sofa. The attitude he'd had was gone. He needed help and he'd answer every question, try whatever Dr. O asked—pretty much anything to stop the brain freezes.

"How are things going at home?"

"Better. Mom and Dad were at my game. That's the first time that's happened."

"Good. You seem pleased."

"Yeah. It was cool."

"So tell me what's been going on other than that."

Justin took a deep breath. No sense sugarcoating it. He was here to get help. "I've been having these freezes."

"Can you describe them?"

"It's like an out-of-body experience or something. I don't know. It's crazy. One minute I'm fine and then bam—my brain takes me to the night Mom tried to kill herself. I freeze. It's crazy. My brain shuts down or locks. I can't make sense of things around me. My dad thinks it's PTSD."

Dr. O wrote a few notes on his pad and looked up. "Tell me what happened the first time you experienced this freeze."

Justin told him what had happened that night in his truck.

"How often are you experiencing this sensation?"

"It happened once at my girlfriend's house and again during a game."

"Do you know what triggered each of these events?"

"At my girlfriend's, it was seeing Austin McCoy. He's dating her sister."

"He is the boy who texted Chelsea when the accident happened?"

"Yeah. It was like all of a sudden I got it. I mean really got it, that he had nothing to do with Chelsea's death. It was Chelsea's fault. She killed those other girls. That's big, right?"

"Very big." Dr. O smiled, but it didn't last long. In the next breath, his face fell back to its normal neutral expression. "Go on."

"It was crazy—almost like my brain was shouting that it was her fault. And then it happened. Brain freeze. My mind went from the accident to the night I found Mom with the gun."

Dr. O wrote on his pad. "Tell me what happened at the game."

"That was weird. I was reminded of one of Chelsea's paintings and then it happened." He slumped back into the sofa.

Dr. O'Malley set his notepad on the chair next to him. "Let's go back to the night you found your mom with the gun. Take me through that night."

Justin didn't want to visit that memory. But the thought of having another freak-out scared him more. His chest tightened just thinking about walking through the door that night. "My dad was at work, but he knew something was wrong. I was out with Ryan."

"Ryan?"

"My girlfriend. When I got home I knew things weren't right." Sweat beaded across his forehead.

"Take your time, Justin. I'm going to give you some tools to reground yourself. Put your feet on the floor, your back against the sofa. Take a deep, slow breaths. When you're ready, continue your story."

Justin concentrated on the feel of his feet against the floor. He breathed deep and slow. Then he kept his gaze on Dr. O'Malley and finished his story. He had to stop a couple of times and practice the regrounding techniques, but he got through it. When he finished, he was exhausted.

Dr. O'Malley smiled. "You were very brave to go after that gun. You've been under a lot of stress since your sister died. You've cared for your mom, taken on household duties, and managed to perform in school and athletics. It's going to take some time to work though this. Do you feel the relaxation and regrounding tools are helpful?"

"They seem to be. But what do I do if I'm on the football field?"

"The key is to recognize triggers. As soon as you feel the anxiety building, reground yourself. If you're on the field, focus on the seams of the ball, on the number of another player—anything to keep your mind focused on the here and now. But the other part of it is to allow yourself to remember in the appropriate venue."

"What do you mean?"

"When it's safe. Here with me. With your girlfriend, your parents. A best friend. Over time, the memory will be easier."

Justin nodded and promised himself he'd do all of those things. He couldn't imagine talking about that night over and over. He didn't want to be like his mom—stuck reliving the memory. Dr. O'Malley discussed relaxation techniques with him and more "tools" to reground himself. He wasn't sure he bought into all that stuff, but he'd give it a try.

When the session was over, Dr. O'Malley talked to the family, reviewing with them the same things he'd told Justin. Then he asked Justin and his dad to step out—it was his mom's turn.

"Fell better?" His dad took a seat in the waiting room next to him.

"Yeah. At least I know it'll probably get better."

"It *will* get better."

Justin nodded. He sure as hell hoped so. He pulled his phone from his pocket. Today was Ryan's big day—the introduction of Teens Against Violence. She'd said she was scared to get up in front of the school. He'd hoped he would make it back in time to be there for her, but it was going to start in fifteen minutes, so that wasn't happening.

Justin: Good luck. You'll do great.

Ryan: Thanks.

*

I can do this. She sat on the stage with Braden McGuire and Mrs. Bettis as the last of the students took their seats in the auditorium. Ryan took a deep breath as Mrs. Bettis stepped up to the podium.

Mrs. Bettis spoke softly into the mic. "Thank you for coming today."

Somebody from the back yelled, "We didn't have a choice." Laughter filtered through the crowd.

Mrs. Bettis continued, "Bullying has been an issue in this country and in our school. It's not just about picking on kids at school. It takes other forms too. That's what we're here to discuss today." She pointed to the large screen behind her. "Please focus your attention on this short video."

The film threw out statistics. One in ten teen girls are victims of dating violence. One in five teen girls and one in seven teen boys have experienced rape or sexual assault.

Ryan watched the audience for a reaction. Nobody seemed to get it. They were texting or talking or sitting there with glazed looks on their faces. How could they not care?

After the video ended, Mrs. Bettis nodded to Ryan.

She stood on shaky legs. The note cards had gone soft from the sweat in her hands. The click of her heels echoed as she walked to the podium. She looked at the bored faces below the stage, cleared her throat, and a heard a snicker from the audience. She set her note cards down and gripped the sides of the lectern. She had to make them listen, to make them understand.

"I am a victim of violence. But it didn't begin at the fountain. It began three years ago, in Chicago, at a party. I was excited to be invited to this party—all the popular kids were there."

As she spoke, the memory of that day flooded back to her. She'd been attending the Fine Arts Academy magnet school for a few weeks and was getting noticed for her work. She'd climbed to the top of the cool ladder in a matter of days. The invitation to Lauren Butler's party was sure to secure her place in the high school hierarchy. "I begged my mom to let me go. I wish now that my mom had never given in." The whispering around the room stopped.

It was easier when they ignored her. She took another deep breath.

"It was one of those parties like you see in teen movies. There were so many cars, we had to park down the street. The parents were home. They took our keys at the door and served all the alcohol we wanted." Her stomach turned as she got to the next part. "It was the first time I'd had a beer, but I met a guy who encouraged me."

Alex Butler. He stood next to the tap laughing at something. He had dark, almost black, curly hair, and perfect skin. She tried not to stare at him as she closed in on the keg, but it was hard not to.

He looked Ryan in the eyes. "I've got to do something, but I'll be in the basement later. Come find me." He jogged down the patio steps leading to the pool and high-fived some guys.

Her friend Kat smirked. "He's hot for you, girl."

Ryan swallowed another sip. "You think so?"

"Yeah—so are you going to go to him later?"

"Should I?"

"Of course you should. He's Alex Butler."

Ryan felt giddy. "Yeah, he is, and he flirted with me. How long should I wait?"

"I don't know, but let him get there first."

"Ha. Ha. Very funny." Ryan topped off her cup the way she'd seen Alex do it.

Kat looked at the guys gathered by the pool. "Think he'd share his friends?"

"There are lots of guys here. Fill your cup and let's mingle."

They melted into the crowd, not veering too far from the keg. Ryan tried to keep up with Alex, but by her third beer she'd lost track of him. She leaned toward Kat, who was talking to a blond hottie from Saint Monica's. "Come with me to the basement."

"I'm good here." Kat gave her a look that said go away.

She was about to go into beg mode when Blondie tipped his chin toward Kat and said, "Come on, let's get another beer." He slipped his arm around her and led her away from Ryan.

Ryan took another sip from her plastic cup. So what if Kat left her standing on the patio by herself? She was going to meet Alex Butler in the basement. She roamed around the house until she found the stairs to the basement. Her heart raced as she began her descent. She heard guys' voices, but couldn't see them until about the fourth step. She stopped on that step and probably gawked.

Three gods played some shoot-em-up video game while taking hits from a bong.

Beer was one thing, but weed? She started to retreat to the party above when Alex noticed her.

"Hey, it's the girl from the art school." He set his controller down and a soldier on the huge screen blew up as he stood.

Ryan waved. "Hi, I didn't mean to interrupt your game." She backed up a step but Alex jogged up them toward her.

"Don't go. I was hoping you'd find me." He took her hand and led her down the steps. "Guys, this is..." He waited for her to supply the answer.

"Ryan."

"Ryan. This is Paul and Jason." He pulled her down to sit next to him on the cushy couch. "Ever play Call of Duty*?"*

"No. I suck at games."

He stretched his arm across the back of the sofa behind her. "Maybe you haven't had the right inspiration." He picked up the bong from the coffee table and handed it to her.

"I've never done this."

He grinned. "Watch and learn." He stuck his face over the cylinder and inhaled. He held his breath and let it out slowly. He pushed the bong toward her.

Her heart pounded. Drinking was one thing. She'd known there'd be alcohol at the party, but this... She bit her lip. "I'm not sure."

He moved closer and wrapped his arm around her. "Come on, it's just weed. Most people don't get high their first time."

One time—just to see what it was like. She covered the cylinder like he'd shown her. She took a deep breath and felt like she was sucking in fire. The smoke burned her throat and she coughed like mad.

He laughed and pulled her against him. "Hey, it's okay. First timers always cough. Try again."

She did and managed to cough a little less. They passed it around and when the bong came back to her she sucked the smoke deep into her lungs. She leaned back on the sofa cushions and for the first time realized Paul and Jason had left the room. She was alone with Alex Butler.

"How do you feel, rookie?"

"Chill, completely chill." She looked at his curls, brown eyes, and full lips. "I really want you to kiss me."

"Yeah?" He lowered his mouth to hers. She relaxed into the kiss and found herself floating back on the sofa seat. He went with her and continued to kiss her. Somebody was laughing from the top of the stairs. He pulled back and said, "Let's go somewhere quiet."

She didn't speak. She let him pull her up and lead her up the stairs to the second floor and his bedroom. He closed the door behind them and they fell onto the bed.

Ryan let her breath out and focused on the unused cards lying on the sloping top of the lectern. "The hot guy at the keg—the one handing me beer after beer—date raped me." She closed her eyes and shook her head. She wasn't going to talk about the sex she'd had with other guys, or the drugs. She was just now beginning to understand why she'd had sex with those other guys. She'd been searching for some kind of vindication. A couple of times she told herself she was in love and it was okay, but mostly she felt helpless to stop what was happening. Besides, once she was caught up in the moment, she didn't want to.

She wiped a wayward tear from the corner of her eye. "The reason I'm telling you this is because one in ten of you have had the same thing happen. The fallout is ugly. Most of us don't report it. I didn't. I tried to make sense out of it. And, you see, because I'd been drinking I thought it was my fault. I thought I must be broken. But I learned that I wasn't broken. I was a victim. I wanted to hide. I felt if I kept it a secret, if nobody knew, it would go away. Then we moved here. There was no way anybody would know my secret, right? But somehow, it got out. And my *friends* at the Purity Club decided I needed to be punished."

She looked out across the faces staring at her. Some shifted uncomfortably in their chairs. A couple of girls wiped their eyes and she wondered if they'd been victims too.

"Dating violence is real. Physical abuse. Controlling behavior. Rape." Her pulse drummed in her head. She'd run out of words. She picked up the note cards and flipped through them. Maybe she could get back on track. Seconds dragged on. The microphone amplified her exhales like a punctuation mark to her awkwardness. She found the last line on the card and finished in a flurry of words. "Join us in stopping the hurt."

The applause was slow. Then a group of the football players stood and clapped. The rest of the school followed suit. Tears burned in Ryan's eyes. She didn't want this kind of attention. She just wanted to tell her story and hope that someone would be saved from the pain of what had happened to her.

Mrs. Bettis walked to the front and gave her a tight hug. "That's not the speech we discussed."

"I'm sorry, I just felt…"

"You are a very brave woman." She hugged her again.

Braden talked about controlling behavior, and bullying. Ryan tried to listen, but she was still shaking from her speech. And at that moment, all she wanted was to see Justin. She knew he hadn't made it back in time for the assembly. Maybe he'd be home by the time she got out of school.

Mrs. Bettis talked a little more about the Teens Against Violence Club. When the assembly was dismissed, Braden turned to her. "I didn't know you were going to tell that story. Man, I'm sorry that happened to you."

"I didn't really know I was going to tell it either. I hadn't planed to. It just sort of happened."

He stood and shifted from one foot to the other. "Are you okay? I mean, it was a horrible thing…"

"I'm good." She didn't want to think about it, much less talk about it. "So, you and my sister…"

"Yeah?"

"What's the story you two are working on?"

He gave her a smarmy smile. "You'll have to wait like the rest of the school."

"She's been pretty upset lately. In the interest of the assembly we just put together, let me just say, if you hurt her you will get it back twice over."

"Hey, I don't know what you're talking about. But if she's been upset, it doesn't have anything to do with me. I swear."

She nodded. "Just giving you fair warning." Kelsey, Mackenzie, Austin, and Travis waited for her in the front row of the auditorium.

Mrs. Bettis hugged Ryan again. "Are you okay?"

Ryan shrugged. "Yeah."

She looked into Ryan's eyes. "If anybody so much as whispers something ugly, I want to know about it."

"Yes, ma'am." She clunked down the steps to the auditorium floor.

Kelsey wrapped her arms around Ryan and hugged her tight. "My God, what you did was insane and unbelievably brave."

"I don't know what happened to me. I wasn't even planning to go there. Maybe it'll help somebody. Who knows?"

Mackenzie hugged her twice as hard as Kelsey, but she didn't say anything. Ryan finally pulled away from her. "Hey, let's get out of here."

She texted Justin to see if he was home, but by the time they reached the truck, he hadn't answered. Kelsey kissed Austin goodbye through the open window on the driver's side and started the engine. As usual, Ryan sat shotgun and Mackenzie sat behind her.

Kelsey was just pulling from the parking space when Mackenzie burst out crying. Not just tears in her eyes, or even tears streaming down her cheeks. Loud, uncontrollable sobs.

Ryan unbuckled her seatbelt and turned around to face her sister. "Kenzie! What's wrong? You have to tell us."

Mackenzie jabbed herself in the chest with her thumb. "It was me."

"What was you?" Ryan's mind was racing a million miles a second. *What the hell was she talking about?*

Mackenzie shook her head. "I'm so sorry. It was me. I did it."

Kelsey stopped the truck in the middle of the parking lot. "What was you? You're not making sense."

"I told. I told Macey Brown about you."

26

Ryan's heart pounded in her chest. She had to have heard wrong. "What did you say?"

Mackenzie rubbed her eyes with the heels of her hands. "I told Macey. I'm sorry. I didn't know she was going to do that to you."

Sucker punched. Pain in her chest. A twist in her gut.

Ryan got out of the truck and walked toward the school building. She couldn't be near Mackenzie.

It took a lot of hate to do something like that. Maybe she deserved it. The move here had been her fault—her dad had admitted as much. Of course Mackenzie hated her. For her, it wasn't just about leaving friends. Mackenzie had to give up gymnastics. Training six hours a day for all those years and for what? So that her older sister could ruin it all.

The football players were out on the field, so she made her way to the stands to watch. She couldn't quite wrap her brain around Mackenzie's confession.

Kelsey joined her on the bench. "You okay?"

Ryan looked across the field. "Where's Mackenzie?"

Kelsey indicated the direction with her head. "Waiting in the tunnel. You two are going to have to talk."

"Not now."

"At least come back to the truck. You have to come home. You don't have to speak, but we're expected to be home."

Ryan looked out across the field for Justin's player number, but couldn't find it. Maybe she could get him to take her home. She checked her phone.

Justin: Hanging with my parents tonight. I'll see you tomorrow.

Tomorrow. Surgery tomorrow and she still hadn't told him. And now it seemed she wouldn't have a chance to. And, forget getting a ride from him.

Ryan followed Kelsey down the ramp and through the tunnel where Mackenzie waited. She didn't look at her sister—she couldn't. Too many emotions played inside her. She was full of anger and sorrow and she wasn't sure which was aimed at Mackenzie and which was directed at herself.

During the drive home, the only sound was the country music playing over the radio. When they got home, Kelsey went to the kitchen, while Ryan and Mackenzie each went to their rooms. It wasn't long before her mom appeared in her doorway. "Mind if I come in?"

Ryan leaned against her headboard, laptop on her knees, scrolling through Facebook. Mindless entertainment. She set her computer aside. "Sure."

Her mom sat on the edge of her bed. "How'd the assembly go today?"

Wow, that seemed like eons ago. "It was good. I think we reached at least a few students."

"Kelsey said you didn't exactly stick to the script."

Ryan pulled her knees close to her chest and wrapped her arms around them. "Yeah. Sorry. It just sort of happened. Nobody seemed to get it just from watching the video."

"No need to apologize. It's up to you how much you want people to know. I'm proud of you. You might have made a real difference. There's probably some girl right now going through what you went through."

She shrugged. "I hope I helped." She waited for her mom to mention Mackenzie. If Kelsey had talked to her about the assembly, surely she'd mentioned the drama afterward.

"Are you ready for tomorrow?"

Ryan nodded.

"Any nerves?"

"Some. I've never been put under. That kind of scares me."

"Do you still want to do it?"

She nodded. "Having a messed-up lip for the rest of my life scares me more." She stretched out her legs. "Mom, what happened to those girls? I know they were sent to alternative school, but do you think they're okay?"

"It's a hard lesson for those girls to learn. Their parents have paid for your doctor's visits as we agreed. They are paying for your surgery. It speaks pretty highly of the parents that we didn't have to take legal action against them. For the most part, I think they're good girls. They just got the wrong message. Macey has some issues, but so does her dad."

"I saw Macey at The Grind. She's crazy, Mom. She threatened me."

"If it happens again, we need to know." Her mom let out a deep sigh.

Here it comes. We're going to talk about Mackenzie.

"Well, I'd better get dinner started. Uncle Jack is going to watch the store tomorrow so both Dad and I can be with you." She stood and left. Just like that.

So Kelsey hadn't told Mom what had happened.

Should she go to Kenzie's room and talk to her? What would she say? She hadn't figured out yet whether she should be angry or sorry. The whole thing was messed up. Why had she told Macey? What purpose could it have served? At least Mackenzie's overreaction to all things having to do with the fountain incident made sense now.

She glanced at the wall that separated them. She wasn't ready to talk to Mackenzie, but she needed to talk to someone. Justin was hanging with his parents. She wasn't about to interrupt that.

So Kelsey it was. She found her sister in the coop. "Hey, Kelsey."

Kelsey scattered chicken scratch on the ground. "Have you talked to her?"

"No." She shoved her hands in the pockets of Justin's jacket. "So you didn't say anything to Mom."

She shook her head. "This is between you and Mackenzie."

"The thing is, I don't know how I feel. Part of me wants to slap the crap out of her and the other part wants to apologize."

Kelsey rolled down the top of the bag of scratch and stored it in a heavy plastic tub. Then she sat on the tub. "Don't you think you've done enough apologizing?"

"Okay, where's the Kelsey I know?"

"I admit at first I was angry that we moved. And I won't deny that I still think that what happened at Dad's office had a lot to do with Dad losing his job…"

"I know it did. I asked him point-blank and he pretty much said so. So, really, I took Mackenzie's life away."

"No, you didn't. Mackenzie lived and breathed gymnastics. But she didn't live and breathe anything else. She didn't have friends in school. She didn't do anything but study and train. Look at her now. She has friends. She has two guys who like her."

"Two? Who besides Braden McGuire?"

"Hello? Travis. They may say they're like siblings, but he's crazy about her."

"Yeah, but I think it's one-way." She sat next to her sister. "Has Kenzie said anything more to you?"

"No. After you left, she just cried harder. I made her come with me to find you, but she wouldn't come up to the stands."

Ryan heard the gate to the chicken yard open and looked up to see Mackenzie squeeze through.

Kelsey stood. "This is where I leave." Her gaze flicked up to Ryan's. "She's braving the chickens for you. Hear her out."

Ryan nodded.

Mackenzie made her way over. "I was going for a run when I heard you talking to Kelsey."

A million thoughts swirled in Ryan's mind and she couldn't quite settle on one to express, so she said nothing.

"I didn't know Macey would hurt you."

"Why would you? A normal person wouldn't have done what she did." Ryan looked at the dirt. "What did you tell her?"

"God, it's so stupid. She was trying to get me to join the PC. She went on and on about how great it was that you and Kelsey had joined. It was like she thought *I* was the bad girl."

"Yeah, well, we all know that's me."

"No. Yes. At the time, yes. I was pissed that we'd moved here. Kelsey could bitch about it, but I couldn't. So when Macey pressured me, I lost it. I told her that you'd had sex with more guys than a bag of M&Ms had the color red."

Ryan laughed. She couldn't help it. "That's probably the worst metaphor I've ever heard."

Mackenzie ran her hands over her ponytail. "Don't laugh. What I did was horrible."

"Yeah, it was. It hurts that you'd tell anybody. The whole time I was in PC, I worried that Kelsey would betray me. But you? Never. Then not only did you tell Macey, you didn't tell her the whole story."

"I didn't get a chance to. Eric was with her and he started going on about how he wanted to *do* you. I couldn't stomach it so I left. Macey never bothered me again." She dug her hands into the kangaroo pocket of her sweatshirt. "It was stupid. Can you forgive me?"

The thought of Eric Perez telling her little sister those things made Ryan's stomach roll. So *that* was when Macey had decided she had to pay. She closed her eyes and pushed away the hurt and shame.

When she opened them, her sister was already halfway to the gate. She almost called after her, but she needed some time to think. Of course she'd forgive Mackenzie. But she was damned pissed and not ready to let her off the guilt hook quite yet.

Back in the house, the smell of fried chicken hit her as soon as she walked in. God bless Mom. She was fixing Ryan's favorite. She was about to wander into the kitchen to help when her phone dinged.

Justin: Sorry I couldn't see you.

Ryan: How was the appointment?

He called instead of texting back.

"So, how'd it go?" She smiled for the first time all day.

"Great. I'm not crazy."

"Good to know."

"How did the assembly go?"

She took a deep breath. "Okay." She climbed the stairs to her room. She should tell him what she'd said… but somehow telling her boyfriend that she'd been raped was harder than telling the whole school. She was the crazy one. "How was family time?" she asked instead.

"It was good. Mom is committed to making our family of three work. We went shopping in Spring Creek. Thank God they have a Lowes. Mom wanted to hit all the boutiques on the square."

"Sounds like a fun day." She dropped onto her bed. This was when she was supposed to say, *By the way, I'm having surgery tomorrow*. But she didn't. He'd had a great day with his family. He was happy. The last thing she wanted was to make him worry. She'd call him in the morning.

"It was." He told her about his parents acting silly in a couple of the shops. He tried to make it sound lame, but she could tell by the tone in his voice that he thought it was pretty cool.

They talked until her mom called her to dinner. It was perfect. No drama. Just a conversation about everyday stuff. She'd made the right decision. He needed one worry-free day.

27

Justin couldn't wait to see Ryan walk through the door to Shop class. One day without seeing her was just too much. At least he'd talked to her last night. Things were finally normal. They were an ordinary dating couple without all the extraneous bullshit.

But by the time the bell rang, she hadn't made it to class. He started to text her but Mr. Hesby had already started taking roll.

After class, Eric Perez waited for him in the breezeway between the shop and the main building. He hadn't spoken to Eric since Homecoming and he sure as hell didn't want to now. But Eric, jerk that he was, blocked his way. "Dude, you need to get control of your girlfriend."

"Go suck yourself, Perez." Justin tried to move past him, but Eric grabbed his shoulder. "Take your hands off me."

"I don't know what kind of power trip your girlfriend is on, but she's caused a shitload of trouble for me."

"What the hell are you talking about?"

"That little confession of hers. Brittney is talking about pressing charges against me. But I didn't do shit that she didn't want."

Justin had no effing clue what Eric was talking about, but he wasn't going to let him know that. He knocked Eric's arm off his shoulder. "Like you didn't do shit that my sister didn't want."

"Once we started, she begged me for it."

A month ago, he would have punched Eric. He sure as hell deserved it. But he wasn't worth getting sent to alternative school. He moved around Eric and headed into the building. He waited for Eric to come after him, but he didn't.

He'd almost made it to his locker when Travis stopped him. "Have you heard from Ryan yet?"

"No. I was about to text her."

"Let me know how she is."

"Sure." *WTF?* "Hey, Travis? What happened at the assembly yesterday?"

"It was intense. Ryan told her story."

Her story? "About the fountain?"

"No. What happened to her in Chicago."

What the hell happened to her in Chicago? "Yeah?"

"Rape. That's some heavy shit."

Justin felt the blood drain from his face. "Yeah. I'd better get to class."

She told the whole school but she couldn't tell me?

He focused on his steps as he made his way to her locker. He saw the words on it as soon as he turned the corner. *Die Slut.* He sprinted to her locker. Why didn't anybody care? People walked past it like it was no big deal. He rubbed his hand across the words, smearing the lipstick. His heartbeat thudded in his head.

He would *not* let his brain go into lockdown. He had to think. This was about her, not him. Yesterday she'd told the school she'd been raped and today she was absent. That was not good. He needed to see her. He needed to know she was all right.

Justin: Are you okay?

By the time he reached his next class, she hadn't answered. He thought about ditching school, but he was already close to having too many absences to play football. Ditching would get him suspended for sure.

After second period, Austin stopped him in the hall. "Heard anything from Ryan yet?"

Justin shook his head. *What the hell is going on?* Obviously everybody thought he knew. He should ask, but pride wouldn't let him. She was his girlfriend. He should know what was going on.

Then it hit him.

Maybe she didn't want to be his girlfriend anymore. It made sense. She'd been vague about the assembly. He thought their conversation was just normal guy-girl talk, but looking back, she'd sounded distant. That was it. She didn't want to be with him and couldn't tell him.

Panic rose in his chest. He couldn't imagine losing her, but he didn't want her to feel obligated to be with him. Shit, he needed to see her. He had to talk to her. If she didn't want to be with him he had to let her go.

He looked at his watch. By the time football practice was over it'd be after five. That seemed a long way off.

*

Ryan had almost texted Justin about her surgery a dozen times. She just couldn't tell him in a text. Besides, this was a simple one. She'd go home later in the day. But her nerves were still on edge.

Things happened—even with simple surgeries. Didn't they say that the closest you could get to death was during anesthesia? And, she had to resolve this thing with Mackenzie before she went under.

She looked at her family standing around her bed. It wouldn't be long before she was whisked behind those double doors. She had to talk to her.

"Hey, could everybody step out for a few minutes? I want to talk to Mackenzie, alone."

Her mom raised her brows. "Oh... okay." She turned to Kelsey. "Let's give them some privacy."

When they'd cleared out, she stared at Mackenzie and tried to decide what she was going to say. "Hey." She reached out and Kenzie took her hand. "I've spent a lot of time trying to figure out how I feel."

Mackenzie bowed her head and let her hair fall forward, covering most of her face. "I'm sorry."

Ryan squeezed her hand. "Don't be. Okay, so I wish you hadn't said anything to Macey. But you are not responsible for what those girls did to me—not even a little bit. Macey is unhinged."

Mackenzie bit her lip. "I was so angry. I felt like my whole reason for existing had been snatched away from me."

"I know. And it was my fault. As much as Mom and Dad wanted us to believe it wasn't and as much as I tried to deny it, it was my fault. I can't take back everything that's happened. I can't undo those things I did. I wish I could. I wish I could forget the person I was even existed. I hope you'll be able to forgive me for ruining your life."

Mackenzie leaned down and hugged Ryan. She whispered in her ear, "You didn't ruin my life. I think you saved it."

The nurse came in then, followed by the rest of the Quinn family. "Okay, Ryan, I'm going to give you something to help you relax. It's going to make you very thirsty and a little loopy. It's time to go back." She turned to Ryan's mom. "You and Dad can follow us to the double doors."

*

It was nearly three before Ryan got to come home. She was still groggy from the anesthesia and her mouth had begun to hurt. Dr. Cooper warned her that her face would be swollen for a few days, but she was still disappointed when she looked in the mirror.

Her mom set her up on the sofa with pillows, water, and the remote. She brought her the pain pill the doctor had ordered, but Ryan hesitated. "My mouth isn't hurting that bad."

"Yet. Dr. Cooper said to stay ahead of the pain for the first twenty-four hours."

She swallowed the pill and hoped she'd stay awake long enough to call Justin. She'd texted him several times, but he hadn't answered her. He'd have a break between school and football practice, so she planned to call him then—if she could stay awake. She tried to form in her mind how she was going to explain everything, but her thoughts were too groggy to be coherent.

She clicked on the TV just as her mom brought her an ice pack for her mouth. "Time for your ice pack. I'll set the timer. Leave it on until you hear the timer go off. I'm going to check on the chickens."

The ice felt good on her face. She nestled into the pillow and let the ice and pain medicine do their job.

It was after five when she woke. She hadn't heard the timer, but someone had removed the ice from her face. She grabbed her cell from the end table to find that Justin had texted five times and called twice.

She called him back, but he didn't answer. *Crap.* How could she have slept through this call? "Mom?"

Her mom poked her head into the den from the kitchen. "Do you need something?"

"Yeah." Her mom hovered over the back of the sofa. "Will you wake me if my phone rings? I missed Justin's call."

She nodded. "Do you want me to keep your phone with me?"

"No." All she needed was for her mom to see her texts. "Just listen for it."

"I'll try."

She flipped the channel to a rerun of *The Big Bang Theory* and tried to stay awake. But she couldn't fight the effects of the meds and leftover anesthesia. She was going to miss his call again.

"Ryan." His beautiful voice was calling to her. She opened her eyes. He sat on the coffee table across from her.

"You came." She tried to smile and instantly regretted it. Pain shot through her mouth and up her right cheek.

Her mom appeared next to Justin. "Are you hurting?" She nodded. "It's time for another pain pill—and how about some ice?"

"Yeah. I could use something for pain." She struggled to sit up.

Justin helped her. "You don't have to sit up for me."

"I want to. I need to be awake. Sit next to me?"

He scooted over to the sofa. "I hope you don't mind me coming."

Oh right, she hadn't told him she was having surgery. "I'm glad you're here." She leaned on his shoulder and wished he'd put his arm around her. She felt his muscles stiffen and sat up straight.

He studied his hands. "Everybody at school kept asking me if I'd heard anything. I had no freaking idea what they were talking about. I didn't want anybody to know because—well, you're supposed to know things about your girlfriend. My dad left a message that your mom had asked him to call and tell me you were out of surgery. It seems I was the last to know."

Ryan's heart hurt. She was an idiot. "I'm sorry. I wanted to. It just never seemed like the right time. Either you were having such a good day I didn't want to ruin it, or you had so much stress I didn't want to add to it."

"I don't need to be protected." He took her hand and sandwiched it between both of his. He flashed those double dimples at her, but his eyes were sad. "Everything that's happened between us has been a little crazy. I don't want you to feel you can't tell me things because you're worried about ruining my day. Being with you makes the most screwed-up day better. "

Between the pain meds and the leftover anesthesia, her emotions were on edge. Her heart raced and she tried to blink the fog from her brain. A couple of tears spilled down her cheeks.

He put his arm around her and pulled her to him. "Shhh. It's okay. Shh. Don't cry. I didn't mean to make you cry."

"I need you, Justin. It scares me how much I need you."

"I need you, too. Please trust me that you don't have to protect me from things in your life."

She nodded. "I promise."

Her mom handed her an ice pack and a pain pill with a glass of juice.

"Thanks, Mom."

Then she turned to Justin. “Have you had dinner?”

“No ma’am.”

“We’re ordering pizza. What do you like?”

He looked at Ryan. “What do you like?”

“Don’t ask me. I have to eat Jell-O and soup.”

To her mom he said, “Anything is fine.”

“Okay.” She retreated to the kitchen.

Justin looked at her. “Are you comfortable?”

She moved the ice. “I think I need to lie down.”

He scooted back to the coffee table and helped her onto her pillow. Her sisters blew in the front door and Kelsey pulled her jacket off. “It’s freezing out there. What the heck—it’s only September.”

Mackenzie pulled off her jacket too. “It’s not that bad. You’ve gotten soft since we left Chicago.”

Kelsey shook her head. “I can’t deny it. I love the warm weather. The hotter the better.”

“I love it here too.” Mackenzie looked at Ryan. “How are you doing?”

Ryan gave her a thumbs-up. She knew Kenzie’s statement had been meant for her. It was good to see Mackenzie smile. She hoped her little sister would find her way out of the shyness that seemed at times to paralyze her.

She looked at Justin. They needed to talk more. He needed to know about the assembly. But that would have to come later. “You don’t have to sit there and stare at me.”

“I like sitting here staring at you.”

“I have a better idea.” She sat in the middle of the sofa and pointed to the end. “If you sit here, I can put my head in your lap.”

“Okay.” He moved to the spot she’d indicated and she put her pillow in his lap and lay down. “Better?”

"Much." She tried to watch TV, but her eyes grew heavy. But it was okay. She felt Justin stroking her hair as she drifted in and out of sleep. He joked with her family and she smelled pizza. When he laughed, she felt the vibrations. She wondered if she was smiling on the outside as much as she was on the inside. She was just where she wanted to be.

The luckiest girl on the planet.

Epilogue

Ryan studied her face in the mirror. It had been two weeks since the surgery, and her lip looked perfect. She smoothed her palm across her cheeks. The scars had almost completely healed. Dr. Cooper had said that time would tell if she was going to have permanent scars, but right now, what was left was covered easily with makeup.

She hesitated before spreading foundation across her skin. Battle scars. She felt like she'd gone to battle. The nasty words still appeared on her locker. Nobody could figure out who was doing it. But it was so commonplace now that nobody really noticed. She'd heard that the PC girls were going to be allowed to return to school next semester. Part of her dreaded seeing them. The other part of her didn't care. She was a different person now and maybe they were too.

She finished putting on her makeup and fluffed her hair. It was growing out too. New face, new hair, new girl. She smiled and applied lipstick to her perfect lips.

As she walked downstairs, she heard Justin joking with Austin, Travis, and her dad, so she stopped halfway down and listened. It warmed her heart to hear her boyfriend, who had become a fixture around the house.

When she stepped off the last stair, Justin stood. "You look pretty."

"Thanks."

When they were in his truck, she took a deep breath. Tonight was the night she was going to talk about what had happened. It had been the elephant in the room that neither of them had mentioned. But it was time.

"So I'm sure you've heard about my speech at the assembly…"

He nodded.

"You've never asked me about it."

"I figured that when you were ready, you'd talk about it."

"I'm ready."

"Okay. Do you want to go somewhere?"

She shook her head. "Not really." He drove to the movie theater while she told her story. She didn't know what to expect, but it was weird—as if she were telling what had happened to someone else. She couldn't imagine the girl who had been broken. That girl was still a part of her—she always would be. But Ryan was so much stronger now. When she finished, she gazed at Justin.

He shook his head. "I'm sorry that happened to you. It makes me want to beat the crap out of that guy."

She nodded. "Me too." She took a breath. "Does it freak you out to date me?"

His gaze didn't falter. "No. The only thing that freaks me out is how much I love you."

It was an ordinary date. A movie—complete with popcorn, soda, and hand-holding. It was perfect. Afterward, Justin drove to the trestle. She expected a crowd to be there partying, but they had the place to themselves even though it was a warm evening for early October. They got out of the truck and walked to a grassy area surrounded by a grove of trees. He spread a blanket on the ground and they sat.

They both lay back and looked at the stars—for about an instant before he turned to face her and they kissed. As soon as his mouth touched hers, she caught fire. He ran his hands up and down her back and she snuggled against him.

He broke the kiss and looked into her eyes. She could see the same fire in his eyes that she felt. "Ryan, we'll only do what you're ready for."

She kissed him. "Here under the stars with nobody around but the guy I love? This is the perfect place."

He smoothed her hair from her face. "Are you sure?"

"Very."

"If you change your mind, I'll stop."

"I won't."

He kissed her again and his hands found their way under her shirt.

Headlights illuminated the bridge. "Shit." He pulled away from her and they both sat up. They watched as a couple got out of an SUV, leaving the headlights shining on the bridge.

Ryan squinted. "That's Mackenzie and Braden."

The couple couldn't see them from where they stood, but they could hear them talking as they walked to the bridge.

Braden said, "This is where it happened. It's far enough down to kill someone."

Mackenzie stood next to him and looked over the rail. “Maybe. But I’m telling you, my dad didn’t do it.”

“Somebody killed Cassidy Jones. Your dad was the logical one.”

Kenzie gave Braden a shove. “Shut up. Just shut up.” She ran to the SUV. “Let’s get out of here.”

THE END

NOTE FROM THE AUTHOR

Thank you for joining the Quinn sisters as they settle into small town life. I hope you enjoyed Ryan's story. I thought you might like to read about another one of Hickville High's own. Here's an excerpt of Hickville Horseplay.

1

Had fun last night, babe. Let's do it again. Smooches. Not exactly what you want to see on your boyfriend's Facebook page. The words captioned a picture of my boyfriend--make that ex-boyfriend--Josh Richards making out with Brandy Owens. It wasn't just that she had sat in his lap, facing him, with her legs wrapped around his waist. It was what his hands were doing all over her body. I couldn't get the image out of my mind, not a good thing when you're about to face a line of complicated jumps on horseback.

I pushed Maggie, my horse, forward but my timing was off throwing her off. She clipped the pole with her back feet knocking it off the standard. Dad started yelling before we landed. Nothing new. He made an X with the poles and I took her over them again. An easy exercise for both of us, which was good since my brain was not on my training session.

It wasn't like I didn't confront Josh. I gave him a chance to beg for forgiveness. It didn't happen, not even a little bit. He said *I* was controlling. What's a girl to do? I did what any self respecting

Queen Bee would do. I threw his letter jacket at him, called him a few names and stormed off. We were Josh Richards and Penny Wilson, Spring Creek High's most adorable couple. It's what I always did when we fought. And he always came after me. Except, this time, he didn't. And then, things got bad.

All sorts of pictures and rumors surfaced about various girls he'd been with—you'd think he was in politics. It was horrible, mostly because I still loved him. I know it was wrong, but I couldn't help it. It was one of those times when a girl needed her mom, only my mom died two years ago. I got into such a funk I spent a whole weekend eating Oreos and peanut butter. If our housekeeper, Gabby, hadn't forced me to take a shower I might have actually managed to eat myself into oblivion. I tried talking to my best friend, Megan, but let's face it, the ditz in that girl runs deep. She was too interested in her nail color to listen. So I resorted to my back up friend, Holly. She's one of those people who's always around, but you don't really think about asking to do things with unless it's convenient, or unless everybody else is busy. You know the type, everybody has one. Holly listened to me cry night after night, and even slept over a couple of times. Day after day, I'd look at the way my red swollen eyes distorted my face and vowed to not waste another tear on Josh Richards.

2

“I’m telling you, Holly. I’m officially over Josh. I have cried my last tear.”

“For real this time?” She cocked her head toward me and I’m sure if the wind hadn’t chosen that moment to blow her mass of platinum curls across her face I would have seen skepticism etched in her perfect pimple-free visage. I couldn’t blame her though; I’d made this declaration on a daily basis for eight weeks.

“I burned his pictures.”

Holly filed behind me as we cut between a black Ford Focus and a Blue hoopdi. “Holy crap, the world is coming to an end.”

“Very funny.” I brushed my nondescript brown hair from my pimple-on-the-chin and freckles-on-the-nose face. “I starting thinking about what he did and what he said and I just got pissed.”

“He cheated on you.”

“He said I was controlling.”

“And he cheated on you.”

"He accused me of planning every minute of our time together."

"What an ass, WHO CHEATED ON YOU!"

"And yeah, he cheated on me. That ass cheated on me with Brandy slut-o-the-month Owens!" I thought I'd managed to get past the anger last night during a tough training session with my horse, but it came back with a vengeance. At that moment I felt hate, my eyes burned with it, my muscles drank it up tensing in anticipation of a fight. I scanned the parking lot, searched the courtyard for signs of Josh. "Where is he? I want to rip him a new one."

Holly pulled on the shoulder of my sweater dragging both of us to a stop in the middle of the parking lot. "Whoa--slow down horsey girl."

If you do, you'll look like a total freak. Everybody knows he cheated on you with Brandy, he's coming off as the jerk. If you confront him in front of his friends you'll just look like the bitch that deserved it."

I took a deep breath and calmed myself. "You're right. I can't believe I wasted tears on that ass not to mention dating him for the past eighteen months."

"Ah well we all have our psychotic moments." Holly dropped her backpack on the blacktop and placed her hands on my shoulders. "Okay, you need to make an oath."

"For what?"

"To prove that you're really moving on this time. Raise your right hand."

"What? You're crazy."

"Raise it and repeat after me."

The bell signaled five minutes to get to class. I was never late for class. "Later, we need to go."

"We'll cut through freshmanville. Do it."

I juggled my books into one arm and managed to raise my right hand.

"I, Penny Wilson..."

I echoed. "I Penny Wilson..."

"am totally and completely over Josh Richards."

"am totally and completely over Josh Richards."

Holly smiled and gave me a hug. I did feel better. Holly sort of hung on the fringes of our group and she had a way of seeing things differently. Like when my mom got sick, Holly just seemed to know when I needed to be with someone and when I needed to be left alone. I never asked her--she just knew.

We eased our way into school through the freshman hall door. Ninth-graders loitered by their lockers, hanging on the fringes of high school society. The nerd–herd gathered around the computer lab gawking at the up-and-coming fashionistas primping and preening as they vied for their future places as upper classmen. As we edged past them, I could almost see the wheels turning in Holly's brain. "Let's see, you dated loser-boy for what a year and a half? We need to get you back in circulation."

"Ha, ha. I think not."

"Come on. The best way to prove to J-boy and the rest of the school you've moved on is to get back to dating."

"The best way to prove to Josh and the rest of the school that I've moved on is to *move on*. I don't want to date anybody right now. I'm sick of the games."

"You can't be serious. It's all about the games."

"Not for me. No games. No guys. No dating. Period."

We rounded the corner to the main corridor and my shoulders tightened sending ripples to my suddenly queasy stomach.

There they were. Josh, who didn't have the decency to break up with me before hooking up with the biggest slut in Spring Creek, Texas and Brandy--said hook up. Josh and Brandy. Together. Or should I say Brosh? She was plastered so close to him they looked like they had morphed into one big blob of Abercrombie and Fitch with their perfect blonde hair, perfect bronze skin, and perfect white teeth. I made my declaration and was over him. Completely. Except tears welled anyway. I would not cry. Crying equaled total humiliation and I just couldn't give Brosh the satisfaction.

As they neared us it was like they moved in slow motion and I couldn't take my eyes away. Brandy did a little head flick hair flying thingy. A definite *he's mine* signal. My mares make the same move when I walk them past the stallion pasture. "Penny!" She actually stopped and called out to me. Josh tightened his hold on slut-girl but didn't look me in the face. The wuss.

I stopped and I'm sure my mouth hung open. I stood there looking like a total moron with teary eyes. I probably had drool hanging off my chin. "What?" I managed to say.

"You left this in Josh's pocket." She pulled her hand from the coat pocket and handed me a tube of lip-gloss.

I looked at it and in a flash of brilliance said, "This isn't mine. It must be some other girl's." I did my own head-flick-hair-fly thing--only when I slung my hair a hank of it got stuck in my super shiny lip-gloss and I spent several un-cool seconds spitting it out.

By lunch, however, I was completely over the lip-gloss drama. Our cafeteria was arranged in long rows of rectangular tables. The jocks sat on one end and the girls next to them in descending order of popularity. Before I got dumped, I sat with Melanie and her boy-friend on the high end. Since dumpage, I've been pushed to the opposite end of the table teetering precar-iously close to a whole new social stratum.

I sat next to Holly on the low end and tried not to look at Brandy laughing, flirting and being one with the jocks. It was stunning to realize how fast they replaced me. I had been to every football game my show sched-ule would allow, most of the practices, and I knew the jocks better than their girlfriends. Watching them, it was if I'd never been allowed into their inner sanctum.

Holly must have noticed my misery because she banged the saltshaker on the table and cleared her throat. "Okay, Penny needs an intervention. She took the official 'I'm on the market' oath today. After eight-een months of jerkdom, she needs dating help."

I wanted to bang my head on the table. "Ah-h, no-o. I'm finished with relationships for a while."

Emily rolled her eyes in Holly's direction and ran a hand through her nearly black spiky hair. She was four foot nothing and weighed zilch. "Look, the last thing you need is to get tied down. Date around, have fun…"

"Get a reputation." I sighed and studied my plate. "I just want to chill for a while. My show season is coming up and I need to concentrate on training my horse. I am *not* going to get disqualified in The Annie this year." The Annie is a charity horse show to raise money for cancer research named in memory of my mom. I've sucked since it began four years ago. I just couldn't let that happen again this year.

I looked up from my grilled cheese sandwich and saw a cowboy heading toward our table from the other side of the cafeteria. This was definitely going to be one of "those" days. I knew he was coming to talk to me and I had some 'splaning to do. Our group didn't exactly hang with the rodeo crowd. "Ah, Dad hired a farm hand to help out with the chores though. You'll never guess who." The words had barely tumbled from my lips when my view was filled with wrangler jeans and an oversized belt buckle. "Ty Jackson."

Flashing an "aw shucks" kind of grin, said farm hand straddled the bench across from me. "Hey, my dad said you needed a ride home."

"Ah--yeah." I wanted to get this little meeting over as quickly as possible. We were the smart-populars and a vast chasm separated us from the Wranglers--members of the rodeo team. "My dad thought since you're going to be working for us we could ride together."

"Makes sense." He drummed his fingers on the metal seat; apparently completely unaware his time at our table was up.

We all stared at him but he just kept looking around. One by one we shifted uncomfortably like you do when the sermon is too long in church or when you're waiting for the bell to ring and the teacher is still talking. He didn't get the hint.

"Is there something else?" I asked.

"No. I've just always wondered what the view was like sitting at the beautiful-people table."

Determined to not let his snide remark get to me, I rolled my eyes. "Where do you want me to meet you, Ty?"

"Back parking lot."

"Okay, I'll see you then."

He stood and shrugged. "Later."

As he left our table, Holly stared after him practically drooling. "Did you have to rush him away?"

"You can't be serious."

"Have you ever looked at Ty Jackson?"

I nodded to her in a "duh" kind of way.

"No. I mean since the seventh grade?"

"Why?"

She pushed her platinum curls behind her ears. "Hel-lo, he's totally hot! Like Dirks Bentley hot."

"So, he's got curly blonde hair…and I guess his face is nice to look at…"

"I bet his stomach is ripped. He's built like a god."

"…who wears wrinkled shirts. Besides, Holly, he's a *Wrangler*."

"Yeah, and don't they fit his butt nice."

My gaze focused on Ty's backside as he walked away from our table. "Hol-ly."

"So he's a *Wrangler*. *You* have horses, *you* drive a Dooley."

"Hello, cowboy equals bubba," Emily said waving her hand in front of her.

"Maybe, but I can definitely appreciate him for the fine specimen of one-hundred-per-cent drool-worthiness that he is," Holly shot back.

"You can have him. I don't like cowboys, their big buckles, or their stupid pearl snap shirts. I hate the way they hang around their trucks after school spitting to-bacco onto the parking lot," I said.

Holly sat there all dreamy-eyed and smiled. "Ty doesn't dip."

"What?"

"Ty doesn't dip. Look at his pocket, no Skoal ring."

I tore a hunk off of my grilled cheese sandwich, popped it in my mouth and focused on his rear. Not a bad sight, but I'd never admit it.

Megan pulled my attention away from Tyler Jack-son. "So what's this about your dad hiring Ty any-way?"

"Can you believe it? It's been two years since Mom passed away and he's just now realizing our farm is too big to run alone."

"So hiring Ty should be a good thing," Holly inter-jected.

"I guess--except Dad decided it didn't make sense for me to drive my truck home after school when Ty is coming anyway. So--my truck has been grounded and I've been reduced to riding the bus in the morning and home with Cowboy Ty."

"Eww," Em and Megan said in unison. Then Emily, the queen of digging up past embarrassments, wagged her index finger at me. "Didn't you date him?"

"It was seventh grade, you can't exactly call it dating."

"You and Ty Jackson?" Megan, having lived in Spring Creek for only a year and thereby missing the trauma of my past, raised her eyebrows. I wasn't sure if she was questioning the match or judging it.

Holly shook her head. "Not a good topic. Let it go."

Great Holly, you might as well have shouted "ask her."

"That bad? What happened?"

I swirled a French fry in a puddle of ketchup. I didn't really want to dredge up my past with Ty but I figured Emily would tell Megan her version if I didn't. "It's not that big of a deal. He was my best friend. Right after Mom got sick, things changed. He joined the rodeo team and the next thing I knew he was wearing pearl snap shirts and hanging out with the Agg kids."

Megan swirled the ice in her Dr. Pepper with her straw. "You broke up because he joined the rodeo team?"

Holly rolled her eyes. "You had to ask. You see, Meg, Penny rides English and Ty rides Western and apparently never the two shall meet." She gave a talk-to-the-hand gesture and went into drama overdrive. "I know, I know, it's a mystery to me too. As far as I know the horses eat and poop the same but apparently there is a big disparity between the sophisticated world of the equestrian and the redneck world of the cowboy. I don't know maybe one rides frontwards the other backwards…but you must never say the "c" word around Penny."

"Ha. Ha. Very funny, Holly." I drew in a deep breath and continued. "When Mom had her first chemo treatment she had a reaction to one of the drugs and was in ICU. I found out during school and while I waited for my dad to pick me up, I looked for Ty. I found him hanging all over Misty-Dawn Barns."

Megan choked on her coke. "You're kidding? Misty-Dawn?"

"Yeah, go figure. Anyway, I told him Mom was worse and I needed to talk to him. Do you know what he told me?" Bitterness seeped from deep within my chest. The feeling grew as it traveled up my throat threatening to consume me. *He's not worth it.* I took a long sip on my D.P. and willed the sensation under control. "I've never told anybody what he actually said to me--not even Holly." I looked at my table companions. "He said…" My throat felt tight, but I was not going to cry. Crying would give meaning to the words he seared into my brain. Deep breath. "He said being friends with me was exhausting--he couldn't deal with the drama in my life--that he couldn't date someone whose mom had cancer. I don't care if he rides English, Western, or a freaking goat, I can't forgive him."

Megan stirred the crushed ice in her drink with her straw. "What a jerk."

"Did he ever apologize?" Emily asked.

"He called once or twice, but after what he said to me I wasn't about to talk to him." I popped the ketch-up-laden fry in my mouth and dipped a second one in the sauce. "I'm over it," I lied. "What bugs me now is that Dad hired somebody who knows nothing about Eventing. I need to step-up training with my horse, and he hires a cowboy to work on our farm? What could Ty know about jumping?"

Megan sighed. "Well, not that I'd ever date him, but having eye-candy like Ty Jackson around can't be all bad."

"You are so bad, Megan." I tossed a fry at her and the table broke out in laughter.

For some reason, I saw Ty about a million times more than normal. And if didn't see him, I always knew where he was because Josh and his Neanderthal buddies mooed, oinked, or made some other barnyard noise every time they passed him in the hall. By the end of the day, it wasn't just the jocks that were moo-ing him, half the school was in on it.

After school I rushed to the back parking lot hoping we could leave before anybody saw me with him. The last thing I wanted was to be the recipient of the barn-yard serenade. But, of course, Ty wasn't there. So I had to stand around waiting for him like some pathetic cowboy groupie.

Oh and get this, instead of his grey F-one-fifty truck, we rode in a twelve-passenger van. Now there's an experience every girl must put on her to-do list. Not.

Imagine a van that has been in the hands of a family with nine kids. An assorted collection of pro-life bumper stickers peppered the rear door and wash me was etched in the dirt on the back window. I silently wondered if the Old English script was an indication of how long it had been there. The dings in the door panels and faded blue paint completed the look. I couldn't imagine what the inside was like, and after I opened the door I couldn't believe it.

I'm not sure where the spoiled milk odor was coming from, but I'm pretty sure it was one of the car seats buckled in the second row. A mangled box of animal crackers lay on the floor with headless hippos, broken bears, and legless lions scattered around the perimeter. A mixture of Lego's and Barbie dolls were strewn throughout the van.

Ty grabbed a nude Barbie off the passenger seat, tossed to the back, and shrugged. "My truck is in the shop."

As I snapped my seat belt, my stomach roiled. In three weeks I had gone from dating the quarter back of the two-A district champions to riding through the school parking lot in the ick-mobile with cowboy Ty. I propped my elbow on the window seal and shielded my face with my hand hoping nobody would recognize me. Ty, on the other hand, lowered his window and felt compelled to talk to everybody he saw. It was time to set a few ground rules.

"Look Ty, not that I don't appreciate the…" I caught a whiff of sour milk and my gut lurched a little. I swallowed and continued, "…the ride--it is better than the bus--somewhat--but do you think you could resist calling attention to us and just get us out of here?"

"Oh. You don't want anybody to know you're riding with me?" He placed a hand across his heart. "I'm shocked and wounded."

Ty stopped to let a group walk in front of the van. He poked his head out of the window and yelled. "Hey, do you mind stepping it up. I'm driving Penny Wilson and she doesn't like to be kept waiting."

The group looked at him like he was crazy, but he didn't care, he continued with. "Did you hear? Penny Wilson is riding with me, Ty Jackson. Tell your friends." Ty weaved his way up and down every aisle. He gave everybody he saw a subtle nod and said, "I've got Penny Wilson in the van." I slunk as low in the seat as my seatbelt would allow. When he signaled to exit the parking lot I thought my humiliation was over but nooo. His grande finale was an all out head-out-of-the-window shout, "Penny Wilson is riding with Ty Jackson!"

When we were on the main drag he glanced at me and smiled. "I'm going to pull through the Chicken Shack and get a sweet tea, ya want one?"

I glared at him. "How could you do that to me?"

"Easy. I don't play your games. I don't give a crap if you're popular and if you turn your nose up at my ride again, you can take the bus."

What a jerk. I tried to think of a snappy response but couldn't so I looked out the window and ignored him.

He pulled to a stop at a red light and faced me. "Now do you want a sweet tea or not?"

I reached for my purse, and he put his hand on my arm stopping me. "I got it."

I jerked my arm away. "I can pay for it myself."

"You can get the next one."

I pulled a dollar from my billfold and slapped it on the dash.

Ty tossed it back at me as he entered the drive-thru line. I forgot about the money when we pulled up behind a beat-up black Chevy with a decal of a little boy peeing on a Ford symbol. That would be Josh's truck, and who would be plastered next to him? Brandy.

I wanted to duck, run to the back with the naked Barbie, anything to avoid being seen by Brosh. What happened next sent arrows straight into my heart. After the happy couple in front placed their order, Josh pulled Brandy to him and they started making out. A new surge of pain crushed my chest. Tears stung my eyes. Argh. I couldn't believe I was letting him get to me. Determined not to cry, especially in front of Ty, I tried small talk. "You ever work on a large horse farm before?"

"Geez, they should get a room."

"Remember we have a pretty big place. It's not like cleaning a couple of stalls and you're done. We have twenty-four stalls and that doesn't include the horses that live out."

Ty shot an irritated glance toward me. "I think I can handle it."

A gap in the line formed in front of Josh, but he was too engrossed with Brandy to notice. Ty honked which got Josh's attention. He looked back, flipped Ty off and pulled forward. Pretty much double humiliation for me. Not only did Josh see me, he knew I saw him.

Which was confirmed when he stopped behind the next car, looked back at us and grabbed Brandy again.

"What a jerk," Ty muttered.

In spite of my resolve not to lose it, a tear slipped from my eye. "Damn."

Ty cocked his head in that totally-annoying-David-Caruso-CSI kind of way and said, "You know, he's not worth it."

I wanted to say that I wished people would quit telling me he wasn't worth it. I got it! Of course he wasn't worth it. If he were, he wouldn't be making out with slut-o-the-month. But knowing that didn't make it hurt any less. If anything, it made me feel more like a loser for wasting so much of my life with him. I spat out, "Just get us out of here."

He looked at me like he was going to say something, but instead he shoved his truck in reverse and pulled out of line, muttering, "As you wish."

When we pulled onto the highway he punched in a Rascal Flats CD and sang along. He had an amazing voice and listening to him washed away the vision of Josh and Brandy playing in my mind.

I closed my eyes and swallowed hard. I just wouldn't let it bother me.

ABOUT THE AUTHOR

Following a career as a nursing instructor, Mary earned an MFA in Writing Popular Fiction from Seton Hill University in Pennsylvania.

A native Texan, Mary loves horses, dogs, cats, and small town diners. Although she has recently relocated in northern New Mexico, her heart remains in the Lone Star state.

*

Book layout courtesy of PressBooks.com
Images from Shutterstock.com, used under license
Cover design by SeedlingsOnline.com

AVAILABLE NOW

Welcome to Hickville High
Hickville Confessions
Hickville Horseplay

COMING SOON

Hickville Redemption
Faery Story (Sithiche)